For my late Father...

Known to some as; *'The Velvet Hammer'*

He lived life on his own terms,
but left us much too soon.

Thanks Pop.

Car Store – Preface

I have a song that gets on everyone's nerves and this is how it goes:

I have a song that gets on everyone's nerves and this is how it goes:

I have a song that gets on everyone's nerves and this is how it goes:

I have a song that gets on everyone's nerves and this is how it goes:

I have a song that gets on everyone's nerves and this is how it goes:

I have a song that gets on everyone's nerves and this is how it goes:

I have a song that gets on everyone's nerves and this is how it goes:

I have a song that gets on everyone's nerves and this is how it goes:

I have a song that gets on everyone's nerves and this is how it goes:

I have a song that gets on everyone's nerves and this is how it goes:

I have a song that gets on everyone's nerves and this is how it goes:

I have a song that gets on everyone's nerves and this is how it goes:

-LFW

Chapter One

Love will find a way.

I hadn't walked three steps from my car, fumbling with yet another of my outdated ties, when I heard a scathing voice.

"You can't park there!"

I looked up to see an angry looking little man in a three-piece suit. He stood stock-still in the middle of the parking lot, hair pasted to his head as though it were cemented there.

"I'm here for the…"

"I know who you are." The little man scowled. "Go park that piece of crap in the employee parking."

I looked around stupidly, feeling massively under-dressed.

"It's over there," he pointed with two fingers across the seven acre expanse of the lot, "past the used car building. Then come back up here and report to Brick. He'll get you to the conference room."

"Yes sir," I said almost without thinking. "right away."

Trundling across the lot in my old Subaru, I squinted through the pitted glass, smeared dirt and bird crap. Passing the laser straight lines of shiny new vehicles I felt that I'd slipped into a realm for which I was not quite ready. I could almost feel the disgust with which my new 'little general' eyed my thirteen year old sled. Then I saw him shaking his head in my rear-view mirror as I drove slowly across his killing field.

'Did he have a pink shirt on?' I tried to remember as I found my way to the 'employees' lot.

Finding an unobtrusive spot amongst the other not-so-nice vehicles, I exited my car for the second time in five minutes. I cupped my hand over my mouth to check the smell of my breath, and then made the trek back across the lot. I tucked my shirt in tightly as I passed the used car salesmen in front of their little fortress. It was a low, hexagonally shaped building with a blue metal roof that was the same color as the countertops in the showroom. A skylight sat plunked on top as though it were an afterthought, gleaming viciously in the shade-less morning sun.

PRE-OWNED was emblazoned on the front of the building in what appeared to be 'light-up' letters. It was like a Navajo Hogan on steroids.

Most of the used cars seemed to be Nissans also, with a few other brands of cars mixed in; I guessed to offer a broader selection. They were equally as clean as the new cars although not quite as neatly matched. There must've been at least a hundred of them. The used car guys watched me as I made my march, silently smoking beneath their sunglasses, eyeing up the fresh meat. I just kept walking.

Making it past the building, I found myself on the 'New' side again. Veering from my path slightly I crossed over to the front line to check out the goofy-looking 'XTERRA'. There were at least twenty of them parked perfectly next to each other. Reaching the end of the line, I stopped briefly to look at one of the window stickers. The vehicle was an ostentatiously loud color called 'Solar Yellow'. It looked like a smaller version of a Tonka truck to me. Maybe the one 'Road Worker Barbie' would drive. I peered through the glass at the interior.

"Stapleton!" I heard my name yelled from the giant cement porch.

Looking up, I saw Brick standing at the high metal railing that surrounded the porch, or 'point' as I would learn it was called. The railing must've been four-and-a-half to five feet tall and was painted the same royal blue that seemed to be Centennial's signature color. Thick metal wires had been fed through the vertical posts every foot or so and had those weird double ended tightening things attached so they could be pulled extra-taught. Brick's dry cleaned frame was cut into sections by these and it made sort of an optical illusion of his body. I thought of that old Snickers Bar commercial, you know the one where they kept singing about how, *no matter how you slice it, it always 'comes up nuts'?*

"What are you doing?" He yelled down at me through his perfectly trimmed goatee.

Again, I found myself acting completely without thought. Pointing a bent hand at myself I arched my eyebrows up at him.

"Let's go, come on!" he said with mock intensity.

I trotted over to and up the stairs then stood next to him.

"Am I late?" I started to ask.

Curling his hand around the back of my upper arm he shuffled me inside. The sliding doors opened with a whoosh and he stalked me into the showroom then surreptitiously led me back into the first cubby.

"I see you met Gavin already." He said as we found our way into yet another office cube.

"Gavin?"

"Gavin Johnson, the guy that just jumped your shit this morning."

"Oh yeah, I assume he is also my boss."

"He's the General Manager." He stated, putting the emphasis on 'General'. "Just try to steer clear of him for the first few weeks if you can."

He smiled again, it looked like a grimace.

"So here's the deal; there are three other guys coming to this training today. Probably only two of you will make it."

The fear on my face was difficult to conceal, I was nearly broke.

"Don't worry;" he cajoled, "with your sales experience I'm sure you'll make the cut. Just try not to talk, two ears, one mouth. Gavin thinks the world of this trainer. Okay let's go."

He stood up and walked to the door of the cubby office and looked out.

"Wait five seconds then walk down to the used car building and find the conference room." His wedding ring clacked nervously against the metal frame of the sliding glass door.

With that he slipped out of the cube and made his way across the floor to the tower. His gait seemed stilted, like he had something stuck up his ass maybe. His heels clicked annoyingly on the floor like that Manny character's had over at the Toyota store. His toes pointed outward slightly as he walked and his shoulders were pushed just a little too far back. He reminded me of a little guy that I'd played football with in Junior High School. He was really too small to play football, by eighth-grade most of us stood a head taller than him and outweighed him by twenty-thirty pounds. But what he lacked in stature, he more than made up for with dedication and tenacity. Perhaps Brick was like him. I got up and walked back out the front doors.

Making a third trip across the lot I checked my watch and noticed that it was eight minutes to eight. I broke into a brisk walk and headed for the door of the used car building. Reaching for the handle, I was nearly plowed over by a rather disheveled man with wispy wild hair; he had a salesman trailing behind him. The salesman was at least five years my junior but clearly already a seasoned professional. He was trying to explain something to the used car manager; but the tall, portly man was storming away like a startled buffalo.

"I don't have time for this Milo!" I heard him say, his irritation evident.

"But, I told him I'd call him by nine." Salesman Milo protested.

"Later, Milo!"

"But,"

"Later!" he snorted back, wheeling off to what appeared to be a very important meeting.

"Fuck!" Milo spewed, clapping his hands together and kicking the pavement simultaneously.

I was still standing at the door, holding it open, gaping at the exchange.

"You're letting all *zeee* air conditioning out green-pea." A velvety voice commented behind me.

"Oh, sorry." I said looking back through the portal. There was nothing but the hum of the soda machine and a couple coffee makers standing sentinel inside the door.

"Who said that?" I asked, closing the door behind myself.

"*Eeeen* here." The shadowy voice continued.

I looked further around the corner and saw a man sitting in an oddly shaped office. The outer wall was made of cinder-blocks that were stacked half the way up, the top half was glass windows. A number of small black-lacquered wooden plaques leaned against the glass with '1st Place' etched onto their chintzy metal top sheets. Mostly bald and very dark-skinned, he sat at a small desk with a linen handkerchief spread out before him. On top of this was a medium-sized bunch of purple grapes. With one of his skeletal claws, he plucked a juicy orb from its stem and plopped it into his extruded maw. A large onyx ring was positioned on his middle finger between oversized knuckles that had clearly been cracked too many times. What looked like a GM insignia was attached to the face of the stone.

"I'm Victor." He pronounced it *Veeg*-tor with the guttural rattle of man that clearly smokes two packs a day.

"Hi Victor, I'm late. Can you direct me to the conference room?"

"It's around the corner." He pointed with his thumb disinterestedly over his shoulder. His voice had a very round quality, like a ball of dark chocolate.

"Thanks Victor, catch 'ya later."

"Not *eeef* I catch you first…" He smiled up at me from over his glasses, which were slid down nearly to the end of his nose. His teeth were freakishly white, outlined with purple stains from the grapes. I smiled back uncertainly then took my leave.

'What the fuck'sa Green Pea?' I thought as I found my way into the conference room.

The door opened as though it were vacuum-sealed. Seated amongst a sea of thinly padded chairs were the three other guys Brick had told me about. One was a black kid, nicely dressed, he looked like a younger, slightly balder (and fatter), Danny Glover. The other two guys looked like they had just gotten off a bus. I decided to sit next to Sgt. Murtaugh. The front of the room was covered with two giant dry erase boards, a third one stood off to the side. All three of them were bigger than I'd ever seen before. The back and sides of the room were the same as Veeg-tor's office except the cinder blocks had been painted a sort of orangey-tan. Several fluorescent lights hung solidly from the oddly angled ceiling. They were the sort that looked like radiators with long tubes running through them to throw the maximum amount of light; like you might see in an old high school classroom, or a police line-up viewing chamber.

Murtaugh looked up at me disinterestedly as I found the chair next to him. His red and navy blue striped tie cascaded over his round belly and trailed off to the side of his clean white dress shirt. Again I felt a bit out of touch as I settled uncomfortably into the metal framed chair in my friend's old tie and khaki slacks.

"You know what time it is?" I asked him, although the clock high on the front wall clearly showed 7:58.

Random, as I would come to know him, shook his watch from under his cuff, looked at it, then let his arm flop back down to his side before answering.

"S'almost eight." He stated flatly. Hanging sideways in his chair, a pair of red-rimmed eyes expressed a boredom with life that was much too young for his age.

"Thanks." I whispered back. He shot me a wan look and turned toward the front of the room to stare blankly at nothing.

"I'm Joey." one of the kids in the second row said behind me. I turned to see a maybe nineteen year old holding his hand out to me. "This is my cousin Deano."

My eyes fell immediately to his shoes, which were of the heavy metal rocker high-topped variety. He and his cousin were both wearing them; I was almost surprised to see that they had been laced up. Joey was wearing a short sleeved, striped shirt with a skinny tie that had apparently skipped the nineties and found its way into the new millennium. The jeans he was wearing, although they matched the shoes, made him look even more like an idiot and his hair was cut in classic mullet style, business in the front, party in the back. Deano hadn't even bothered to wear a collared shirt. I gave Joey's hand a cursory shake and turned to face the blank dry-erase boards myself.

Another door opened on the other side of the room with a loud, metallic click and a freshly scrubbed gentleman entered with his briefcase. He had what was almost a buzz-cut and his fair skin had the pinkish hue of someone who'd never worked a hard day in his life. I sat up in my chair a bit straighter; Random just traced the man's steps with a calculated roll of his eyes.

"Hi." The man said, setting his briefcase on the long, white folding table in front of us. We were silent. "Okay," he continued. "Let's get started."

Opening his briefcase, he pulled out several nine by six inch spiral notepads and handed one to each of us.

"I'm sure you all brought pens, but I have some extras if you need one."

I detected a bit of a southern accent in his voice, probably Texas or Oklahoma. It definitely wasn't twangy enough to be from the 'true south'.

"I'd like to start today's training by going around the room and getting to know one another. I'm Gary and as you might've already guessed, I'm not from Colorado."

He pronounced it 'Colorada'. I cringed slightly at his pronunciation; I hated it when people said it that way.

'He must be an Okie.' I thought, irritated.

"I'm actually from Tulsa."

'Bingo.'

What the fuck am I doing here? I thought again. My forehead began to itch at the scalp line and a dull headache was forming on the underside. It was like someone had scribbled it there with a Husky pencil. Reaching into my pocket for a pen I fondled my cigarettes briefly before pulling it out.

"I've been training people how to sell cars for about fourteen years; I have two wonderful children and a lovely wife..."

I glared up at the clock; already wanting a smoke... or maybe a college education.

"...Janet." He smiled at us with what he'd clearly hoped was a comforting smile but in reality seemed a bit condescending.

"Who'd like to go next?"

We started at him blankly.

"Okay," he hummed. "How about you?" He pointed at Murtaugh with two hands pressed together in prayerful style.
"Well, I'm Random Hughley. I've worked as a lot tech for O'Calla Nissan for the last two years and I'm trying to break into sales."
"Thank you, Random, and where are you from?"
"Aurora."
"Great... and how about you, in the back row."

"I'm Joey." Joey stuttered, "I've never sold anything before, but I love cars."

"Okay Joey, and where are you from?"

"I'm from Wheatridge and this is my cousin Deano."

"Thanks Joey." Gary continued, smiling his bullshit smile again. "How about you Dean, you love cars too?"

"Yeah," he mumbled, "I guess."

"Okay." He continued, holding one hand up and clearly stifling a laugh with the other.

"How about you Mark? What's your story?"

I guessed that Brick had already made clear to Gary what my name was. I wondered what else he might have shared.

"Well, I'm Mark Stapleton." I said a bit warily. "I was a professional skier and ski instructor for a number of years. I've met with some success in advertising and real estate sales. I'm recently married and have a brand new baby daughter and need to make some real money." Then I spilled without thinking, "Oh and I currently live in Evergreen."

"Good luck Mark, I hope I can help with that." He smiled again and I reached back into my pocket, this time fondling the small bit of folding cash I had to my name.

I tried to convince myself that Gary wasn't so bad after all.

"Now that everyone knows each other, let's get down to brass tacks. My job is to give to you the basics on selling cars, after which you'll have a trial period at this dealership. If you are successful at selling you'll be offered a permanent position here at Centennial Nissan, fair enough?"

"Fair enough." Joey parroted. Random rolled his eyes at me. It was my turn to put a hand to my mouth.

"I encourage you to take notes, as I'll be covering quite a bit of information over the next three days and your sales managers will expect you to have at least a working knowledge of the car business by the time we're done."

Turning to the dry erase board he wrote in large letters the word 'UP'.

"Who knows what this means?"

I could feel the Husky pencil working its way back to the underside of my forehead.

'Uh the opposite of down?' I found myself wishing again that I'd focused a bit more on my trigonometry textbook in high school instead of the glowing bowl of a metallic pipe.

"An opportunity to do business." Random spouted.
"That is absolutely correct, Random. Could you explain that for us?"
"An UP is when you meet a customer on the lot."
"That is partly right, but what else does it encompass?"

'Encompass??'

I knew that Joey and Deano were already out of their depth. But I certainly didn't know the answer Gary was looking for, so I decided to remain dumb. Random's stare had once again become blank.

"A lot of the terms that you'll hear in the car business don't exactly fit. I've always thought that they should call a potential customer an 'OP' or an 'opportunity to do business.' This could mean a customer in front of you, Random; a customer that just left, or a customer on the phone. How do you greet an 'UP'?"
"Hi, welcome to Centennial Nissan, are you here for parts, sales or service?" Random reeled off again.
"You must've talked to a salesperson or two when you were working as a lot tech over there at O'Calla."

Random smiled.

"Mark, how would you handle an 'UP'?

"I guess I'd try to figure out if they wanted to buy a car and then how I'm going to sell them one."

"Good answer, good answer. But I'm looking for something deeper. Let's try a little role-playing shall we."

'Auckkk, let's not shall we?' I thought. *Could this be anymore remedial?*

"Joey, come on up here."

Joey dropped his stuff onto the chair next to him and stumbled his way to the front of the room.

"Now imagine you're a customer that just walked onto the lot and I'm the salesperson that just greeted you."

Gary extended his hand theatrically.

"Hi, welcome to Centennial Nissan, are you here for parts, sales or service?"

"I want a fast ride!" Joey retorted, looking at his cousin.

'What a dipshit!' Random and I shared the thought.

"Okay," Gary continued, unwavered by his attempt at humor. "How fast?"

"Uh…" Joey mumbled.

"Because Pathfinders are pretty fast, but Maximas are really fast!"

"I guess a Maxima?" Joey questioned.

"Okay, would you like a light color or a dark color?"

"Uh… red?" Joey squeaked.

"That's enough, Joey." Gary unhooked him. "You can go sit down now."

Random and I looked amusingly at one another.

"What did I just demonstrate there?"

"Customer service." I answered, thinking anything I could interject at this point would sound smart.

"Okay, what else?"

"Control." Random put forth smugly.

"You sure someone didn't give you the answers before you walked in here this morning, Random? Control is definitely an important part of the sales process. But again, I'm looking for something deeper. Dean? Have any ideas?"

"Ummm... not really." The fear in his was eyes apparent as he looked at his cousin.

"Mark, come up here."

The pull from my seat was like escaping gravity.

The Okie had something, not sure what, but he had something.

"Okay, you be the customer. I want you to go out the door you came in this morning and then come back in as an 'UP'."

I walked over to the door and pressed the horizontal bar, allowing a sliver of natural light into the room. The hallway smelled now of slightly burned coffee and co-mingled cologne, otherwise it was empty. I pushed back through the door and tried to do my best impression of 'Mr. Customer'.

"Hi, Welcome to Centennial Nissan." Gary extended his hand and I took it magnetically. Grasping my hand in his firmly he said, "I'm Gary."

"I'm Mark." I said automatically.

"I love you." He followed matter-of-factly.

"What?" I returned, trying to remove my hand from his as quickly as possible.

"Are you here for parts, sales or service, Mark?" my hand still firmly locked in his.

"Sales, I guess." I stammered,

'Did he just fucking say 'I Love You', or did I hallucinate that part?'

Glancing at Random, I noticed a smile curling on his lips.

"I love you."

He fucking said it again! What the cheese… whiz?

"Great, are you interested in a car, truck, suv?" he still hadn't dropped my hand.

"Truck."

"I love you. Let's go take a look." Mercifully he unclasped my hand and slapped me on the back.

"You can sit down now, Mark. Thanks for playing."

I slunk over to my seat, feeling somewhat violated.

"Who can tell me what I just demonstrated there."

"I don't even have an opinion on what just happened there." Random drawled; suddenly sounding a bit more ethnic. Joey and his cousin we're scared mute.

"Random. Look me in the eyes."

He slumped down a bit more in his seat and then rolled his eyes up to meet Gary's gaze, bulging them out a bit for effect.

"I love you."

"Motherfucker!" Random expelled, standing up to go.

"Hold on." Gary stopped him. "Sit down."

Random slumped back into the seat next to me again, his hands on the armrests ready to push himself up again.

"Relax, man." Gary admonished. "Let me ask you a question. How much does a hard loaded Maxima cost?"

"I dunno." Random answered warily, "thirty-two grand?"

"Thirty-two grand." Gary restated, walking to the dry-erase board again. "THIRTY-TWO GRAND!" he nearly yelled, writing the number enormously on the board, replete with dollar sign, comma and those little zeros that come after the decimal point. "You gonna give thirty-two grand to someone who doesn't love you Random? Mark? Dean?"

"No fuckin' way!" Joey answered.

"NO FUCKIN' WAY!" Gary yowled again, writing the words on the board in uppercase lettering. Then right next to that he wrote the words:

Love will find a way.

"NOBODY!" he said loudly to the wall, "Nobody," He restated softly, "cares how much you know, until they know how much you care."

He stood the dry-erase marker on end on the table in front of him, deliberately punctuating the statement.
"Okay," he said, "let's take a ten-minute break and then we'll address some nuts and bolts stuff."

I looked up at the industrial strength clock. It read 8:48.

Car Store – Chapter Two (Flashback)

How it happens.

I was nearly three decades old and not quite two years sober when my first daughter was born. She swallowed a bunch of amniotic fluid during the birth so she was having trouble breathing from the start. Barely three minutes old, I scooped her tiny body up in my arms as the nurse rushed us down to the NICU. In the intensive care, we placed her on a little bed and they covered her head with a Plexiglas bubble that pumped fresh oxygen into her struggling lungs. I'd never been more scared in my life, but the nurse assured me that this type of thing wasn't uncommon. Nonetheless, my wife and daughter had to spend a couple-three weeks in the hospital while she found the strength to start her new life.
Fortunately I'd been let go from my lousy landscaping job just prior to her birth so Medicaid paid for pretty much everything. This was auspicious because we were almost totally broke and couldn't have paid the medical bills even if we wanted to. One evening as I stood in the recovery room

cradling my newborn in my arms, her sleepy eyes looking up into mine, I heard the voice of my mother behind me.

"You're going to take care of me aren't you?" she stated sweetly in the third person. She might just as well have banged a gong in my ears. The gravity of the situation fell upon me like a ton of Chicago bricks. I needed to get my shit together... like yesterday!

Shortly thereafter, my wife and child returned home to our little duplex in the comfortable mountain town of North Evergreen, just west of the city. I sat in the living room pouring through the want ads in the paper, trying to find some sort of job that my skill set would afford me. What types of careers were available to an ex-pro ski-bum, ex-ad salesman, ex-bartender, ex-chumpsucker, and recovering alcoholic? I needed money and I needed it fast. Then I saw a boxed ad, among many others, that offered a guaranteed $1,500 per month.

Sell cars!!

I'd sold things before; people generally liked me; how hard could it be?

I had no idea.

Off I went in my 1987 Subaru GL wagon, wearing my nicest patterned shirt with a collar and my cleanest pair of khaki slacks. It was early May; the day was dreary and misty. Low clouds hung across the foothills like soggy blankets. Acrid blue smoke belched from the back of my shit-box gray wagon and mingled with the bruised, purple day.

The first store I stopped at was a gigantic Toyota dealership. I drove around the immense lot and looked at the merchandise. I knew it was a popular brand, especially in Colorado. They had rows and rows of little trucks, shiny SUV's, economy cars in every color imaginable. Glistening in the wet spring like steel-clad candy, who wouldn't want one? I found an inconspicuous place to park and pretended to be a customer, wandering from window sticker to window sticker trying to display a disconnected interest. It was a good fifteen minutes before anyone approached me.

A young man finally emerged from the gigantic showroom and shuffled slowly up to me beneath his umbrella.

"You like 4-Runner?" he asked in broken English. His accent was thick and blurry, like the misty rain... like my future.

"Yes." I answered, still trying to perpetuate the ruse of being a potential customer.

"You want light color or dark color?" the tone of his voice round and curt. Eastern European I guessed.

"Dark I guess. I live in the mountains, so I don't want it to show dirt."

"You want white. I be right back." And off he turned, not waiting for my response. So I stood in the drizzly morning watching water puddle around the tires of the cars, not really sure what to do next. Fortunately my new Baltic friend was back quickly with a set of keys and a magnetic license plate in hand.

"Let's go on test drive," He announced, slapping his plate onto the back of a white SUV, "here's keys."

'What the hell,' I thought, *'let's see how this works.'*

With that, I was on my first test drive, learning the ropes of what would prove to be a minimum of an eleven-year commitment. My initial foray into the heart of the beast, the self-devouring monster known by those in the know as simply: 'a car store'.

Five minutes into the process and I had to admit to the salesman that I was actually looking for a job and not interested in purchasing a vehicle. He seemed a bit relieved and directed me back on the quickest route to the dealership.

"Just go inside and ask for Manny." He said as he dropped me near the front door. "He can get you an application."

I could hear the Carpathian curses as he drove the SUV back to the line.

Walking into the hushed showroom, I looked about for the man in charge. No one greeted me upon my entrance. There was no receptionist at the front desk or any salespeople around at all. Glad to be out of the rain I wandered the tiled fishbowl looking for a manager, or at least some coffee for chrissake.

After about ten more minutes of gawking about, someone finally approached me.

"Can I help you sir?" the completely forgettable salesperson asked.
"I was actually hoping to apply for the sales job." I replied politely.
"You need Manny. I'll get him."

The sales manager materialized from some back room down a seemingly hidden hallway. His hair was very short, but somehow still slicked back. A crisp white shirt failed to hide his pudgy form and a gold wedding ring gripped his too chubby finger.
"Can I help you?" He half-asked; half-accused.
Turning to face him I extended my hand with all the politeness I could muster.
"I'm Mark Stapleton." I stated more flatly than I'd intended. "I'm interested in the sales position?"
"Come on back." He returned curtly, spinning on his heel and flicking his index finger behind his ear in a half-assed 'follow me to the killing room' gesture. Before I even heard the clicking of his heeled shoes on the tile, I knew I hated this fucker. Sucking in a breath quietly, I followed him into a small cubicle sized office that didn't have a real door, but a sliding glass one. 'Weird', I thought, but what the hell did I know.
Manny sat behind the metal desk and intertwined his fat little sweaty hands in front of him. An oversized watch bulged from the cuff of his shirt and clunked onto the Formica

desktop. I noticed the brand name on the face, Rolex of course. The wedding ring he wore was embedding itself into his fleshy phalange. It sported a diagonal stripe of small diamonds, three maybe, or was it five? He was clearly perturbed about something and didn't mind displaying it on his brow, a brow that was beaten and wrinkled by years of feigned disbelief. Obviously used to telling people how it is, he began the interrogation.

"So why would you come to an interview for a job where you know you need to wear a tie, without a tie on."
"I didn't know you needed a tie to sell cars." I retorted.
"Look at how I'm dressed." He continued.
"I have some ties at home." I murmured.
"Have you ever sold anything before?'
"Yes…" I started.
"Did you even bring a resume?"
"Yes I have one in my car."
"You come in for an interview with no tie, wash-n-wear slacks, no resume…"

I stared at him blankly. Not sure how to respond.

"I tell you what." He snorted, exhaling angrily through his nose. "Why don't you fill out an application and if it looks like we can use you, we'll give you a call."
"I actually have quite a bit of sales experience."
"Oh yeah?" he spouted, "Like what?"

'What a first-class jackass!' I thought to myself. *'What the fuck did I do?'*

"Well." I started again, "I sold advertising for several years, worked in real estate sales for three years after that…"
Manny rolled his eyes, leaned back in his chair, and looked at me like he'd just woken from a coma.
"Real estate, huh, so how'd that work out?" his tone was growing exceedingly acidic.
"Not so good actually," I responded, "pretty cutthroat."

"Yeah," he paused pensively, "cutthroat." he said it more to himself than me. "So do you expect that the, uh, car business will be any less, uh, cutthroat."

Not sure what to say, I mumbled something incomprehensible.

Manny's eyes bulged again, as if he had numerous important things to get done and interviewing me was clearly at the bottom of the list.

"What was that?" he asked curtly. "I didn't hear what you said."

"I'm not sure, I've never sold cars."

"Yeah, that's for sure."

"I'm sure given the opportunity…"

Manny exhaled strongly through his nose again.

"…I could rise to the occasion."

His fish-eyes bulged again at my statement; so far out this time that I could see the broken vessels that held them inside his skull… just barely.

"You know what," he said in an unquestioning tone, "I'm done."

"What?" I asked in disbelief.

"What? You didn't hear me?" he mocked, slapping his sweaty mitts on the desk, leaving greasy paw prints as he pressed himself up from the chair.

"I don't think we can help you here."

"So you don't want me to fill out an application?"

"Sure, fill one out. Go up front and ask for Sharon."

"So that's it?"

"Yeah, that's it."

As he clicked down the hallway, back to whatever cave from which he'd emerged; I turned on my rubber soled shoes and crept to the front desk.

The girl-woman at the front sat insipidly at her raised semicircle shaped desk. A gigantic phone sat to her right and an equally large notepad rested on the desktop in front of her. I shuffled up to her and asked for an application. Her indifference bordered on the edge of hatred as she reached into a file drawer somewhere beneath her ridiculous phone.

"Here." She stated flatly, slapping the several page packet on the counter.

"Okayyyyy…" I said, mostly to myself as I turned from her desk.

'These people are fuckin' psycho.'

Finding a small round table in a forgotten corner of the showroom floor, I perused the pages. The first couple were standard, you know; name, address, phone #, followed by the 'are you an American citizen page'. But as I delved into the packet, the pages grew darker and more insidious. Page 4 began with a series of questions that I really felt were no one's business. What is your marital status? How many children do you have? Do you currently or have you ever smoked marijuana? How often? Have you ever committed or been charged with a felony?

'Have you ever had anal sex…? In prison or elsewhere?'

Okay, so the last two weren't on the application, but regardless, there was no way I was going to waste another minute of my fucked-up life in this place. Flipping the packet closed, I wandered slowly back to the receptionist's desk.

"That was fast." She spouted disinterestedly.

"Yeah," I returned, "I don't think I'm cutout for this place."

"Well, okay then."

Taking the packet from off the counter, she turned back to stone. I circumnavigated her desk, pushed through the glass doors and back into the grayish-white day.

Chapter Three (Still Flashing Back)

A copy of the Home Game...

Awakened by the cries of my baby daughter, I stumbled one eyed to her tiny bedroom to see what was the matter. The pungent stench from her diaper opened my other eye for me, as well as my nostrils. Lifting her tiny frame from the crib to the changing table, I removed the offending diaper and stuffed it, tightly wrapped, into the robot-like diaper disposal bin. Cleaning her up with an overtly aromatic wet-wipe I slid a new diaper from the drawer and buttoned her tiny little jammies around it. Gathering her gingerly up from the table I rocked her slowly back and forth, praying for her sleep to come again quickly.

As luck was still not with me, I brought her quietly to our bed and laid her between us. At a loss for lullabies, I sang an old Bob Marley tune to her. My wife shifted in her sleep. I sang a bit more softly. My little peanut fluttered her giant eyes then stuck her pudgy hand into her mouth. Sucking on it sleepily she found her solace and soon after was sleeping, well... like a baby. Me, I was not so lucky. Lying in our bed staring at the popcorn ceiling, my mind groped for its next move. That first interview had gone very poorly. I felt that I'd lain there for hours, but it was probably only about fifteen minutes before my worried mind found sleep as well.

Up again with the dawn, I found my way upstairs to the kitchen and started a pot of coffee. Impatient for the brew to start, I used an old restaurant trick from back in the day and stuck a mug right under the filter. Turning quickly, I fumbled for a pack of smokes. Caffeine and nicotine would become my new drugs of choice; fuel for the wicked, vices of the damned.

Pulling the mug from under the persistent stream and deftly stuffing the pot back into its place, I spilled only a drop or two onto the sizzling burner. I dumped a pile of milk into the morning glory and exited through the sliding door onto our ridiculously small deck. Rumpled want ads clenched in one hand I lit a butt with the other, cringing as the hot smoke billowed into my eye.

Slapping the paper open angrily, I scanned the ads with my good eye and squeezed bleary tears from the bad one. Anyone watching from below might have thought I was a pirate, all squinty and bedraggled as I was. They wouldn't have been too far from the truth; as I would soon have to make semi-public knowledge. Setting my cigarette on top of the overflowing ashtray, I looked over the want ads a bit more intently. Tracing the page with my finger I came upon what would prove to be the one. Centennial Nissan was seeking professional sales people, 'experience preferred but not necessary'.

'Now that was a bit more my speed.'

Circling the ad I crushed out my butt and took a large swig of coffee. I pulled the sliding door open and crept back into our kitchen/living room.

My wife and daughter had risen in my absence.

"I think she's scared of flowers." My wife stated through her laughter.
"What?"
"Our daughter, I think she is scared of flowers."
"Really?" I asked.
"You know those roses you got for me?"
"Yeah?"
"Well every time I get near them with her, she cries."
"Huh," I chuckled, "weird thing to be afraid of."
"Yeah." She said, "Did you find another dealership to apply at yet?"

"Yeah, there is a Nissan dealer down the street from that Toyota store."

"Cool."

"I wonder if I should call first."

"Maybe," she offered.

"You know, set a real appointment."
"Maybe." She said again.

"Yeah, I'll call first."

Pouring myself another mug of coffee I sat down with the paper. Looking up at the clock I noticed it was about eight.

"Wonder what time they open?"

She was occupied with feeding the baby.

"I guess I'll just call now."
"What?" she asked disconnectedly.
"I said I'll call now."
"That's my sweet little stinky-butt." She whispered to the baby.

I decided to call the dealership now.

"Centennial Nissan?" the pleasant woman answered, "How may I help you?"
"Hi," I returned with my most professional voice, "This is Mark Stapleton. I'm inquiring about the sales position?"
"You need to speak to Brick, one moment please."
'Did she say Brick?'
"This is Brick."
"Hi…" I responded, taken a bit off guard. "I'm um, interested in the sales position."
"Can you come down now?"
"Well I live in Evergreen."

"Okay so you can be here by nine?"

The clock read 8:08.

"Ummm, sure I guess I could be there by nine."

"Great, see ya then."

I was left with a dial tone.

"So you got an interview?" My wife asked distractedly.

"Yeah, have to leave like right now."

"Okay," she said more to the baby than me, "Good luck, Daddy."

*　*　*

The day was roofed with a bluebird sky as I trundled up the driveway in my old piece of crap. Ponderosa pines lined the tiny paved streets of my North Evergreen neighborhood, their needles glistening in the morning sun as if coated with rainbow-colored diamonds. I peeled the goofy bug-eyed sunglasses off my head and slid them over my ears. Feeling my optic nerves relax, I lit another cigarette and squinted through the blue smoke and badly pitted windshield. Small white clouds hung like a mobile above Mean's Meadow. It felt good to be back in my old hometown, regardless of the reasons.

Leaving the relative safety of the foothills, I merged onto I-70. It seemed that traffic was already moving at a frenetic pace. Pushing my thirteen year old Subaru to the limit, I managed to weave my way into the current. Fortunately the ten mile stretch to Lakewood was a downhill run. Letting the vehicle roll more than drive, I pushed the odometer needle past the eighty mile per hour mark. Other drivers flew past me as though I were standing still. Thank the gods my dashboard was only shaking a little bit. Pressing an old Soundgarden CD into the player, I drowned out the ludicrous morning.

It wasn't even fifteen minutes before I reached West Colfax. I hadn't remembered people driving this fast when I was kid. Of course when I was a kid I had my Grand Pa Pa's old muscle car, and much less respect for the law. Passing the malls and office buildings, I wondered how I'd ended up back here; I fuckin' hated cities.

Things were different now, though. I had a baby and a wife now, people that depended on me to find my ball sack every morning. Chris Cornell wailed through my worn-out speakers. My hand clutched the steering wheel, glossy with over a decade of use. My eyes scanned the west urban skyline, which was not quite so glossy, regardless of the years of use. I lit another smoke and cracked the window a couple inches. The exhale was grayer now, dustier.

'I can do this.'

Chapter Four (Still, Still Flashing Back)

<u>Larceny in your heart...</u>

The Nissan sign rose above the pavement like Japan from the ashes of Nagasaki. I couldn't cross directly into the dealership because the median ran the length of the block. Cruising to the next stoplight, I whipped an illegal U-turn and chirped the tires briefly in the process. Passing the first entrance to the lot, I opted for the second. The glare from the hu-normous windows of the showroom glimmered up my windshield. I slowly passed beneath the watchful eyes of no less than eight salespeople. They stood on the elevated cement porch like magpies.

Finding a space in the area marked 'Customer Parking' I killed the engine. Sliding a stick of gum from a fresh pack of Wrigley's, I straightened my Dad's old tie in my rearview mirror. It was too wide, but at least the polka dots were small. The warmth of May felt good on my face as I climbed from the driver's seat and headed across the small parking lot. A long cement ramp led down from the double doors of the showroom, a royal blue railing traced the edge with perfect symmetry. I felt each step through the soles of my worn out shoes as I traversed the small parking lot.

"Welcome to Centennial Nissan." A perfectly groomed man of my approximate age stated confidently. His clean hand extended to greet mine, fingers slightly down, thumb cocked, poised to collect me.

"Hi." I returned boldly. "I'm here to see Brick."

"Cool. Here for the sales job?"

"Yep."

"I'll introduce you."

He climbed the ramp slowly, stepping methodically. I met his gait and climbed along with him.

"Ever sell cars before?" He asked.

"Nope, first time."

The double doors swooshed open automatically and a blast of cool, clean air filled our nostrils. It was full of new leather and tire rubber sheen. Tiles like dinner plates were polished to godliness. Three beautiful new cars waited patiently on the floor, perfectly spaced, impossibly clean. A nicely tanned receptionist sat to our right in front of a wall of keys, to our left was a tall counter, walled with glass. Two men sat behind the counter, thoroughly disinterested in our presence.

"Cherie here can get you an application." He stated as if he owned the place, doing a double handed point at the receptionist. "I'll tell Brick you're here."

"Good morning." I said to the dark skinned woman with a slight frame.

"Hello," she returned sweetly, "You need an application."

"Yes, please."

"Ok." She smiled, setting the package of paper on the blue Formica countertop.

"You must be Mark." a self-confident voice stated firmly from behind me.

"Yes, Mark Stapleton." I returned quickly, turning to offer my hand. He took it in his rotating mine vertically and pulling me away from the counter.

"Thanks for coming down so fast. Let's find you a place to fill that stuff out."

"Great."

Leading me to a small grey office that was again fronted with a sliding glass door, he had me sit behind the desk.

"Try to fill out the application as completely as possible then bring it up to the tower. Got a pen?"

I held up the pen I'd brought in front of me.

"Perfect."

'The tower?' I thought to myself. *'What the hell is that supposed to mean?'*

I filled out the ridiculously long application with my best block writing. Then I came to the part about ever being arrested. I was pretty sure that my record had been expunged.

Back in my drinking days, my girlfriend had gotten popped for stealing some art from a gallery. Unaware of what was actually transpiring, I'd found myself unwillingly driving the 'getaway' car. Well I wasn't actually driving, more just sitting in the parking lot in a drunken stupor. The judge had taken pity on my stupid alcoholic ass and allowed me to enter a treatment center instead of the prison system. It had been almost two years since the infraction and I'd met all the terms of my probation. Sitting in the glassy grey box I stared nervously out through the door at the showroom, my pen stalled over the application.

About five minutes had passed before I decided I better just come clean. Rising from the desk I tiptoed to the giant glass walled area that I could only assume was the 'tower'. An 'Employee's Only' sign hung from a couple wires that extended down from the ceiling. I stood in front of the sign, not sure what to do next. Brick sat at the far end of the counter behind the sign and a dark haired gentleman with a bushy mustache was to his left. He was squawking at the salesman in front of him. It was something about 'skating' and the 'up log'. He might as well have been speaking an ancient Scandinavian dialect. I stood squeamishly in front of the glass like an English orphan, the application clutched in my hands an empty bowl. Ned, as I would come to find out was his name, looked up at me through the glass and his bushy eyebrows rose questioningly.

"I have a question about this application." I said through the glass.

"We're done." He stated curtly to the salesman in front of him. "Don't fuckin' do that again!" Ned's face curled into a slightly sideways smile and the salesman came out from under the dangling sign and slinked out through the whoosh of the sliding glass doors.

"Come on around." He said, motioning with two fingers in a 'come hither' gesture.

I stepped quickly into the area in front of the desk, knocking my head on the sign and sending it bouncing back and forth on its wires. Grabbing it quickly, I steadied it back into place. Brick looked up from his computer screen with a bit of a snicker. Ned smiled knowingly back.
"Did you get it all filled out?" Brick asked with a slightly patronizing tone. I looked down at him from over the counter. His gaze was piercing, pupils the size of pinheads. My eyes fell to the application,
"Um... I'm not sure how to fill this part out." I mumbled.
"Which part?" he asked again sardonically, his bluish-green eyes flicking over to Ned briefly. I sensed the sideways smile forming on Ned's face even though I wasn't looking at him.

"Well…" I started, "this part about ever being arrested."

"Let's go back into the office again for a second." Brink intoned secretively.

Brick and Ned followed me into the first of five 'offices' and slid the glass door shut behind them.

"Have a seat." Ned said comfortingly, motioning to the chair behind the desk. Brick sat on the corner and Ned placed both hands on the desktop, leaning in over the desk to my right. I felt about three feet tall, all that was missing was the spotlight.

"Let me see your application." Brick demanded calmly. He read through the first two pages intently but quickly. His studious eyes scanned the pages with the efficiency of a cougar scoping out his prey. He looked up at Ned and smiled. I did actually have a lot of customer service and sales experience. Perhaps my application would speak for itself. Ned smiled back at Brick, crow's feet burst out like sunbeams around the corners of his eyes. He turned his face back to mine, closely, but not too close.

"What'd'cha do?" he asked.

"Well it wasn't actually me so much as my girlfriend." I exhaled. "We were at a birthday party at a bar over the pass from where we lived…"

"Sounds familiar," said Brick, "go on."

"We were leaving town and my girlfriend saw an art gallery and told me to pull over. So she could, you know, look at the art. I was pretty drunk and just wanted to get home so I stayed in the car. Then I heard the sound of breaking glass…"

They were both listening intently now, seemingly more interested in the story than my indiscretion.

"A few minutes later the crazy bitch was loading art work into the back of my wagon. Turns out we were pretty much right across the street from the police station. So of course we got busted. Let me just say this though, that was two years ago and my record has been expunged. I don't drink anymore and I've got a baby daughter now so I really need a good job."

Brick smiled. "I don't drink anymore either."

"Just leave that section blank." Ned said.
"Leave it blank?"
"We've all made mistakes." Brick assured me, "It helps to have a little larceny in your heart in this business."

I looked at him with what must've been disbelief.

"So the next training session starts Monday, right." Ned asked Brick.
"Yeah, next Monday."
"So can you be here next Monday at 8:00 sharp?" Ned asked me.
"So I'm hired?"
"If you do well in the training I think we can find a place for you here."
"Really?"
"Be here next Monday." Said Brick, arching his arm over the desk.

I shook his hand automatically, not really sure what had just happened.

"Welcome to the team."
"Welcome to the team." Ned parroted.
"Okay," I said in a faraway voice, a voice that didn't quite seem like mine.

"See you Monday."

Chapter Five – (Present Day)

Follow the Gold Brick Road.

The frost had nearly melted off of all the car windows and beads of water were glistening on their roofs as we found our way into the steel morning sun. It wasn't even nine o'clock yet and we'd already had a full day. Random and I reviewed our morning over little Styrofoam cups of coffee and Camel Lights.

"That guy is kinda intense, hey?" I started.
"I can't believe you didn't punch that freak." Random jabbed.
"He was just trying to make a point."
"Yeah well he better just keep his point away from my ass."
I laughed, taking a long pull from my smoke and pushing on my sunglasses.
"So you worked at a dealership before?" I switched gears.
"Yeah. Those fuckers at O'Calla wouldn't give me a shot at sales, so here I am. I probably know as much about Nissans as most of the guys workin' here."
"That should help."
"Yeah." He hot-boxed his smoke, dropping ashes down the front of his tie. "Shit," he exclaimed brushing them away frantically.
"Jesus bro," I chuckled again, "you're as nervous as a long-tailed cat…"
"In a room full of rocking chairs?"

"You got it." I smiled, feeling a bit like that weird boogery character in *'Risky Business'*. "Let's go back in there and see what else this freak has to say."

"Might as well," Random droned, "got nothin' else to do."

"What the Fuck?" I punctuated, trying to do my best Tom Cruise impression.

Random looked at me, his face an empty chalkboard.

When we reentered the back room of the 'Hogan', Gary had already set some new paperwork on our respective chairs. The cousins were trying to read through their packets together and looking very confused.

"Random, Mark, thanks for joining us again. Have a seat."

Gary had also erased the board, except for the word 'love'. Random looked up at the board and immediately turned sideways in his seat again.

Writing quickly across the top of the board we saw the words, 'The Steps to the Sale' come into view.

"Random, tell me the first step to the sale." Gary said without turning around.

"Meet and Greet." He answered flatly.

"That's right." He wrote the words next to a number one, which he circled. "Meet and Greet. Or perhaps we should say greet then meet. Of course until you greet someone, it is difficult to really meet them. So we know that you are supposed to welcome them to the dealership then get to know them.

"How do you get to know someone, Mark?"

"Tell them you love them Gary?"

"Very glib, Mark, very glib, but you are partially right."

"How do you get a girl to have sex with you Joey?"

"Get her drunk?"

"Well that's one way, but how do you get a girl to have sex with you twice."

"Make her breakfast?" Deano piped in, high-fiving his cousin in the meantime.

"Good answer, but no. You ask her about herself, get to know her. Build a relationship."

"Find common interests." Random tried.

"Good point, Random. How do you find common ground with someone?"

"Ask what they like to do?"

"Very good, Random. People love to talk about themselves. They don't care if you're broke, used to be a pro-skier, listen to Black Sabbath, etc. etc. They want to talk about themselves."

"Who knows what active listening is?" Gary continued.

Silence.

"Great."

"What?" Random asked.

"Active listening is when you shut up and listen to what a potential customer is telling you and then respond accordingly."

My hand was already growing tired from scribbling notes. It felt like school and it had been a long time for me.

"Mark, how did you get your wife to marry you?"

"I'm not sure I'm going to give you the answer you're looking for."

"Okay, let me ask the question a different way. Why did your wife marry you?"

"Um, because she was pregnant."

"So she married you because she was pregnant?"

"Well you see she is from Georgia and she's a Baptist and..."

"Stop right there." He wheeled around and pointed at me.

"Do you think your wife married you because you knocked her up?"

"Well it's as good a reason as any, I guess."

"Bullshit!"

'Here he goes again,' I thought *'this guy has got a lot of damn gall!'*

"Do you love your wife?" he asked accusingly.
"Do you love your wife?" I retorted.
"Yes. But that isn't what I asked."
"Uh Gary, you're getting little personal don't you think?"
"I'm not paid to think, Mark, I'm paid to act. Just answer the question."

'Fucker!'

"Do you love your wife?"
"Yes! Jesus!"
"Do you love your baby daughter?"

'Holy bitch-weasel, this guy doesn't hold anything sacred!'

"What do you think, Gary?" I was beginning to get angry now.
"I think you do, but that's not what I'm asking."
"Of course I love my daughter!"
"Okay then, perfect."

He returned to the board and started scribbling again.

Married – loves wife
Has Daughter – loves daughter

"What did I just do Joey?"
"Pissed off Stapleton?"
"Random?"
"Found common ground."

"Yes, exactly," Mark and I are both married and love our wives and children. "Bingo, active listening."

"Huh." I realized aloud.

"You like this shit, Stapleton?"

"I guess I do Gary."

"Good, go sell a car."

"Right now?"

"No not till Thursday, I still have to get paid. But I'll buy you lunch for being such a good sport."

*****

The burger joint across the street was jammed between a porn store and a bowling alley. I sat with Gary and Random at a high table that hadn't been thoroughly cleaned in probably twenty-thirty years. The place was a flurry of activity and packed to the gills. A few of the other salespeople were running in and out, taking their lunches to go. The snowy television above Gary's head showed a picture of George W Bush. It was the year 2000 and he was running for president. I'd never cared much for politics as politicians had never seemed to care much about me. It didn't really seem to matter which party was running (or not running) the show.

"Think Bush is gonna win, Mark?" Random asked.

I looked over at him; there was shredded iceberg lettuce all down his tie.

"Are you seriously asking me that question?'

"Yeah," he asked and then, "Fuck!" as he brushed the lettuce off, smearing thousand-island dressing into the fabric.

"You know his Dad was down with the CIA since before it was even called the CIA right?"

"Yeah," Random fumbled, "I mean, no. What the crap does that have to do with anything?"

"Dude, it's all set up." I hissed arrogantly. "There is not a doubt in my mind that Bush will be president."

"I don't think he's gonna win."

I looked at Gary as if to say, *help me out here*.

"You're not really that naïve are ya', Random?" Gary asked.

"What?"

"They're like royalty, Random." I warbled, "Except way worse."

"It's all set up." Gary said.

"It's all set up." I agreed.

We sat in silence for a while and ate our lunch. I dipped my fries in mayonnaise doused with black pepper. It felt good to have a nice, hot lunch especially since I didn't have to pay for it.

"It's kinda like the car business if you think about it." Gary said, glomming down his own pile of fries.

"What?" Random questioned.

"It's all set up so that we win."

"You mean like a casino?" I inquired.

"Well it's not quite that easy, Mark. But think about it. Everyone needs cars. The dealership has what, like two hundred of them, three-hundred? They are all perfect, or at least appear perfect. You're situated on the busiest street in the Denver Metro area, your boss has virtually unlimited funds. All you gotta do is show up. You can't lose."

"So what do we need *you* for?" Random chided.

"Good question." Gary mused.

"Care to answer that question?" I prodded.

"I'm like Glinda."

"Glinda? Who the fuck is Glinda?" Random asked.

"The good witch of the North." I said.

"The good what of the where?" he drawled.

"Very astute, Stapleton." Gary interjected, "Care to enlighten our young friend here?"

"You ever see the Wizard of OZ?"

"Yeah, everybody's seen that shit?"

"Glinda is the one who shows Dorothy the Yellow Brick Road."

"Exactly Mark, only this road… this road has bricks of gold." Gary punctuated profoundly.

"I hear that!" Random cheered. Raising his soda cup, "Here's to the golden brick road!"

Raising my cup I looked up at George W on the set. I wasn't sure what he was talking about, but he sounded like the adult's voices on the old Peanuts cartoons. I just glad to hear from Gary that I might not get a rock in my trick or treat bag this year.

"Salud!" I cried.

"Cheers." Gary added.

Chapter Six

Making it happen.

I awoke to the sound of my hungry daughter crying in her crib. My wife was already sliding from under the covers to retrieve her. The red digital numbers on the alarm clock glared 2:22. Throwing the covers over my head, I knew I wouldn't find sleep again that night. I heard the soothing clicks and clucks of my bride and she pulled our daughter from her crib. Her crying reached a higher pitch as her diaper was changed. Then her sobs were muffled against my wife's breast. I could feel my bloodshot eyes beneath my tired lids. The training session had gone well. Deano didn't show up the second day and Joey never found his way back after lunch, so Random and I had earned our positions mostly by default.

The second day and a half of training went by with a minimum of '*I Love You's*' and a maximum amount of information. I lay in bed for another ten minutes then pulled myself up and tiptoed upstairs. Retrieving the spiral notepad that Gary had given us, I reviewed the dog-eared pages. 'Make a Friend' on one of the pages was underlined. *'Easy enough.'* I thought to myself. 'S P A C E D' read the headline on another page. I strained my memory to remember what the acronym signified. Safety, Performance, uh, Economy, uh....

'Ben Franklin', the next page read. Next to that I'd written 'Needs Analysis'. *'Oh yea..'* I recalled. Ben Franklin used to make a list of pros and cons before making a decision. 'Sell yourself, sell the dealership, sell the car.' Another line read. The Husky pencil was beginning its scribble again.

Setting the notepad down on the couch we'd borrowed from my sister, I lifted myself again and stared out the window. Floodlights dotted the hillsides of the surrounding homes. North Evergreen was an interesting amalgamation of old summer cabins, 80's duplexes and nicer homes that had been built during the various boom times. It was a funny mix. I wondered what kind of person each of the floodlights represented. Did these people go to college? Did the garbage man live in that one; a doctor perhaps... in the one on top? Maybe marijuana dealers in that crappy old cabin with the split log siding, the bark still peeling from its slats. I wondered what they might all be doing at this hour; the garbage man at his breakfast table, smoking a Pall Mall and drinking Navy coffee, the doctor cradling his sexy young wife, the dope dealers drooling on their pillows in their comatose slumber. Who knew? But there they were, leading out their lives with no knowledge or concern for my own.

Green digital numbers glowed forth from the crappy little microwave positioned on the corner of the kitchen counter. Sliding the small coffee maker from its place next door I quietly opened the cabinet above. The giant metal can caught the orange glow of the lonely streetlight that streamed in through the tiny kitchen window. The scoop was buried deeply in the grounds so I found a filter and sifted them into it directly from the can. The pot clicked audibly as I unstuck it from the grimy burner and slipped it under the faucet. Turning it on to only a small trickle I watched it fill slowly. As I poured the water through the grate on top of the Mr. Coffee, nearly a third found its way onto the counter.

"Fuck." I whispered under my breath, searching for a dish towel.

Soon enough the element was heating up and the machine sighed with familiar puffs of steam followed by the blissful gurgling sounds. I heard my wife downstairs shuffling back to bed from the baby's room. Ripping the filter from a smoke, I slid the glass door back and emerged onto the porch. The glow of the city lights traced the thin horizon of the black foothills to the east. It was still chilly in the wee hours of the May morning. Flicking my lighter aflame, I pulled the coffin nail to life. Exhaling hard against the briskness, a cloud of blue smoke peeled out from my lips.

'*You should've finished college,*' my mind taunted.
"But you didn't." I said aloud.

Thoughts swirled in my brain about the new career I'd chosen.
How would I learn this game? The people I'd met so far seemed so full of shit, so cynical. Was this me? Had I become that person already, not even yet a full three decades young?
"Wait a minute?" I whispered aloud. "What day is today?"
Setting the cigarette down on the railing, I stumbled back into the darkened duplex. I opened the fridge to avoid turning on any lights and looked up at the calendar on the wall to my right.

"No fuckin' way." I whispered.

It was my birthday. My twenties were over.

****

The sunglasses were barely blocking the glare from my eyes as I made my way back onto I-70. The pot of coffee I'd already downed was weighing heavily on my bladder as I raced into West Denver with the rest of the psychos. The radio announcers were cackling crows, pushing their fake laughter out onto the airwaves. I was wishing they'd play some goddamn music. It was just after eight o'clock and even though I'd been up since just after two, I was somehow in danger of being late. My foot innately pressed down on the accelerator and soon the car was weaving its way into the fast lane. It hadn't taken me long to join the flow of traffic in their morning commute. As I crested the first hill, the flat city lay before me, nestled under a brown blanket of smog.

Mercifully the radio began to play a little Zeppelin. I think it was one of the more obscure songs off the Physical Graffiti album... the one that started out like a swarm of locusts. Spinning the volume dial up several decibels, I leaned my head back and glared out through the bottom of my shades. Plant was yowling something about '...your wheel sinkin' low.' I felt every bit of thirty. Fortunately traffic was light for a Friday morning so I could enjoy the tune without being fronted by a bunch of angry travelers. The trip to Lakewood normally took about twelve minutes on the interstate, but within eight, I'd found my way to 6th Avenue. In five more I'd be at the dealership. The Eagles followed Zeppelin with 'Take It Easy'; so I was feeling slightly more relaxed and less old by the time my balding tires found their spot in the employee parking.

The first few salesmen were milling about in front of the used car Hogan as I made my way over. Steam rose from the frosty grass on which I walked. I shuffled my feet a bit with the hope the moisture would remove some of the dust from my un-shined shoes. Random was already there, smoking of course.

"I thought I was late."

"Naw," Random replied glancing at his watch. "It's only 8:17."

"Cool." I breathed back, shaking a bent smoke from my own crumpled pack.

It seemed that everyone was smoking and nobody was standing still. It struck me rather comically as I scanned the group. They were all moving their hands about, or shifting from foot to foot, or flicking invisible specks from their shirts. Not so much nervous as really more… agitated.

'City people.' I thought to myself.

"You ready?" Random said.
"Ready for what?" I answered crankily.
"Our first day."
"It's my birthday." I said absently, searching my pockets for a lighter. Random reached over and offered his.
"Happy Birthday, how old is you?"

"Thirty."

"Jesus," he blurted, "You're old. I mean I thought you were like twenty-five or something."
"Thanks a pant-load, Random; and I didn't think I could be any more depressed than I already was."
The loudspeaker blared to life above us.

"ALL SALES PERSONNEL TO THE CONFERENCE ROOM, ALL SALES PERSONNEL TO THE CONFERENCE ROOM."

It was a phrase with which I would become all too familiar. Stubbing our smokes out on top of the ashtray/garbage cans we entered the Hogan.
We filed into the back room where we'd had our training and found our seats amongst no less than twenty-five other salesmen. Most of them were in their early twenties. I felt old again. Brick stood at the front of the room with three other managers, one of which was an Arabian looking gentleman I'd never seen before. He wore an odd looking, multi-colored tie that had what looked like an earring attached to it in a weird spot. It resembled one of those gold studs that the junior high school girls wore around when they first got their ears pierced. It was knotted around the white collar at his neck; the rest of the shirt was a ribbed lavender color. Clearly

expensive and neatly pressed; it somehow still looked cheap and out of date. The room smelled of cologne and smoke. At the edge of the seating arrangement sat two older people, one woman and one man. They both seemed annoyed and thoroughly disinterested, as though they had at least a million other places they'd rather be.

We sat like river rocks as the managers surveyed us, quietly joking with one another. I had the distinct feeling that everyone was in on something to which I was not privy. There was a comfort level these guys were bathing in, like a welcome breeze at a tailgate party. I wasn't really sure I liked it, but I wanted to know more. The side door clicked open and the room went silent. Gavin Johnson strode in with a paper towel clutched in one of his smallish hands. His brow was knitted behind his giant, eighties style horn rimmed glasses. A gray three-piece suit armored his little Saxon body. He tore off his suit jacket, finished wiping his hands on the paper towel then crumpled it up theatrically and chucked it into a nearby waste basket.

"How many cars you got out, Tristan?" he challenged the nearest salesman.

"Eight." Tristan returned.
"How many cars you got out, Milo?"
"Five."
"How many, John?"
"Three."

This went on with every salesperson in the room until he'd singled out each and every one. Then he wheeled around and put his suit jacket back on, smoothing the collar down and shooting his cuffs. With his back to the room he said something to Brick just loud enough for everyone to hear.

"Fix this shit."

I sat up a bit straighter in my chair and looked at Random with an expression that said something like,

'What the fuck was that?'

He rolled his eyes back at me as though he'd seen it a million times. The other salespeople shifted nervously in their chairs as Brick positioned himself in the center of the room. Ned and the other two managers flanked him, shifting their knowing gazes from one another and then out at the staff. After a second look I realized that there were no less than thirty salespeople arranged about the room, including Random and I.

"What day is today?" Brick began, to no one in particular. The silence was palpable. Brick's yellowy, blue-green eyes scanned the room, the only sound the dull hum of the overhead lights.

"WHAT DAY IS TODAY?" he repeated, making it clear that the question was not rhetorical. The salespeople looked around at one another, nobody wanting to be the first to talk.

"The seventeenth." I offered, too green to know the difference. Ned smiled at one of the other managers behind Brick. It was the disheveled one that I remembered from the other day. His woven leather belt was strained beneath his protruding belly, the buckle pushed off to one side as though it were put on in a massive hurry.

"Thank you Mark," Brick nearly yelled to the room. "At least someone knows what day it is."

"It's his birthday." Random added.

Brick's expression softened briefly. He reminded me of Harvey Keitel's character in 'Pulp Fiction', right after Tarantino gave him that cup of coffee.

"Happy Birthday." He chided, "We'll be sure to get you a cake later."

I felt my complexion turn about three shades of crimson as the entire room chuckled at my expense.

"The seventeenth." Brick continued. "So how many selling days do we have left?"

The room again fell silent. Some of the salesman would've clearly rather danced across hot coals then answer.

"Anyone?" Brick kept on.

Obviously no one wanted to speak.

"Eleven." He answered his own question. "I guess that means you need at least a car a day to make the board, John."

The salesman that had only three cars out slunk down in his chair a bit further.

"Five cars, Milo? Maybe I should see if my sister can come help you."

Milo glared past him at the shoddily dressed used car manager. The harried man reciprocated the glare with an equal ice-blue intensity.

"You got something to say, Milo?" Brick challenged.
"No sir." Milo stated evenly.

"Good."

Brick began to pace slowly back and forth in front of the staff, his perfectly pressed slacks just brushing the tops of his two tone loafers.

"We need to pick up the *picante*, boys and girls."

I looked around the room, there was only one woman. She seemed to be somewhere in her mid-fifties, but her once blond hair was showing some signs of gray.

"We've got eleven selling days left and except for Tristan, I'd guess that no one in here is tracking their goal."

The nervousness of the salespeople took on an audible quality, like a bear waking in his den. Even the other managers we're sharing shaky glances at one another. Random surveyed Brick's speech with his disinterested gaze, a long finger rested pensively across his upper lip. Brick spun on his heel and stood stock still, again at the center of the room.

"We've got thirty-two used and fifty-six new out as of today. We need forty more by the end of Saturday."

Brick turned to the used car manager with mock dismay.

"You want to take over, Mik? I'm feeling sick."

The used car manager grabbed a plastic chair and strode front and center. Brick faded back like a white James Brown, shoulders hunched, his hand over his mouth.

"This is a chair." Mik started. His speech flustered. Wispy hair clung to his rapidly balding dome like milkweed.

"It has a four-leg suspension, an orange polymer top…" his speech was excited yet exasperated. The bottom buttons of his barely tucked in shirt were sticking out oddly over the top of his wrinkled pants.

"Look at these rivets;" he kept on, "they're completely flush with the top." His large, thick hands brushed the seat of the molded chair. It suddenly began to seem less ordinary.

"These vents in the back provide for maximum air flow without sacrificing adequate support for your lumbar."

I felt myself wanting to sit in the damn thing as he painted the picture of comfort and functionality.

"Look at the color; classic racing orange… I'd buy one." He added with a bit of red-neckky twang.

A few snickers rippled through the room. He took a couple steps back and viewed the chair lovingly. It sat quietly in the center of the room. Morning sun streamed through the high windows as we viewed it in silence. Sensing the point was made, his tone became slightly less comedic.

"Do you think you could maybe apply some of this to selling cars this weekend?"

He turned to the room. His stare was again ice-blue, bordering tungsten gray, and far away… far, far away. With his striped tie cocked to the side he resembled a hybrid of Gene Wilder and Yogi Bear.

'Smarter than the average bear.' I mused.

"I'm done." He said to no one in particular, stepping back to let someone else have a turn. I felt a little like clapping.

Ned sauntered in from the side, shaking something from his pocket and tossing it into his mouth. Chewing whatever it was as he talked, he stopped just short of the center of the room.

"Guys," he whispered loudly, "This isn't rocket science."

His hands rose to either side of his shoulders, his fingers splayed out for effect.

"It's all set up so that we win. Just get out there and find a customer today. When you get that customer, put a tack in their foot and don't let 'em go until you get a commitment. When you get the commitment, get a deposit. When they give you a deposit, fill out a credit app. We'll take it from there, I promise; it's just that simple."

A cricked smile crept out from under his bushy but neatly trimmed mustache. His were eyes alight with something that bordered on fascination, as though he were sharing some sort of ages old wisdom wrapped with a bow.

"It's so simple, it's practically criminal."

Stepping back to the side, he kept his crow's footed smile trained on us. I was strangely calmed and nauseous at the same time.

"You got anything?" Brick said to the Arabian looking man.

"No," he said in a deep, tired tone, "nothing." His expression as he glared out from his profile displayed anything but nothing. He looked a little like Billy Joel on the back of that old record. You know the one, where Billy's bedraggled face was staring coldly out through a broken window. I could almost see the jagged glass framing his face.

"Ok." Brick summated, "Let's go."

Chapter Seven

"What's the matter with the car I'm drivin'?"

Random and I stood at the back of a little Sentra on the showroom floor. He was explaining to me how the rain channels on the deck lid would keep the rain from running into the trunk by directing the water around the sides, down behind the bumper and onto the ground. His explanation was very smooth and somehow interesting, even though I couldn't imagine how or why I would ever need this feature; nor would I choose the valium shaped compact as my ride. Brick noticed what we were doing and shuffled up next to us.

"Whatcha doin' boys?" he asked with a note of sarcasm.
"I'm showing Mark how the rain channels work." Random replied.
"I don't think *I* even know how those work." Brick said, "Show us again."
Random did the presentation again, using his hands a bit more for theatrical purposes.

"Well done, Random." Brick said pleasantly, "That was a brilliant presentation. I just have one question."

"What's that?"

"Is Stapleton gonna buy a car from you today?"

Random's face crumpled, not sure how to answer.

"First lesson today guys," Brick continued, unmoved by Random's obvious consternation. "The customers are out on the lot."

"So I guess we should be outside." I answered.

"Good guess." Brick stated flatly. And with that he wheeled on one of his tiny heels and headed for the tower.

Random and I b-lined it to the double doors and emerged onto the giant cement porch.

"Kiss ass." He muttered.

"You really know a lot about these cars." I returned, trying to sound sympathetic.

"Yeah."

"Maybe you could help me out here?"

His expression brightened a bit at this and we found our way past a gaggle of sales guys and down the ramp to the lot. The rows of cars were gleaming in the Friday morning sun.

"Tell me about Pathfinders." I said sheepishly, "I used to date a girl in Winter Park that had one. She let me drive it one time, pretty awesome."

"What year was it?" Random asked, his pleasant demeanor returning slowly.

"Not sure, '93 I think."

"Shit, that thing was a toy compared to the new ones."

"Oh."

"Yeah," he continued, "the new ones have a micro-polished V6 with a direct ignition system that produces 235 horsepower!"

"I'm sorry," my expression clearly confused, "a pusha-flugen what?"

Random shook his head at me slowly.

"You really don't know shit about cars, do 'ya? Not that I couldn't tell by that piece of shit Subaru you drive."

"I once made a radiator fit into it at a salvage yard outside of Gunnison. It wasn't from the same model year, but I'm pretty good with a hammer."

"Christ, Stapleton. You really do need my help." He smiled broadly with rows of giant whitish yellowy teeth.

"I guess I do." I smiled back.

As we were talking, a large, somewhat portly young man waddled his way up to us. His tie was curled in his hand oddly, like a security blanket. He stood a few feet from us as though not sure if he should interrupt or not. Random looked in his direction and lit up a smoke, saying nothing.

"Are you Mark Stapleton?" he asked in a matter-of-fact tone that computer geeks use.

"Yes."

"I guess I'm your office partner." It sounded more like a question than a statement. "I'm Jeremy Speck."

"Nice to meet you, Speck." I said darting a pointed hand forward.

Reaching into his pocket, a fat hand emerged with a set of keys.

"Brick told me to show you guys how to do a demo drive."

"Let's go." I said, lowering my unshaken hand.

He walked us down the line to a gold colored Pathfinder and slid his large, round body behind the wheel. Pulling the vehicle from the perfect row he got out and opened all the doors, including the hood and the rear lift-gate. Not sure what he was doing, I watched quietly.

"The first thing you wanna do is *explode* the car."

I felt like we were playing with matchbox cars for a minute. All the doors sat open, just waiting for us to insert a few 'Black Cat' firecrackers or maybe even an M-80.

"Then you start at the front. The first thing I show people is the crumple zones and breakaway engine mounts. See these creases in the metal, in the event of a front-end collision, the front of the vehicle acts like an accordion and…"

Random broke in, "The engine mounts break away sending the engine underneath the car instead of back into the main cabin."

"Very good, Random." Speck said, clearly annoyed by the interruption. "What do you suppose is the benefit of these features, Mark?"

I stared at Speck, not sure if the question was rhetorical or not. He looked back at me blankly, curling his tie in his hand again.

"Safety, I guess?"

"Good." Speck continued. "Next I like to bring the customer around to the driver's side and show him the door."

"The door." I said flatly, wondering what could possibly be interesting about a car door.

"Yes. Nissan manufactures a one piece door on the Pathfinder with a twelve-gauge steel construction and pipe-style interior beams for added safety."

"Wow," I said sarcastically, "that's really interesting."

"Yeah," Speck went on, oblivious to my sarcasm. Random rolled his eyes at me again and we shared a smile.

Slamming the door firmly, he trumpeted proudly, "Try that with a Toyota!"

The morning sun was beginning to glare down on us with its high-altitude intensity, I was glad I had my shades. Reaching into my pocket for my smokes, I lit up and tried to pretend I was still interested. The Husky pencil was starting its scribble again. Speck pointed out the rear door handle, it was built smartly into the side of the door instead of on front like most vehicles and he described it as *'airplane style'*. I took another long pull off my smoke. He lifted himself into the rear seat by grabbing the *'oh shit'* handle that was attached to the inside somehow. I could see a rather large pit stain was forming under the short sleeve of his purple JCPenny's dress shirt, XXL no doubt.

"One of nicest features of the Pathfinder," he droned on, "is that the back seats recline." He demonstrated this by flipping a hidden lever on the side of the seat and easing it back about two inches. I couldn't think of a reason why anyone would give a shit about the back seat reclining, but again, what the hell did I know.

"Now I'm 6' 3; but as you can see I fit very comfortably in the rear seat."

Jammed into the back seat as he was, he looked far from comfortable. Raising the butt to my lips I took another long drag and exhaled through the side of my mouth. He wrestled himself out of the seat and slammed the rear door also, punctuating again the 'solid' construction of the vehicle. Walking us around to the rear he began rambling about cubic feet of cargo space, tie-down hooks and some other features of little interest.

My mind began to wander. I could hear David Byrne's faraway voice as he started warbling in my head;

"Letting the days go by, let the water hold me down..."

My cigarette didn't seem long enough all the sudden.

Walking us around the passenger side of the vehicle; Speck continued his encyclopedic description.

"What's the advantage of a pipe-style door beam?" I heard him ask to neither one of us in particular.

"In the event of a side impact, a pipe-style door beam…" Random began.

Byrne crowed again in my head.

"And you may ask yourself, where, how did I get here?"

Listening to Random and Speck carry on about door beams I realized how much these guys were actually into this shit. The Husky pencil was in full scribble now, the dull headache forming again on the inside of my forehead. Looking up at the cement patio, I noticed that a number of other salespeople were watching us over the blue railing. Leaning into one another, huddled shoulder to shoulder like pigeons, they were obviously enjoying the show with great amusement. I finished my smoke and looked around at the blacktop. Realizing that there were no other butts on the ground, not a one, I crushed mine out on the bottom of my shoe and deposited it in my back pocket. I could almost hear the chattering snickers of the pigeons. Random and Speck were back at the front of the vehicle again discussing something about 'jewel-styled' headlamps and the benefits thereof. I was bored stiff and anxious for some air-conditioning. When Speck finally reached up and shut the hood I realized that we'd been circumnavigating the vehicle for nearly twenty minutes.

"Letting the days go by..."

"Okay." Speck summated, "Let's go drive this thing."

I felt like taking a nap.

"Hop in the front seat, Mark."

'Thank the gods.' I cheered inside my aching head.

Random scooted to the middle of the back seat and we buckled ourselves in. I immediately began searching for the A/C. The dashboard was like a goddam spaceship, fifty *buh-jillion* buttons and nothing that looked like a 'cold' knob. Speck wanted to talk about the stereo.
"Both the SE and LE models of this car come equipped with a BOSE Premium Sound system…"

"Where's the fuckin' A/C dude?" I asked curtly, too hot to be polite.

Speck deftly punched a few buttons on the dash and cool air began to flow mercifully forth from the vents. I noticed that both the driver's and passenger's sides had their own controls. It must've been obvious that I'd never seen anything like this newfangled contraption before, because Speck diverged from his canned stereo speech and began to talk about the dual climate-control system. It was an equally boring explanation but I was blissfully enjoying the blast of cold air so I sat quietly and feigned interest. Random was fumbling around with the gadgetry in the back seat. Leaning back into the headrest I closed my eyes behind my sunglasses.

"Letting the water hold me down..." Byrne continued in my head. I smiled briefly, relaxing to sound of Speck's not so melodious voice.

After a couple minutes the car began to roll forward and we were finally driving. It had only been half of an hour since Speck said we were going on a 'demo' drive. Turning right; past the employee parking, instead of left onto Colfax; Speck started in again with his pitch.

"The first thing I want to show you is the turning radius." He announced, rolling slowly past the customer parking and down into a hidden alley that traced the back of the lot.

A chain-link fence topped with three barbed-wire strands bordered the edge of the lot. I could see now from our vantage point that the used car Hogan was actually a two story building that housed several garage doors on the lower level. From the front of the lot, one could not see that this part of the building even existed. A retaining wall rose to our right as we trundled toward the building; it now resembled a Keep more than a Hogan. After about eighty yards the alley broke into a sizeable, triangle shaped piece of cement just in front of the garage doors. Speck veered the SUV to the right and followed the retaining wall for a few feet. It had risen now to a full twenty feet above us. Spinning the wheel to the left sharply he spun the truck into a tight circle. It easily spun around on the triangular cement pad. As if to accentuate the effect he did the circle three times, coming dangerously close to the large, textured bricks of the retaining wall and the impassable links of the fence.

"You'll notice," Speck continued, "that the Pathfinder has the turning radius of a much smaller vehicle." Random looked out the window with his standard disinterest, but I was thoroughly impressed.

"Due to the unibody construction there is also a limited amount of body sway." Before I could ask what a unibody was, we were headed back up the alley once again, this time at a considerably faster clip. Rounding the corner past the customer parking, we pulled up to Colfax. Dozens of cars raced past us of all shapes and sizes. I began to look at them a bit differently. They all seemed so much newer than mine, shinier, somehow... better. The A/C continued its calculated whirr as they flew by. Speck finally saw a gap and shot into the flow. We weaved our way through the traffic as the Navajo sun blared down on us from above. Cresting the hill just past the Taco Bell and a small, old import dealer, I caught a glimpse of my mountains resting comfortably on the horizon, shimmering slightly behind the smog of the city.

"Into the blue again..." Mr. Byrne continued.

"Where you goin'?" Random asked.

"Well," Speck almost drawled "Most people like to loop their test drives back to Sixth Avenue, but I like to take 'em up I-70. You know show 'em what these babies can do."

"I'd like to see what it can do." I stated robotically, still a bit comatose from his encyclopedic 'walk-around' and the ensuing spin cycle demonstration."

"Okay!" Speck answered excitedly, turning onto Denver West Boulevard.

Within a couple minutes we were motoring up I-70 toward the mountains.

"One of the best features of the new Pathfinder is that it has a micro-polished V6 that produces as much horsepower as a Jeep Grand Cherokee does with a V8."

He might as well have been speaking Swahili.

"What's the diff'?" I asked.
His expression seemed confused.
"What do you mean?"

"I'm sorry," I said, realizing that he obviously didn't speak *'Dude'*. "What's the big difference between a V6 and a V8?

Random guffawed from the rear seat.

"The Nissan engines are very advanced, Mark." He continued condescendingly, "They have a direct ignition system and micro-finished parts that reduce friction and help to burn the fuel more efficiently. This produces as much power as many V8's without sacrificing the better mileage that you get from a V6."

"Oh."
"Allow me to demonstrate." Speck said, mashing his oversized foot down onto the gas pedal.

The vehicle began to accelerate, smoothly and quickly, slipping through the gears without so much as shudder. I felt my shoulders pull back into the comfortable seat. Billboards and other vehicles stood stock still as we sailed past them. The giant highway climbed before us and the city melted away behind.

"After the money's gone…"

As we continued our ascent, I grew more relaxed and increasingly impressed with the power of the vehicle. My neck rolled forward and I glanced over at the speedometer, it read 108mph. It felt as though we were doing maybe sixty.

"Wow." I exclaimed.
"Yeah." Random agreed.
Speck just smiled and pushed the power button on the stereo.

We rode silently for several minutes, enjoying the sun and the sky and the music. Red Rocks Amphitheater appeared down the valley to our left, then disappeared behind the scrubby foothills as we climbed still further up the interstate.

"Just hit a buck-ten." Speck announced in his now classic computer geek speak.

"Nice." Random said, "I'm gonna sell a million of these things."

"How fast are we supposed to drive these things?" I asked.

"Not this fast." Speck returned, "I'd appreciate it if you didn't share this little experience with Brick."

"Right."

"I usually get off at the next exit and let the customer drive."

"Makes sense." Random agreed.

"How fast are the customers allowed to go?" I jibed.

"Very funny, Stapleton," Speck answered, "just have 'em keep it under ninety if you can."

Veering off onto the exit ramp, he let the physics of the incline slow the vehicle organically, rolling gently to a stop at the top. Clicking on the pleasantly metronomic blinker switch, he turned onto the frontage road and into a gravel parking area.

"Who else wants a turn?"

"Dibs." I said automatically.

"Whatever." Random replied nonchalantly, "I've driven plenty of these."

Nearly jumping from the passenger's side I cruised around the front and took the wheel. Reaching down to adjust the seat I realized that it was electric. After a few small adjustments, including the radio station and volume control, I was ready.

"I usually encourage the customers to take the frontage road back down to the hogback." Speck shared, "This way they can check out the handling."

"Sounds great." I retorted.

Reaching for the gearshift I went to pull the beast into drive. Speck put his hammy palm on my shoulder. I looked up at his boyish face.

"Try to keep it under ninety." He smiled.

"No problem."

I spun out on the gravel and lurched up onto the asphalt. The handling was quite impressive, more like a car than a truck really. I'd driven the frontage road many times before and felt quite comfortable.

'You may find yourself, behind the wheel of a large automobile...'

The handling *was* equally impressive. I took the turns like a downhill racer.

"Cops like to hang out on this stretch." Speck warned as I took a rather sharp turn at close to seventy-five and hit the accelerator instead of the brake.

I looked down at the speedometer and realized it had crept well past eighty. Slowing slightly I asked,

"What the hell's a unibody?"

Random decided to field my question quickly,

"A unibody construction means that the body of the vehicle is welded to the frame instead of just bolted on. That's why the Pathfinder feels more like a car than a truck."

"Sure does." I agreed, taking the next corner at close to eighty again. "Whoooo, yeah!"

"It also makes your repair bills exponentially higher if you get into a collision." Speck added.

"Do you share *that* with the customers?" I asked smart-assedly.

"Not if you actually want to sell them the vehicle." Random commented with his sunny darkness.

Speck just curled his tie in his meaty claw.

As we neared the interchange that would get us back on I-70, I noticed a Conoco station coming up on our left.

"Who wants a pop?" I asked rhetorically, trying to do my best John Candy impression.

Pulling to the front I asked again, "Who wants an Orange Whip?" I pointed comically at Speck, "Orange Whip?" then at Random, "Orange Whip?"

They both stared at me blankly.

"Okay." I giggled, "Three Orange Whips."

'Children,' I thought as walked into the little store. *"They've probably never even seen The Blues Brothers."*

The gas station was run by Indians, dot not feather, and smelled pungently of curry and body odor. I walked quickly to the refrigerated section and grabbed three orange sodas. As I headed for the counter my bladder informed me how much coffee I'd already had this morning and I veered into the disgusting bathroom. After I'd *'hung the llama'*, I decided to wash my hands and face. The cool water and pink soap was surprisingly refreshing amidst the squalor. Looking at myself in the mirror, it occurred to me that my hair was considerably longer than either of my two new compatriots. I ran my hands under the water again and slicked my mop back a bit further.

Holding my breath as I paid for the sodas, I wheeled quickly and sprung through the front doors. Random and Speck were sitting quietly in the truck, clearly not conversing. Opening the vacuum sealed door, I handed them each a soda and slid into the driver's seat again.

"We're not supposed to drink sodas in the vehicles." Speck commented nervously.

"Oh," I chittered sarcastically, "but it's okay to drive up a federal highway at nearly twice the speed limit, huh?"

"Orange Crush??" Random nearly shouted. You sure you've always been a white boy, Stapleton?"

"Go Broncos!" I answered.

Random opened his soda with an audible hiss.

"Uh-huh." he returned flatly, taking a long drink of the soda and rolling his eyes out the window.

"Okay," Speck said, opening his soda much more slowly, "but we've got to get rid of these bottles before we get back to the dealership."

"Lighten up, Specker," I said sarcastically, "its okay to get thirsty."

***

Upon our return to the dealership, I noticed that Brick and Ned were standing at the railing. Ned was enjoying a smoke but Brick watched us like a hawk as Speck pulled the truck back into the line. Inching forward slowly, he checked the mirrors on both sides to make sure the vehicle was perfectly in line with the others. We popped the doors open and emerged back into the heat of the day. Both Brick and Ned's eyes were upon us as we sauntered back up onto the porch.

"How many appointments do you have today, Jeremy?" Brick asked acidly before we reached the top. Speck curled his cheap tie again in his fist and said nothing.

"Show Stapleton your office," Ned said calmly, "then hit the phones again."

"K." Speck answered, averting his eyes from Brick's icy-hot gaze.

*****

The doors whooshed open again and we slid across the off white tiles to the center cubicle. Except for a couple-three 2nd and 3rd place plaques from varying years, the office was rather Spartan. Three chairs surrounded the metal and Formica desk. They matched each other in a completely forgettable grey. A not-so-new phone sat on the corner next to a square leather box filled with black pens. The walls were covered with some type of woven burlap like material also in a bluish grey shade. The husky pencil began its scribble again. Jeremy sat gingerly down in the chair behind the desk as if he might accidently sit on a tack. Yanking open a drawer he removed a pack of gum and slid out a piece. He didn't offer me one. His eyes seemed a bit far away as he peeled away the foil wrapper and bent the stick into his mouth.

"So this is where it happens." I stated, trying to lighten the mood.

Speck just looked out the door of the office and into the void of the showroom.

"You need some pictures up in here." I said.

"We're not allowed to put up anything on the walls," he started, "except for a calendar."

"What about those plaques?" I asked, hoping to ease the palpable tension.

"Oh yeah," he said "and those."

I could feel that he'd won far too few.

"So we'll share this office," he continued, "this is where you bring the customers after the test drive. If one of us is using the space, you are allowed to use any empty office."

"What if they're all full?" I asked, noticing earlier that there were only five.

"Then you take the customers to one of the tables on the floor."

"Oh."

Reaching into the top drawer of the desk, he pulled out a small spiral notebook.

"This is a 3 x 5."

It looked to me like it was at least a 9 x 6, but who was I to argue.

"We use these to track our customers."

Flipping to a blank page, he traced a big cross. It divided the entirety of the page into four boxes. In the margin at the top, he wrote the date.

"When you get an Up, you write their information in one of these boxes."

"So like name, phone #, the kind of car they want, etcetera?"

"Yes."

"You're a quick study." I heard a cheery voice behind me say. I looked up to see Ned leaning in the doorway of the office. His pasted-on smile curled beneath his salt and pepper mustache.

"Come with me, I'm going to introduce you to a couple more of the guys." Then turning to Speck, "I'm sure you've got some calls to make." He cocked his head and raised an eyebrow slightly. The tips of his freshly trimmed hair wavered like miniature, fiber-optic tentacles, the glow of the overhead fluorescents giving the black strands a deep purple hue.

I rose from my chair and followed him back onto the showroom floor. He walked me down to the office on the end and introduced me to a couple of young guys, one of which didn't look a day over sixteen.

"Jaime, Cortland, this is Mark. Mark, Cortland and Jaime are gonna show you how to work a 4-Square."

I felt a bit like I was back in elementary school as I reached out and shook each of their hands.

'Wasn't 4-Sqaure a game we'd played back then?'

I could almost smell the giant red rubber ball and hear the weird *'sproing'* sound it made as it bounced off the blacktop.

"Nice to meetcha." Cortland said after Ned took his leave. His accent was clearly southern, sounded like Tennessee or perhaps a bit more north, like Kentucky or West Virginia maybe.

"Hey dude." Jaime said; he was clearly from West Denver.

Both were freshly scrubbed and clean shaven. Their shirts were clean and their ties were pressed. Cortland looked as though he even had the money to have his clothes dry cleaned. Jaime was sporting his nicest button down and a tie that would've been at home at Colorado Academy or Kent Country Day.

"Ever sell cars before?" Jaime asked.
"Nope," I answered, "first time."
"You're gonna love it." Cortland stated sunnily.
"I hope so."
"You from Colorado?" Jaime asked.
"Yeah, well, I was born in Chicago but I grew up in Evergreen. You?"
"Yeah, grew up here in Lakewood."
"I figured; how about you Cortland?"
"Danville, Kentucky." He proclaimed; his southern drawl displayed a bit more patriotically.

'Figured that too.' I thought; a little surprised at my divining abilities.

"So what's this 4-square all about?" I asked.

Cortland looked down at his desk, a large legal sheet of paper laid upon it with a bunch of informational lines at the top and another big cross below.

'What's with the crosses?' I wondered.

"So," Cortland started, "When you bring the customers in after a test drive, you sit them down in your office and ask them how they would like to title the vehicle."
"Isn't that a bit presumptive?" I interrupted.

Jaime looked at me blankly.

"It's called assuming the sale." Cortland continued. "After you get their names and addresses, then make sure you get their phone numbers."
"Yeah," Jaime warned, "especially their work numbers."

"Yeah," Cortland agreed, "Brick'll have your nuts in a Tupperware bowl if you forget the work number."

I snickered a bit at this.

"I'm not kidding," Cortland kept on, "he keeps a big Tupperware bowl under his desk. Just like the one your Mom used to put the extra cookies in!"

"Yeah," Jaime said, "it used to have like salad or something in it, but now it's just full of fuzzy, little satchels."

"We're pretty sure that's where your office partner's family jewels reside." Cortland drawled on.

I was full on stifling a belly laugh. Speck was only two offices down.

"Anyway, so you've got all their personal information, now you're ready to go to the tower."

"Get the first pencil." Jamie added.

'Pencil?' I wondered. *'They do this shit in pencil?'*

As if reading my mind, Cortland smiled then continued with his explanation.

"So the desk guy will put the sales price here." He wrote a bogus price in the upper right-hand corner of the page. "The trade value goes here," another number appeared on the upper-left. "Then he'll put the down payment here and the monthly payment over here." The bottom two boxes were now filled in. "Okay, so now you're ready to work your deal."

Spinning the page around to face me, he presented the deal.

"Okay Mr. Stapleton, so the Xterra you're purchasing is 29995; with 600 dollars for your trade and 7500 dollars down you'll be at about 685-695 per month…"

"Okay." I hummed back.

"So does that work for you?" Cortland asked.

"Sure?" I answered.

"What a lay-down!" Jaime exclaimed.

"What?"

"Nothing," Cortland sneered at Jaime, "Nobody wants to put that much down usually."

"So what am I supposed to say?"

"Most customers don't want to put any money down, or very little." He explained, "So when you present the first pencil, you're just trying to get a commitment."

"The three-c's." Jaime blathered forth again.

I looked up at his teenage face questioningly.

"You wanna tell me what the hell language you're speaking?" I chided.

"Don't listen to him," Cortland said calmly, "he doesn't know what he's talking about. All you're trying to do is get a commitment."

"Okay."

"So if the customer doesn't want to put any money down, what do you think you do?"

"Turn him upside down and shake?" I asked.

"Well maybe not quite that hard edged. You show the customer that if they put less down, the payment goes up," he replied.

"So it's like a scale?"

"Eggs-actly." Cortland drawled.

"So tell me you want to put 2000 down."

"Okay," I said, starting to enjoy the role-play.

"I can only put two grand down."

"Perfect. So now I'll start to illustrate the math." He crossed out the 7500 number and wrote in 5000. In the lower right-hand box he crossed out the payment and wrote in 775-789."

"So with 5000 down your payment should fall in the high 700 range."

"Five grand!" I retorted, trying to pull off my best John Belushi, "Five grand, man? I've never even seen five grand!" They both looked at me blankly; the inference was clearly lost on them.

"Okay," Cortland kept on, "so can you do 4800?" writing down the number below the 5000 figure. "4500?"

I shook my head silently as they watched me intently, studying my every move. The silence was palpable; it almost felt like I was actually buying a car. Cortland stared me eye to eye, dead in the face. His finger held the page to the desk as if it might suddenly fly away. He was clearly expecting me to answer, even though we were role-playing. I leaned back in my chair and folded my arms, exhaling loudly. This wasn't my first rodeo.

"2000," I said sternly, "that's all I can do."

"Ok," Cortland wrote the number down quickly. "So with 2000 down your monthly payment should be in the low 900's. Does that work for you?"

"Nine-hundred dollars a month." I stated flatly.

Sproing!

The role-play was losing its appeal. "Does any customer agree to that? It seems more like a mortgage payment."

"You'd be amazed." Jaime interjected, leaning back up against the grey burlap wall. I looked up at him; then scanned the wall behind Cortland, both him and Jaime had a number of more little black-faced plaques than Speck. Mostly 2nd and 3rd place ones, but the dates seemed newer and there were definitely more.

"Okay," I said to neither one of them in particular. "now what?"

Cortland looked back down at the 4-square. It looked kind of like the one on a playground, a playground where idiot-savant children had been doing crazy calculations. I felt a shadow emerge behind me and Jaime abruptly stood up a bit straighter. Cortland's green eyes rolled upward, above my head. I turned to see Brick standing on the opposite side of the glass.

"How's it going?" he asked.

"Well Cortland's trying to get me to agree to a mortgage payment on an Xterra." I joked.

"Let's see." he requested; reaching a hand out for the scribbled page. "Hmm. 2000 down, 900 per month... So you agreed to this?"

"He's a total lay-down." Jaime interjected again through nervous laughter.

"I didn't agree to anything."

"That's good Stapleton, 'cause you'd have a firm grip on this ride. Getting the gist of how this works though?"

"Yeah," I returned, "It seems to work a lot like the Spanish Inquisition."

"Yeah, well, nobody expects that." he smiled wryly, nonchalantly recognizing the reference to Monty Python.

"Just remember, it costs money to buy new car. Your job is to get as much of that money as possible."

Chapter Eight

Where's that confounded bridge???

I sat on the floor of my duplex surrounded by brochures. My baby daughter lay upon a fleece blanket staring up at nothing in particular. Everything about her was unbelievably tiny. Miniature toes dotted the ends of her fat little feet, her chubby little legs kicked jerkily at the air. Small mittens covered her china-doll hands in order to protect her soft cheeks from the scratchiness of her nails. Her nose and mouth crinkled into silly expressions under glassy new eyes. I wondered what she might be thinking of this whole thing, just barely a month and half old. My wife had set her in a sunny spot because the doctor had told us that she might be a bit jaundiced. I was just glad that she was home and breathing easily.

Trying to concentrate on the benefits of a dual-overhead cam engine, my eyes were continually drawn to my little creature on the floor. I mean I'd been around babies before, but you never really get to hang out with them much when they're this small. Usually if you see someone with a newborn, they're all wrapped up like a burrito. She was so... not helpless really, but... needful. Lying there as she was, so fragile and perfect in every detail. I felt dizzy and excited and overcome with joy all at the same time.

It was like that feeling you have when you get off that rollercoaster for the first time and all you want to do is get right back on... run through the steel maze of handrails; sometimes leaping right over them or swinging under them... champing at the bit to get another taste of that terrifying freedom and then... you're in that rickety old wooden car. The bar clamps down over your thighs, locking you in, committing you to the wild ride. That first clunk as the chain engages, the click, click, click as it strains to drag you and a bunch of people you don't know to the top of that first big hill. Then you crest it and your stomach leaps into your throat...

My daughter was starting to wail. That angry 'meet my needs' cry that opened her toothless maw into a breathless gape. Her need bordered on rage. Scooping her up my arms I rocked her gently. There was no smell that suggested she might need a change. Padding down the staircase I quietly entered our dark and messy bedroom. My wife was trying desperately to steal a few winks. The sheets were tangled about her and the pillows were stuffed both under and over her head.

"I think she's hungry."

She slid the pillow to the side and sat up, zombified with lack of slumber. Her arms rose to collect our child. Scooting back against the headboard-less wall she drew out her breast, her tousled hair falling around my daughter's slight body. I stood in silence for a little while, awestruck by the miracle of watching my bride nurture our first born. Then my eyes turned to the glaring numbers on the digital bedside clock, it was 3:33 in the afternoon. Pulling the door to our bedroom closed I quietly tiptoed back up the stairwell to the great room. Collecting the strewn brochures into a pile, I dropped them on the hearth and lay down on the couch. My head was swimming with an overflow of information.

My wife shook me awake some four hours later. Rays of orange light were blasting through the kitchen window and sliding glass door.

"You should eat some dinner." She said softly as I blinked into the dusty evening sun.
"What time is it?" I asked groggily.
"Almost eight," she returned.
"Jesus, I don't even remember falling asleep."
"Come eat."
"Where's our sweet pea?" I asked through a stretch.
"Sleeping like a baby." She whispered in her sweet southern way.
"Cool."

The corner of the table was set with two plates of food. Stumbling my way over, I noticed that she'd made a shepherd's pie. Curling my fingers about a fork I shoveled the steamy potatoes and corn and beef into my mouth. My stomach grumbled with satisfaction as the warm, buttery lumps found their way over my tongue and slid down my throat. We sat silently at the table and ate slowly, both too tired to converse. My t-shirt and sweats were still rumpled from my unscheduled nap. I grabbed our empty plates and began rinsing them off in the stainless steel sink. Before I'd finished, my wife's hands found her way around my mid-section and I felt her head resting between my shoulder blades. Dropping the dishes and shutting off the water I turned to face her.
Her hair was clipped up in the back with one of those giant, spring-loaded types of hair thingies that left strands poking off at odd angles. An old college sweatshirt was draped about her shoulders, just barely concealing the milky swell of her breasts. Her full hips filled out the tight fitting sweats below her waist. I encircled her in my arms and held her

gently, swaying her tall frame back and forth. Her exhausted arms clung to me and her head rested heavily on my shoulder. After what seemed like hours, my lips found hers and we kissed briefly. Her hand slid down to mine and she led me toward the couch. Sitting down in front of me, she slid the elastic waistband of my sweats down onto my thighs and took me into her mouth. I exhaled at the ceiling and closed my eyes.

****

It was the Friday morning before Memorial Day as I sat in the low grumble of the meeting room. The dusty, morning sun was streaming through the upper windows as we waited for the managers to lay us low with yet another *'rat-whipping'* session. Friday morning meetings were very crowded, as all the salespeople were required to attend. Random was at my right and another green pea was to my left. They both sat slumped in their chairs with the defiance of youth. My right leg was folded up onto my left, my right ankle resting on my left knee. I could hear the elder salespeople behind me chattering about past Memorial Day events and 'spiffs'. There was an air of anticipation this morning and the room felt much different than it had before.

The left door clicked open and no less than eight managers filed into the room. They stood at the front, eyes fixed on the staff. Ned stood with his legs slightly apart, hand clutched over his wrist in front; Brick paced. Crazy-hair, disheveled man leaned one hand on the counter and cocked his thick soled dress shoe around his other ankle, *Mik*, I think they called him. The Arabian guy stood quite still, simmering behind his bug-eyed stare. The rest were guys I had not yet come to know, Gavin was nowhere in sight.

"This is gonna be a short meeting today guys." Brick started. "It's Memorial Day weekend."

He paused theatrically, the statement hanging in the air like smoke.

"We are nowhere close to where we want to be, but I don't need to tell most of you that." His fingers splayed and curled as if his hands were tired from throwing bales of hay or perhaps a thirty hour stint of crab fishing. Wheeling and pacing as he spoke, the left side of his face revealed a painful grimace.

"We need no less than fifty cars out to make forecast this weekend."

Again he paused; the significance of the number was lost on no one.

"There are roughly twenty salespeople in this room. That means each of you needs two and a half car deals by nine o' clock Monday night."

'Two and a half?' I asked myself.

"You've got eight managers here. We will be here from bell-to-smell until we hit 50!" his tone was growing steadily more acidic, bordering on bellicose. I could tell by his stilted gait that Gavin had probably rammed a rather sizeable and stiff pole up his ass earlier this morning. He stopped abruptly and faced the group. I could now see the full breadth of his grimace. The two toned loafers he wore seemed to constrict his feet as he rolled slightly from his heels to his toes.

"We will hit fifty cars this weekend, failure is not an option." He stared at us with his hellcat eyes, smoky and sulphur-green, ringed with bridled fury. A few of the senior salespeople squirmed in their chairs.

"Your shift isn't over until you sell a car. If you don't sell a car today, I suggest you come early on Saturday. Do not leave until you sell at least one car. If you decide to leave before you sell a car, you might as well bring any of your personal belongings with you because you will not be welcome back."

The squirming became audible shifts and stifled groans. Brick turned slowly to look at his team of managers. They were stoic.

"Any questions?" the pall fell over us like a giant flag. "Good." He punctuated and walked boldly to the edge of his captains. I wondered if he had any French lineage, or possibly Austrian. When he reached the end of the line, he turned and folded his arms over his chest.

"Ned, tell 'em the good news."

Ned sauntered forward with his staticy charm.

"Okay," he puffed optimistically, "You heard the man, fifty cars by the end of business on Monday."

The number seemed slightly less imposing when Ned said it, as though it might actually be attainable. The Arabian man I would come to know as Z (for Zaheed), wrote the number largely on the dry erase board behind him as he spoke. Ned turned and smiled with mock nervousness at him.

"So to reach that goal, were going to offer you some incentive. This weekend we're doing dice rolls."

The room exhaled.

"Yes." I heard someone hiss from the back row.

Ned reached into his pocket a pulled out a slab of cash. From the top he slid off a ten dollar bill and held it up for illustrative purposes.

"Ten bucks a spot, and you can double-down against the house, cash in fist."

Cheers and hoots filled the room, briefly. I had no idea the fuck he was talking about.

Zaheed stepped forward and looked coldly at the group, his round chin turning up slightly as he waited for their silence. As the ruckus subsided he nodded to Ned as if to say;

'Continue'.

"If you sell more than three cars in the next three days, the fourth gets you twenty bucks a spot and the fifth gets you thirty."

The response was enthusiastic but muted. Zaheed turned his head only slightly then proceeded to write the info on the dry erase board.

Ten $ / Spot
Double Down
After 4 then $20/spot
After 5 then $30/

"Let's make it a positive weekend guys!" Ned exclaimed, his eyebrows arched on his forehead like seabirds. "If we all work together we can make a lot of money and hit the store's goal!"

Stepping back slowly as though he just recited "St. Crispin's Day", he fished a mint from his deep, pleated pocket, popped it into his mouth, then craned his neck back at Zaheed.

"You got anything?" he asked.

Zaheed paused dramatically.

"Guys." He breathed through a forced whisper, audibly clicking the cap back onto his marker. Taking another few seconds to place the pen deliberately in the tray of the dry-erase board, he turned slowly and walked in an effete yet erect fashion to the forefront.

"We have to, somehow, someway..." the words were drawn out, as if he had feathers in his throat, or sandy marbles in his mouth. "...find a way to sell someone a car today; not tomorrow, not next week, but right now, today. The 'be-back bus' doesn't stop out front every morning to drop off all the customers that you didn't sell cars to yesterday. These customers are all coming here to buy a car. If we don't sell them one, there are eight dealerships down the street that will be happy to."

Extending his left arm to the west I could see the garishly textured gold ring on his finger, an equally flashy watch emerged from his white cuff. Turning his head back to the slumped group of salesman and leaving his hand extended, he continued.

"Go out there and get a customer, sink your teeth in and don't let go until they buy a car from you." He let his arm flop back down to his side, slapping his thigh for punctuation.

It was the most I'd heard the man say in the ten-something days that I'd worked there. A quiet fell over the room. Ennui and fear simmered beneath the buzz of the overhead lights.

'Is that it?' I wondered.

"Mik?" Zaheed asked, not making eye contact, turning his head only enough to speak his one word question.

"No," Mik-crazy-hair returned, "They know what they need to do."

They both gave deferential glances toward Brick, Brick shook his head slowly, arms still knotted across his chest.

"Okay then," Z finished, "Go make it happen."

****

Walking out into the blazing western sun, I was still trying figure out how one could sell 'half a car' and nervously shaking a cigarette from a crumpled pack of smokes. I hadn't yet sold a whole car and was feeling pretty worried about when I might actually get a chance to dip my beak. As I lifted the bent nicotine delivery system to my lips and pinched a matchstick between my fingers, Milo and Tristan rushed out the door from behind me and blasted through my elbow. The smoke, match and matchbook flew down into the grass in front of me.

"Sorry, dude." Milo yelled back, his arms outstretched, tie flung about his neck, "didn't see 'ya there."

I was just about to lean over to collect the mess when I heard the familiar scratch of a flint-wheel and saw a cigarette being offered to me from a fresh pack of Marlboro Lights. It was the guy I'd first met when I was applying for the job.

"Fuckin' kids." he growled, squinting through the smoke of his cigarette.

"How old are *you*?" I asked, shaking off Milo and Tristan's trespass and sliding the smoke from his pack.

"33."

He handed me his lighter and I lit up as well, taking a long pull and hurling the smoke from the side of my mouth.

"I just turned thirty."

Pulling out a pair of designer shades, he slid them over his eyes.

"Divorced yet?"
"Nope, just got married and have a new baby girl."
"Good luck with that, bro. I've got two myself... kids, not wives." He smiled wryly.
"Are you a Mormon?"
"Not anymore."
I put on my shades and smiled back.
"Mark." I said finding my hand and offering it to him.
"Joe." He said back, taking my hand firmly. "Welcome to Purgatory."

Chapter Nine

<u>Swim.</u>

I stood on the cement porch of the dealership, my hands curled around the top railing like talons. Just a couple hours before I'd called my wife to tell her that I had not yet sold a car and was therefore required to stay at work until such time as I had. Her sleepy retort was a bit cranky, but she'd agreed that I needed to do what was asked of me. Random had delivered a car around 4:30 and was long gone. Joe had sold two cars already but was working the late shift anyway. He was hanging about because it seemed he had nowhere else to go. Nonetheless, I was happy to have someone next to me as the sodium arc lamps flicked to life and the raging sun buried itself into the mountains behind us. As we stared into the waning heat of the day I was flanked on my other side by another young man, also blond. I hadn't figured out if he was a manager or a salesperson yet but it appeared that he served in some sort of management capacity.

"How's it goin', Stapleton?" he asked out of the black.

At bit taken aback by his impolitic familiarity, I turned to him, the surprise readily apparent on my face. Joe rolled back on his heels, ducking his head between his arms and pretended to stretch his tired back as his claws clutched the railing. Before I had a chance to think, I was answering the young man's question.

"Well I've been here like eleven days and I still haven't sold a car."
"So what's your problem?" he asked sardonically. I couldn't tell if he was trying to be funny or not.
Feeling my eyebrows rise to a peak on my sunbaked brow, I looked at his young face questioningly. He removed an imaginary fleck of tobacco from his tongue and flicked it off

the balcony. We had about a ten-second staring contest before he finally decided to introduce himself.

"Kevin Farmington." He stated curtly.

"Mark Stapleton." I returned tiredly, "But you already know that."

"Yeah, Brick told me. So seriously, what do you think your problem is?"

"I'm not sure man," I started, "the people seem to like the cars. They all wanna drive the cars. But I can't get 'em to buy the cars."

"So let me ask you something." It wasn't really a question.

"Would you rather have half of *'something'* or all of *'nothing'*?"

I looked again at him quizzically. His stern, square brow was set, straight, thick, blonde tufts of hair shot off his seemingly flat head like cactus spikes. Joe groaned from between his arms. Mr. Farmington curled his body around mine like a chicken and looked at Joe, his stern expression unchanged.

"Haven't you already delivered two cars today?"
"Yes." Joe moaned at the ground.
"Go ahead and take off then," he said, "me and Stapleton are gonna sell one tonight."

Joe rose to his full height again and sighed. His large eyes seemed tired in their hollow sockets.

"Okay, Farm." he said with a half-yawn, half-smile. "Good luck, Stapleton."

With that he schlepped past Speck and Jaime, who'd apparently also not yet sold any cars either; then down the cement ramp to the blacktop and off through the orangey circles of light on the lot. I noticed as he wandered off that the streetlamps showering the lot were quite numerous, I'd say at least thirty of them. Five lamps apiece extruded from the top of each ridiculously tall pole. Somehow even with so many, they didn't quite illuminate the entire seven-plus acre expanse of cars and trucks.

"So you never answered my question."

I looked back from the lot at his stern face. He seemed way too wide-awake for after 8 pm. Of course, he had the benefit of youth.

"I'm sorry." I returned sleepily, "Would I rather have all of…"
"Would you rather have half of _something_ or all of _nothing_?" he inquired again, unabashedly talking over me.
"Well I've got a whole lot of nothing right now, so…"
"So did Brick tell you that if we have to pay you your guarantee, we don't really need you?"
"I didn't remember him saying anything to that effect, no."
"Well we don't."

He lit a menthol cigarette and exhaled harshly above my head into the night. His gaze flashed a bit and then softened. Turning his shoulders to the railing, he rested his wrists on the top. His 5' 8", maybe 5' 9" frame required that he reach up slightly to do this. Looking at his profile against the lit up signs of the 'Bowl-o-Rama', his hair looked a bit like 'Max Headroom's' or perhaps 'Foghorn Leghorn's'. I smiled a bit in spite of my depression and fatigue. I lit up my own smoke and exhaled forcefully, resting my wrists on the railing as well.
A small 1980's Subaru hatchback veered onto the lot. The engine was ticking badly as it crept beneath us.
"Sticky lifters." I half-said/half-thought, through another pile of smoke.
"What?" Kevin asked.

"The lifters are sticking on that Subaru."
"Oh, looks like that's *your* customer."

I handed him my cigarette.
"Put this out will 'ya."
"No problem."

As I started down the ramp to the Customer Parking, Jaime and Speck turned their heads from the railing.

"Good luck with that one Stapleton." Jaime jibed out the side of his neck.

I was too tired and frustrated to respond. Locking my delirious gaze on the customer as he emerged from his rusty little car, I continued on.

"Welcome to Centennial Nissan." I stated with as much enthusiasm as I could muster at 8:45 in the pm.

"Hey." The fuzzy thirty-something man returned.

His hand was rough in mine as he shook it and his skin was darkened by a mixture of dirt and suntan. His grip was strong from the clenching of tools. Dirty jeans hung about his skinny frame, ending at his dusty work boots where the steel toes were showing through the worn out leather. For a belt it appeared that he had tied a couple shoestrings together and lashed them about his waist. His sleeveless t-shirt was pocked with threadbare holes and had some old bar's logo on the front, just barely legible from the years of wear.

'Can't judge a book by its cover.' I tried to convince myself.

"I need a truck." He said abruptly.

Looking over my shoulder through the pitted glass of his hatchback, I noticed a tool belt, a couple of cement caked five-gallon buckets and various other power tools jammed into whatever nooks and crannies they could fit. He'd obviously put down the rear seat to allow for more room, but his gear was still pushing up against every window in a jumbled mass. I could almost smell the greasy sawdust that I'm sure was caked across his dashboard.

"Yes you do." I agreed.

"It's gotta be an extra-cab 'cause I've got two kids also."

"Did you want a new or used truck?" I asked, praying he'd say used. It didn't appear that there was any way this guy could afford a new one.

"New." He returned to my dismay. "Definitely."

"Ok."

Walking slowly through the brightly lit lines of cars I saw a Frontier Crew Cab parked by itself at the end. I somehow knew that it was the 'one'. It seemed that my customer was angling toward the vehicle as well.

"How about that one?" I asked pointing to the truck.

"Looks great." He answered.

I looked in the corner of the windshield for the stock number and wheeled to grab the keys.

"I'll be right back." I said robotically. Then I trotted back to the showroom for the keys. Farm was still standing at the railing finishing off his cigarette.

"You got one." He stated as I made my way up the ramp.

"I hope so…"

"You got one." He stated again matter-of-factly as the double doors whooshed open.

Having secured the keys, I jogged back across the lot and began opening the doors like Speck had shown me. The features rolled off my tongue like water droplets. Pipe style door beams, hood safety catches, twelve-gauge steel construction. Practically stuffing him into the passenger seat, we were ready to roll.

"I'm gonna drive it off the lot first just to show you where the controls are and then I'll let you take the wheel okay?"

"Okay." He parroted.

It all seemed just a little too easy; I could feel the Husky pencil starting its scribble again, briefly. Turning onto Colfax, the traffic flow had waned to a trickle in the late evening.

"The nice thing about the Frontier versus other light trucks," I heard myself saying, "is that it has a full ladder rack construction and the body is bolted to the frame. This gives you a bit more torsional stiffness than most light trucks." I was surprised by how much I actually knew.

"Uh-huh." He grunted.
"You like music?"
"Yeah," he said.
"Cool," I returned, flipping on the stereo. "Nissan uses Clarion audio systems in even their most basic vehicles." I continued, leaving the volume control deliberately low. He reached forward, selected a classic rock station and cranked it up.
'Nice.' I thought.
"They also use a 3.3 liter V6 in their trucks so you have more power than most other light trucks as well."

"Yeah." He said, "I know Nissans are supposed to have really reliable engines."

'*Sweet.*' I thought again.

"You ready to drive?" I asked.

"Definitely."

"Cool."

Pulling the truck into the massive K-Mart parking lot, I put it in park and hopped out. We performed a mini *Chinese Fire Drill* in the vast emptiness and then he was behind the wheel. Adjusting his seat a bit to reach the pedals I told him to adjust the mirrors as well then asked him if he wanted to take it up I-70 or the shorter loop onto Sixth Ave. He opted for the short loop. Something told me I had a buyer.

He was a bit out of sorts for a second as he turned back onto Colfax. It was clear that he hadn't driven a truck this nice in a while, maybe ever. I knew how he felt. Directing him to Simms, we made our way through light traffic to Sixth. Now he could really open the vehicle up. It was a manual and he kept popping the clutch as he made his way up through the gears.

"Sorry." He kept saying as the truck lurched forward. "My clutch doesn't work this good."

"It's okay man," I said calmly. "I understand."

Letting him take it up to a little over seventy, I reminded him that this section of Sixth was sometimes a speed trap. He looked down at the speedometer and realized that he was doing nearly seventy-five.

"Holy shit!" he exclaimed, giving away his excitement. "This fucker *is* fast."

I laughed, "Told you, man."

"Sweet." He replied.

I directed him to exit the freeway at Kipling and circle back to the dealership. Stopping at the red light on the corner of Kipling and Colfax, I decided just to go ahead and ask him.

"So," I started tentatively, "If we can make the numbers right, you think you wanna take this truck home tonight?"

"Fuck yeah!" he responded, looking back at me. Noticing me sitting there in my stiff shirt and tie, he answered again a bit less fervently. "I mean yes, definitely."

"It's okay," I said through my laughter. "I've heard that word before."

He smiled sheepishly and flipped on the blinker, turning back onto Colfax and toward the dealership.

"Where should I park?" he asked, turning back onto the lot.

"Just park it next to your car," I said, assuming he was trading it in.

He veered slowly into the Customer Parking and parked a full space away from his old Subaru.

"Perfect." I said as calmly as I could. "Let's go inside and take a look at some numbers."
"Oh," he half-moaned, "The fun part."
"Yeah." I said, just as scared as he was.

The porch was empty as we walked slowly up the ramp to the showroom. I walked him through the double doors and into Speck's office. Seating him in the burlap gray chair I explained I'd be right back.
Farm was leaning up against the high counter of the tower as I strode up and hit my head on the 'Employees Only' sign again.

"Watch that sign, Stapleton." Brick said snidely from behind the counter. "It hangs from the ceiling." I blushed a bit and then found my stride again.

"I think this guy's a buyer." I said softly.

"Is he trading that piece of crap out there?" he asked.

"Um, yeah." I stammered, "I mean I think so."

"Did you ask him?"

"No."

Brick looked at Farm knowingly.

"You want me to go in now?" Farm asked.

I looked at them both with what must've been fear.

"No." Brick said, holding up his palm, and then to me, "Go ask him if he's planning on trading that twenty year-old car."

"It's an '83, I offered."

Farm shifted on his feet, clearly agitated by my stupidity. Brick held up his palm again, a look of warning creasing his brow. Again to me,

"Go ask him if he's planning on trading in that lovely, seventeen-year old, rust-eaten, quasi-moto lookin', worthless excuse for a car."

"Should I say it just like that?" I answered sarcastically, too tired to hold back.

Farm snickered a bit at this, then crossed his arms over his expensive tie and stared out the front glass. Brick looked at me a bit harshly, then his lips curled into his grimace-like smile again.

"Just go ask him." He whispered through a stifled exhale.

I wheeled quickly and just ducking the sign, I strode back to the office. Popping my head in, I asked if he was going to trade the hatchback.

"Is it worth anything?" he asked, "If not I'll keep it for my kid."

"Hold on." I said and walked back up to the tower.

Brick and Farm we're back in their original positions, staring at me like I had three heads.

"He wants to know if it's worth anything, otherwise he's gonna keep it for his kid."

"What do you think it's worth?" Farm spouted, clearly annoyed.

Brick held his hand up again, this time making a 'calm down' gesture toward Farm.

"Grab a four-square and go ask him how he wants the car titled. We'll deal with the trade later."

I turned to the edge of the counter and peeled a worksheet off the top of the large legal-sized pad. Walking lightly on my over tired feet, I almost tip-toed back to the office. I was about halfway there that I realized I'd never even asked this guy his name.

'Shit.' I thought as my gait slowed even further. Baby-stepping into the office, a light bulb went on in my brain.

Sitting down abruptly in Speck's chair I set the four-square in front of me and I asked him for his driver's license, mumbling something about how I was supposed to get a copy before we went on the test drive. Just to make the subterfuge seem real I asked him for his insurance card as well. He dug into his back pocket pulled out one of those eighties style Velcro wallets. As he peeled it open I noticed that it still retained the shape of his hind quarter. After what seemed like several hours, he was able to wrestle his license from the plastic window pocket. He handed me the bent and worn piece of plastic between two fingers. His hand looked as tired as I felt. The buzz of the overhead lights seemed ridiculously loud.

"CHARLIE LIMBURGER" it read.

'Thank the Gods!' I thought to myself as I began to fill out the worksheet.

"So you want the truck titled as Charlie Limburger..." I began, pen poised above the paper in front of me.

"It's Chuck, actually." He offered.

I looked up at him apologetically. "I'm Mark, by the way, Mark Stapleton."

"Nice to meetcha, Mark." He smiled back, offering his hand. I shook his paw again, hoping I wasn't blushing. He smiled again knowingly, "I'm new at this too."

Exhaling loudly, I was having trouble remembering the last time I'd actually inhaled.

"Ok, so Chuck Limburger, 2975 S..." I began again, this time actually writing his name on the page.
"Oh, he said, that's my old address."
"K..." I said, scribbling out what I'd written.
He gave me the correct address. I slunk back to the tower, feeling as dumb as a box of hammers.

"Ok." Brick said curtly, "Let's go."

I handed him the worksheet and he snagged it out of my hands quickly. Farm checked the face of his seemingly expensive watch and then looked at me rather coldly. I checked my own, it was 9:33.

'Fuck.' I thought.

"Ok," Brick said quickly, handing me back the worksheet.

The MSRP price was written in the upper right-hand corner, he'd written 'Sale Price' next to it with a black Sharpie. On the upper left side he'd written ACV and next to that it read $5.00. In the bottom two boxes were the numbers 5000 and then 695/mo.

"His beloved 'snatch-back' is worth about five bucks, with our truck sale-priced at $20,679.00, if he puts five grand down, his payments will be about six-ninety-five a month."

"Snatch-back?" I sniggered back.

Brick almost smiled.

"Just go ask him if that'll work."

I walked back to the office with a bit more verve this time, finally feeling that I might actually be on to something. As I sat in front of Chuck, I spun the worksheet around to face him.

"So my boss says that your car is really only worth about five bucks."

The words came out stilted; I mean the poor fucker actually drove himself here in the thing for chrissake.

"So I guess that you may want to keep that car for your kid."

He rolled his eyes to the ceiling as if to say, 'Duh!' I plowed on.

"So with our truck sale priced at $20,679, if you put $5,000 down, your payments will be about $695 a month."

"I want to pay cash." He said.

"Oh." I said back, looking stupidly down at the worksheet, wondering what to do next.

"Hang on just a sec."

I walked back to the tower, worksheet in hand. Brick and Farm looked at me in disbelief.

"He wants to pay cash." I announced as I ducked the sign yet again.

"How much?" Farm blurted.

Brick flipped the worksheet over and scanned the back. "I don't see a commitment here."
I stared back at him vacantly.

"Farm, show this genius how to get a commitment."

Farm grabbed the worksheet from Brick and started toward my office; my 'deer in the headlights' expression watched him go.

"Come on." Farm condescended as though he were talking to a shy puppy. I began to peel myself away from the counter.

Brick called after me in a scathing whisper,

"Don't say a fuckin' word."

Farm walked briskly as we returned to the office for the fourth, (*or was it fifth?*), time.

"What's he go by?" he asked curtly.
"What?" I half-whispered.
"His name?" he asked again.

"Oh, Chuck."
"Of course, he does."

With that he flew into the office and circled the desk like raptor descending for the strike. In one deft motion he perched himself on the front edge of the chair and slid the worksheet in front of him.

"Hi Chuck, I'm Kevin. Mark is still a bit green at this, so I'm going to help out a bit. He tells me that you want to pay cash."

"Yep." Chuck returned.

"So are you just going to write a check or are you borrowing the money elsewhere."

I was wondering why he asked this, but Brick's warning was still ringing in my ears, so I stayed mute.

"I'll just write a check."

"Okay," Farm continued. "So our truck is sale priced at $20,679 and your trade is worth basically nothing. So does that number work for you?"

"I want to pay twenty grand even."

Farm flipped the worksheet over and began to write,

I will buy and drive now for $20,000...

Pausing briefly over the words he looked up at Chuck over the worksheet and then down again.

"And how did you want to handle the fees and taxes?"

Chuck looked up at me as I leaned against the wall between them. Farm shot me a look a half second after. There was no mistaking the message in his eyes. I remained a statue.

"Uh," Chuck wobbled.

Farm answered the question for him. "It appears that you live in the City and County of Denver, correct?"

"Uh, yeah."

"So your taxes are 7.2% and then of course there is delivery and handling of $249.00. I assume you want to include all of these in the cash purchase?"

"Yeah, I guess?" Chuck half-questioned.

"Great!"

Farm proceeded to complete the sentence he was writing on the back of the worksheet.

I will buy and drive now for $20,000 ++, no trade.

Under the sentence he drew a line big enough for a signature then darted back with the pen and drew a small 'X' at the beginning of the line. Then he spun the page quickly under Chuck's nose.

"Just sign right there, write me a check for $20,000 and we'll start getting your truck cleaned up."

"I can take it tonight?" Chuck asked.

"Of course," Farm added. "We'll even fill it up with gas for 'ya."

Chuck paused briefly over the worksheet in disbelief. Farm nonchalantly set his pen to the side of it, the tip pointing directly at the signature line. Chuck stared at the words for a couple minutes as if re-reading the single sentence over would somehow give it deeper meaning. Then he picked up Farm's pen and signed. I did my best to guard my elation.

"Mark," Farm stated calmly, "Why don't you go grab a deal jacket. Chuck, I just need a check and we'll start getting the truck cleaned up."

Chuck reached into his other back pocket and extracted his bent up checkbook.

I wandered out the office door and trod deliriously to the receptionist's counter to collect a deal jacket. Brick was grinning at me from behind the glass walls of the tower.

'That shit was too easy.' I thought to myself as I came back through the office door.

Farm was standing behind my desk with the worksheet and a freshly written check in his hand. He turned a sharp hand down at Chuck, thumb extended, fingers pointed sharply together. With his arm bowed over the desk, it resembled a bird's wing, although this time it was slightly less rapturous.

"Thank you for allowing us to earn your business." He announced cheerily. "Mark will complete your paperwork and then we'll get you into the business office."

"What time is it?" Chuck asked.

Farm made a cursory glance at his watch and mumbled something about it being around a quarter to ten, but assured him we'd have this done in twenty to thirty minutes. Chuck seemed ok with this as Farm beckoned me to slide under his wings and start the paperwork. As I sat down, I saw that my watch clearly said 9:58.

****

Walking back up to the tower with my deal folder, I was feeling ten feet tall and bulletproof. Farm was leaning up against the counter again, smiling a cat-bird smile and basking in the glow of the giant Nissan sign that was streaming through the gigantic front windows. A third man stood behind Brick's chair. He couldn't have been more than five feet tall and his head was oddly misshapen, like a pale colored eggplant with hair. I handed the jacket to Brick, unable to contain my ear-to-ear smile. He took it from me gently and smiled back.

"Let's look at this work of art." He commented snidely as he set the folder neatly in front of him on his desk.

The cartoonish looking man leaned in briefly over his shoulder, scanning the cover page quickly from behind his huge, bottle thick glasses. Then he looked up at me with a DeNiro-like upside down smile. I felt myself holding my breath again. Brick reviewed the cover sheet then asked me if I'd gotten a copy of his license and insurance. I stammered to the affirmative, not wanting to let on that I hadn't even asked the guy his name up until that point. Something told me that Brick already knew this. He smile-grimaced at me again then initialed the cover and handed the folder over his shoulder. Eggplant-head grabbed it quickly and waddled away through the half door at the back of the tower without saying a word. I noticed that he walked with his large, flat feet to the sides like a penguin. His unusually long arms hung at his sides like wet flippers.

"Don't worry about him," Farm said to me from his casual lean. "He's a total freak of nature."

I looked down at Brick, anticipating his congratulations.

He pawed about on his desk a bit then said curtly, without looking up.
"Go sit with your customer until Mel is ready for you."
"Ok." I said back, turning to toward my office for what seemed like the hundredth time.
"Then come back up here for your dice roll." He stated with a bit more encouragement.
"Oh, yeah!" I remembered, the hop returning to my step.

The ten minutes I spent with Chuck while waiting to get him into the back office seemed like an eternity. Perhaps it was the adrenalin still pumping through my system or the exhaustion in my brain. Thank the gods for the number of winters I'd spent as a bartender. The conversation turned from fishing, to marriage and kids, the weather of course. Finally

Mel materialized at my door and we led Chuck back to what I would learn is called 'The Box'.

"Okay Mark." Mel stated flatly when we reached his door, also of the sliding glass variety. "I'll take it from here."

I shook Chuck's hand again and thanked him and he slid tentatively into the chair in front of Mel's desk. As I walked softly back into the showroom I heard him say something about it being the 'killing room'. Mel didn't laugh. I walked a bit more quickly back toward the tower.

Brick was practicing with a set of dice on top of a newspaper spread. It appeared to be a copy of our ad.

"Good news and bad, Stapleton." He said to me without looking up. "The truck you sold is an 'old stocker', so you get a $200 'spiff' on top of your 'mini'."

I stared at him blankly; he might as well have been speaking Arabic.

"Bad news is, because Farm here had to close your deal, you're gonna have to split that commission."

Other than the fact that I had no idea what he was talking about, I could've cared less. I was just happy that I'd finally sold a truck!

"What's a 'mini'?" I asked, trying to mask my elation. The excitement in my voice was impossible to disguise.

"Minimum commission," Farm interjected, "a hundred bucks. Fifty in this case, 'cause you've gotta split it with me."

"You have to split the spiff also." Brick continued, "But you get to keep whatever you get on this dice roll for yourself, in cash."

Farm smiled at me with what looked like genuine respect. "I told him I wouldn't take half your dice roll."

"Thanks." I smiled back through a relieved breath; "I'm as freakin' broke as *a bone in a paper sack'*." Neither of them caught the reference to the old "Widespread Panic" lyric.

"Okay." Brick said with a bit more excitement, shuffling his butt back up into his chair and rolling the dice in front of him a couple more times. Scooping them up quickly, he slapped them on the counter in front of me with and audible clack.

"Ten bucks a spot then you can double down against the house."

I'd seen the Dead in Vegas a couple times so I knew what 'Double Down' meant. Trying to look cool I shook the dice in my fist and shot a breath over them through my curled fingers. The first roll sent one of the dice skittering off the counter and onto the floor. I chased it down as it bounced off the tiles. I was like a kitten pawing at a wayward butterfly; so much for looking cool. Once I'd collected the offending die I steadied myself back at the tall counter again.

"Sloppy dice, Stapleton," Brick smirked. "do that again and no dice roll for you."

He sounded a little like the 'Soup Nazi.' I could tell that the inference was intended. We shared a smile for a second.

"Don't worry about him, Mark." Farm interceded. "He's just giving you shit for no reason." I think it was the first time he'd called me by my first name. It felt good.

I shook the dice again and softly rolled a 'hard eight'. Although I'd never played craps, I somehow knew that 'double four' was the hard one.

"Hard eight!" Brick announced as if he'd plucked it from my mind. "At ten bucks a spot that's eighty lousy bucks."

Sliding a large wad of cash from his pleated pocket he peeled off four twenties and laid them on the desk in front of him. They looked crisp and new; nearly four times what I currently had in my pocket.

"You gonna keep it or go for the 'Double'?"

I looked again at the money and then up at Brick. He'd turned sideways in his chair and grinned somewhat manically at the grip of cash in his mitt. Farm leaned in a bit too.

"I think I'll keep the eighty bucks." I said reaching over the counter for the bills.

"Oh!" Farm wailed theatrically, wheeling toward the front glass windows again.

"You're such a pussy, Stapleton." Brick needled me quietly as my hand stopped mid-grab. I felt a rush of anger flash up my neck and redden my face. It was as though a gate had been opened in my psyche and a legion of demons was let loose into the open coliseum of my mind. My hand retracted slowly from the meager collection of twenties.

"OK, FUCKER!" I nearly yelled, surprising myself, and Brick, with the volume of my voice.

I put my hand to my mouth briefly and looked around the empty dealership. No one had heard my outburst but us. Farm was leaning against the front window now, coolly sneering at the exchange.

"Fucker, huh?" Brick restated sardonically. "Is that the best you could come up with?"

"I'm sorry…" I started, realizing that I'd just basically cussed out my new boss after not even two weeks on the job.

Brick held up his hand to me just like he had with Farm. "Don't worry about it." He said calmly, "It just shows me that you've got some stones. Wanna go for the double?"

"I'll take that action." I spat forth, somewhere between pissed-off and relieved.

"Okay," he said, the excitement of the game back on. "Here's how it works. You roll again, and then I try to beat your number. You win; you get a buck-sixty. I win, you get nothing."

I picked up the dice again glancing at the twenties still laid neatly between us.

"You can do it, Stapleton." Farm cheered, once again at my shoulder.

I dropped the dice again, making sure to roll them down my fingers so they wouldn't tumble off the counter. They jounced about for what seemed like several minutes, one mercifully facing up a 'four' and the other spinning excruciatingly on one corner and finally resting on 'three'.

"Oh." Farm said again, this time a bit less theatrical.

"Seven." followed Brick; sweeping the dice from the counter and working them between his palms. His eyes were lit up like that bully kid you used to play marbles with that thought he was set up to snag a few of your best cat's-eyes.
I leaned on the counter with both elbows, trying my best to look unconcerned. Seven wasn't a bad roll, but it wasn't exactly good either. At least the odds were with me. Brick let the dice rest in his right hand; then he shook them a few more times for good measure and shot them onto the desk in front of him. He pulled his hand back as if they were hot stones. They tumbled flat almost immediately, both facing up 'threes'.

"Yes!" I nearly yelled again.

Brick inhaled through his teeth as though his foot had just found a sizeable thorn.

"Yeah!" Farm yowled, trying unsuccessfully to contain his excitement.

I stood just quietly and waited.

Brick again pulled the grip of cash from his pocket and peeled off four more twenties then laid them on top of the four he'd already disbursed. Shuffling the bills slowly together he dropped the small stack in front of me.

"Beginner's luck." He jeered; but a smile lingered behind his begrudging eyes.

"Whatever." I said folding the cash neatly into my pocket. My fingers lingered there for a couple extra seconds, the little wad felt nice and thick.

"Over three-hundred bucks for a half-deal," Brick said more to himself than anyone. "Guess you owe me at least two car deals tomorrow."

"How about two and a half?" I answered a bit more smugly than I'd intended. Then, turning to Farm, "I guess half of something *is* better than all of nothing."

My adrenaline powered smile was in danger of cracking my face. Farm grinned back; Brick joined us with his half-grimace/smile also. Had there been any canaries in the room at the time, they would've been overcome with involuntary shivers.

Chapter Ten

How the cow ate the cabbage.

I awoke Saturday morning to the sound of crows cawing from the outside our tautly shaded bedroom window. The clock read 6:41. Peering through the slats of the cheap-ass metal blinds; I witnessed an odd sight. What appeared to be the remains of a ground squirrel sat on the black and red stain of where it had met its end. The gruesome scene played out on the curve of the little driveway that ran by our duplex. Somewhere between thirty to forty crows were gorging on the remains. There must've been another thirty plus in the large Ponderosa pine above their grisly breakfast. The dusty, black birds strutted about on their spindly legs, plucking at the grotesquely twisted corpse. Overfull bodies, replete with their darkness, cackled and flapped at one another as they jockeyed for a morsel. Each one seemed to get its due as they circled the poor dead squirrel in a cockeyed, clockwise dance, flying off in turn with beaks full of flesh and fur. Then, as quickly as they'd awoken me, up they flew in a spiral of black and blue, feathers glinting in the bright morning like fresh ink spewed across the sky.

I let the slats of the shade snap back into position with their annoying clatter, a shimmer of dust trailed off them and dissipated through the geometrically perfect rays that divided themselves into our bedroom. Following them down to the floor I noticed that at least three days of work clothes had trailed around my side of the bed. Collecting them in my monkey arms, I dropped them into a partially filled laundry basket and slumped up the stairs to start some coffee.

The sink was full of partially washed dishes. Cranking the faucet over to the hot side, I opened the dishwasher and began half-assedly rinsing them off and plunking them into the bent racks. When I'd cleared two-thirds of the sink out, I yanked the coffee pot from Mr. Coffee's clutch and filled it with screaming hot water. About two-thirds of the way through the filling, the plastic lid flipped down and blocked the flow, spattering water all over and scalding my right hand.

"Fuck!" I spat angrily, trying to contain myself, so as not to wake the baby.

Fortunately instinct took over and my left hand found the faucet, pushing the weird stainless steel handle over to the cold side. Plunging my enflamed claw under the mercifully cool stream of water, I exhaled through my nose and rolled my head back on its neck. Not switching the temp of the water, I gingerly lifted the lid again and let the stupid, fucking pot fill all the way. After it was full I jostled it back into Mr. Coffee's grip and pressed the brew button.

"Fuck." I whispered again, realizing I'd forgotten to put the coffee into the filter thingy.

Pawing into the cabinet above the coffee maker, I located a filter and some grounds. Plunking the little paper parachute into its plastic receptacle I dumped the coffee directly from the can into it. Slapping the hinge closed I just beat the gurgle and hiss of the heating element, as it began its metronomic coffee making process.

"Yeah!" I whispered maniacally at the little appliance. "Fuck you! Mr. Coffee." I punctuated my victory by flipping it the double American bird of freedom with both hands.

* * *

As I was filling a Ziploc baggie with cubes of ice from our crappy little freezer, I heard the creak of my new bride on the stairs. Reaching the top she stared at me from across the living room. I looked up at her, still gritty from my wrestling match with the coffee maker.

"What happened?"
"I burned myself."
"Oh," she said with just the smallest hint of sarcasm. "Did my precious, punkin' burn his little hand." She cooed, hoping to illicit a laugh.
I held my paw up to her, the top of my thumb and first finger still raging red from the burn. Cradling it in her hands,

she kissed it gently then kissed me. Sliding the baggie from my hand she proceeded to fill it with ice and wrapped it in a mostly clean dish towel. Handing the makeshift ice pack to me she pulled her robe a bit more tightly around her and told me to sit down while she finished the coffee.

"It's done." I heard myself mumble as I found my way over to the couch. The ice felt good on my hand.

"Want some breakfast?" she asked.

"No," I said, "just coffee."

She poured us both a cup and walked one over to me. I set it on the coffee table then got up to grab the milk from the fridge. Pouring a dollop into the mug, I replaced the container into the stinky little cold box.

"We gotta get some Arm and Hammer for this fridge."

"Yeah;" She agreed, reaching around me for the eggs and bacon. "And some food."

"Yeah... sold my first car last night."

"Really?"

"Well, it was a truck actually."

"Cool!" She trumpeted, turning to the stove and laying three strips of bacon into the pan.

"Yeah," I said, the pain from the burn subsiding. "They've got this deal going this weekend that pays me in cash also."

"Really?" she inquired.

"Yeah they do this gambling thing where you roll these dice and they pay you in cash for selling a car, on top of your commission."

"Gambling thing, huh?" she asked in a suspicious tone.

"Yeah, so I won eighty bucks, then doubled down and won another eighty!"

"Awesome!"

"Yeah, can't wait to get back there today and win a fistful more!"

She dumped a couple of eggs right into the bacon grease and they crackled and fizzed.

"Will you put a bagel in the toaster for me?"
"Sure." I said, slurping my coffee as I opened the fridge again.
   Popping the bready little donut halves into the toaster I plunged the lever down and watched the heating elements glow to life. The heat only scared me a little bit.

"I'm gonna go take a shower and get dressed."
"K." she answered disconnectedly.

As I started down the stairs she trumpeted again after me.

"Can I have some of that money to go to the store?"
"Sure." I paused on the landing, trying to remember where I'd stuffed the cash.
"Sure." I said again.

*****

As I pulled out of the ridiculously small, two-car parking space that we were allotted for our rented townhouse, I craned my neck over my shoulder to see if anyone was coming. The blood stain on the pavement had blackened even more in the morning sun, and there was nothing much left of the unfortunate squirrel. Turning my gaze back through the grimy windshield I hit the gas and my ancient wagon shuddered up the steep driveway. My little car seemed averse to working this Saturday morning, I pushed the accelerator a little harder and the shimmy stopped. I looked down at the clock on the stereo, it was 8:08. We opened at nine on Saturdays, I'd be early.

*****

When I got to the dealership, it was quite empty. A large white tent had been erected near the front corner of the new car line. It was just big enough for two vehicles to fit under and someone had done just that. There were Day-Glo green tags hanging from the rearview mirrors inside and they were parked in a sort of sporty way, facing into the lot.

Had the tent been there yesterday and I just hadn't noticed?

I turned sharply and rolled slowly past the vehicles, one was a Pathfinder and the other was a Maxima. They looked expensive and way beyond my reach.

Having parked, I wandered back across the lot past the used car Hogan. Victor stood on the point in front. He was rolling his arches on the edge of the curb; depositing and extracting a cigarette from his thin purple lips. The column of ash dangling from the end was impossibly long. I wondered what he was doing here at just after 8:30 in the morning; I couldn't imagine that he hadn't sold a car yesterday. I veered myself in his direction, shaking a smoke from the fresh pack I'd just bought and lit it with a brand new orange Bic lighter.

"Goood mornick." He uttered in his gravelly voice; taking a deep pull from his cigarette and exhaling a giant cloud. I noticed that his hair was shaved very close to his skull. His skin seemed stretched over the bones in his face, giving away his age perhaps more than he realized, *perhaps not*. His complexion was very dark, darker than a person who was merely tanned by the many hours he spent on the lot. I suspected that his lineage was mixed but it was difficult to place.

"Good morning!" I returned cheerfully, joining him on his perch. "I sold my first truck last night." I announced, still frothed up a bit about finally selling something.

"Guuud…" he said slowly. "I got three out yesterday."

'Wow.' I thought.

"How many cars do you sell a month?" I asked with genuine interest.

"Usually about seventeen or so." He replied modestly.

"Jesus!" I exclaimed before I could catch myself. "That's a lot!"

"Yeah, well here it is. There was a time when I sold twenty-five to thirty. Before all the booolshit."

I could tell by the reflection in his eyes that he wasn't trying to 'booolshit' me.

"Where'd you do that?"
"Back in Illinois."
"Wow!" I said aloud this time.
"That's where I got this." He continued, showing me his large, black-stoned ring with a super-imposed 'GM' insignia. "I was actually the General Manager of that store for five yeeears."

My awe must have been apparent as I eyed the large ring. It was a mix of gold and silver that clasped the giant, rectangular piece of onyx.

"We set sales records for the whole state for three years in a row. That's when the big-wigs in Detroit sent us these rings."

"Cool." I said. "So now you just sell cars?"

"Yes," he mused, "management is a young man's game."

I'd heard through the grapevine that you made more money selling used cars, so I was trying to do the math in my head on how much seventeen might bring you.

"You'd do well to stick with learning how to sell new cars first." He said, as if reading my mind. There seemed to be a lot of that type of *ESP* going on around this place. It was then I heard my name announced over the loudspeakers.

'MARK STAPLETON, REPORT TO THE NEW CAR SALES DESK.' Then again, 'MARK --- STAPLETON, NEW CAR DESK, PLEASE.'

The addition of the 'please' seemed more like a command than a polite request.

"Dooouty calls." He smiled at me with his bony teeth.

I looked at my watch, it was 8:44.

As I turned toward the new car showroom I felt a sudden burst of energy and broke into a trot. Upon reaching the cement ramp, I slowed back to a brisk walk and made my way up. Brick was standing out on the point directly in the center of the railing. He wasn't smoking.

"You rang." I started, doing my best 'Lurch' impression.

He smirked at me and squinted out toward the lot.

"Good job last night."
"Thanks."
"Stick close to Farm today." He said in confidence.
"K..." I said back, perhaps a bit more shortly than I'd intended.
It's okay Stapleton," he condescended, "I won't make you split all your deals with him."
"Is he a manager here?"
"No," he said quickly, "Well, he acts as a 'floor manager' but he is one of the better salespeople here."
"I appreciated his help last night."
"Just remember, when he goes in on a turn for you, don't talk."
"K."
"We're gonna try to get you three deals today."

The excitement in my face was difficult to contain. I opened my mouth to thank him, but he cut me off before I could say anything.

"It starts with one."

And then he said sternly,

"Nobody has an 'up' unless you have one."

I must've looked a little like the RCA dog staring into the gramophone.

He was still squinting out at the shiny lines of cars and trucks. I turned and stared out into the lot as well. Random rolled onto the lot below us. Several of the other salespeople rolled in sporadically behind him.

"You've got a huge leg up on these kids." He said softly, "Don't fuck it up."

With that he pushed back from the railing and stalked back into the showroom. I stood at the railing, still a bit unclear about the earlier statement he'd made. It was only eight simple words, but it felt as though he was trying to impart something more profound. I rolled the words over and over in my head.

'Nobody has an 'up' unless you have one.'

"Oh!" I exclaimed aloud, finally grasping the statement.

"Oh what?" Random asked as he hauled his body up the ramp.
"Oh," I responded, emerging from my meditation, "Nothing. What's up?"
"Nuttin'. Did you finally sell a car last night?"
"Yes, fuck." I breathed, "Well, Farm had to help me, but I doubled down and scored some cash."

"Sweeeet." He drawled back.

"I'm gonna go for three more today."

"Yeah, well good luck with that."

Joe and Tristan were walking up the ramp behind him. Random tried his best attempt at being cool.

"Stapleton popped his cherry last night."

"Did Farm take half your deal?" Joe asked immediately.

"Yeah," I returned bashfully. "But it was an 'old stocker' so I made a little extra there and doubled down for a buck-sixty in cash."

"Nice." He started, and then, "Wait, did you sell that Frontier Crew Cab?"

"Yeah, the gold 2000."

"Fuck!" he exclaimed, mostly to himself, "I have someone coming in on that one today."

"Not anymore." Random jibed.

Joe looked at him acidly.

"Fuck." He cackled again.

Tristan stood coolly for a second, eyeing the exchange. Our eyes met briefly and then he scanned the length of my body as if inspecting my attire. Later I would learn that he was actually sizing me up.

"I'm going over to 'Used." He said to Joe and turned back down the ramp again.

Joe strode up the ramp with his head down, his steps were long but deliberate. His eyes darted back and forth, calculating. Bobbing his head oddly as if balancing his gait; he briefly resembled an ostrich or perhaps an emu. The doors whooshed open and he was gone.

"Good job, man." Random said.

"What'd *you* sell?"

"An Altima."

"Get a good dice roll?"

"Yeah, ninety bucks."

"Nice."

We both turned back to the railing.

"What's up with the tent?" I wondered aloud.

"Those are demos." Random said.

"What's a demo?"

"Man you really don't know anything do you?"

I shot him an irritated look. He smiled and pointed to a row of cars back by the fence between the customer parking and the Hogan.

"See those cars."

"Yeah," I said, still cranky from his earlier comment, "So?"

"Those are demos; all the managers get to drive new car demos, and some of the salespeople."

"Really?"

"It's one of the perks."

I thought of my old piece of crap shuddering its way up the driveway this morning.

"How does a salesperson get a demo?"

"I heard that you have to average like fourteen cars a month for like three months in a row to get one." His tone was suggested that this was a very difficult task.

"Huh." I stated.

"When they get close to like fifteen hundred miles on 'em then we have to sell 'em."

Jaime emerged from the building and joined us at the railing.

"How's it goin' boys?"

"Stapleton is gonna' sell three cars today." Random announced jokingly.

"Good luck with that." Jamie scoffed. "Brick's already on the warpath. He just ripped me a new one for not selling one yesterday."

I thought about what Brick had said to me earlier; glad that I'd managed to sell one. Joe strutted back onto the porch and lit up a smoke. He was apparently over the fact that I'd sold the truck he was planning to sell. An older car pulled into the middle entrance and headed toward the used side of the lot. Victor stopped his curb-sitting and strolled in their direction. I watched him as he leaned down to the potential customer's window, clutching the roof of the car with his right hand. After a short exchange the customer pulled into the used parking, and then the two of them were walking out to the front line.

"You guys are gonna be cupping my ball sack today!" Joe announced out of nowhere.

Random and I looked at him with surprise. Jaime shook his head at the railing.

"I just made three appointments." He continued.

I felt a pang of jealousy. Victor was quietly driving his customer off the lot in a used Sentra, the sale price numbers were still pasted boldly across the windshield. The lot seemed immense and empty. Joe was going on about how busy he was going to be, Jaime and Random glared at him.

Another vehicle pulled into the center entrance and crept toward us along the new front line. It rolled to a stop near the tent and a gigantic black man emerged from the driver's seat. I looked around briefly to see if anyone saw them. Nobody was making a move. I could feel Brick's eyes burning through the back of my skull from behind the glass windows.

'Nobody has an up unless you have one.'

Sliding stealthily to the right of the other salesman, I tiptoed down the stairs on the south side of the cement porch. By the time anyone saw, I was a third of the way across the lot, making a beeline for the first customer of the day.

"Welcome to Centennial Nissan!" I nearly yelled at the customer, still a good ten steps away. His wife had gotten out of the car and was following him to the white Pathfinder. She was tiny in comparison to him. My arm extended robotically as I made my way to greet them. The gargantuan man stood sideways to me, half in the shade of the tent. Turning to face me he reached out his gigantic hand and met mine. Disappearing into his immense paw, the grip of his handshake was surprisingly gentle.

"I'm Mark." I offered.

"Reggie." He returned, his voice was as big as he was. "And this is my lovely wife, Marlese."

She smiled demurely, not offering her hand.

"Hi." I smiled back at her.

"I've always wanted a Pathfinder." He told me flat out. "But I've got to see if I can fit into it first."

"No problem." I said, trying to contain my excitement. "Let me just grab the keys."

I turned and started for the showroom. Then as an afterthought,

"Wait right here."

I trotted up the stairs toward the double doors and past the sideways sneers of my compatriots. The doors whooshed open and Brick and Ned's eyes followed me to the reception desk.

"I need the keys to the white Pathfinder, please." I said sunnily to Cherlie.

"What's the stock number?" she asked politely.

"Uh…" I stammered, realizing I'd forgotten to check the tag on the vehicle. "...the one under the tent?"

"You always need the stock number, Mark." She said with a sing-song warning. I could feel Brick grimacing behind me.

Cherlie glanced down at her desk and found a short list of vehicles.

"That's Glinda's demo." She said more to herself than me.

'Glinda?' I thought comically, *'The good witch?'*

The giant phone lit up in front of her, followed by a muted ring.

She held up one finger, then answered the phone. I leaned on the tall counter and turned to look at Ned and Brick through the glass wall of the tower. Ned was clearing and organizing his desk, Brick was doing his jungle-cat stare out through the glass. I looked out through the doors at Random and company, Joe was still spouting at him and Jaime. Cortland and a few others were milling about on the porch as well. There was another tall, Arabian-looking man amongst them. He was darker-skinned than Z and very nicely dressed. He was smiling at another of the salesmen that I didn't know and his teeth were very white.

"Here are your keys, Mark." Cherlie stated sweetly, dangling them up at me.
"Sweet." I said quickly, snatching them from her fingers.

As I started for the doors, I heard Ned's voice, "First up of the day!"

I turned quickly and saw him smiling up at me from behind the glass. Smiling back, I strode through the doors and out onto the porch. As I jogged down the steps again, I heard Brick's voice again in my head,

'Don't fuck it up.'

I kept my little salesman's jog going until I was within steps of Reggie and his wife. They were already looking all around the vehicle.

"Let me just pull this out for you, so we can take a good look."

"That's okay." Reggie stopped me, "I just want to see if I can fit in this thing."

"Ok," I said dejectedly, opening the driver's side door, "Let me just adjust the seat for you."

I unlocked the door and pulled it open. Reaching down for the controls I powered the seat all the way back and reclined the seat back as well. Keeping the keys, I trotted around to the passenger side. Reggie wedged himself into the seat and closed the door, Marlese hopped lightly into the back. My enthusiasm began to wane as his Yule-log-sized thighs encircled the steering wheel. He just barely fit. I couldn't imagine how he could possibly drive the thing.

"Does this steering wheel adjust?"
I realized that I had no idea.

Fumbling underneath the steering column, his large hand found some sort of toggle on the left-hand side. The steering wheel began to rise slowly.

"Here we go." He said comfortably. I felt my verve beginning to return.

"The seat could probably recline a bit more." I guessed.

Opening the door so he could arch his titanic arm down to the controls, he flicked one of the switches; the seat bottom lowered, and then tucked itself back a bit more. I tried to mask my surprise since I didn't know that the seat could do that either. He reached up and reclined the seat back a bit more. I was amazed that he could actually fit his 300 pound frame into this thing. He was actually probably closer to 320.

"Oh yeah," he purred, rolling his bearish shoulders back and forth into the seat. "This might work, oh yeah." He repeated, adjusting the mirrors. "Let's go drive this thing."

I looked up and noticed that their car was still parked in the middle of the lot, partially blocking us in.

"I'm actually supposed to drive the car off the lot." I squeaked, "And we should probably move your car first."

"Ha-ha." Reggie laughed heartily. "Right, I guess we should."

Opening the door again, he hauled himself out of the driver's seat and fished his keys from his pocket.

"Baby," he said handing the keys to his wife, "will you move the car for us."

"Sure, baby." She replied sweetly. I could tell that they were very much in love.

"Just turn right at the end of the line here and you'll see the customer parking. We'll come pick you up." I directed.

She smiled at me coquettishly and I realized how beautiful she was.

"I know, right?" Reggie said from behind me.

"You're a lucky man, Reggie." I said without thinking.

"You don't have to tell me," he laughed again, "I hit the jackpot with that one."

We switched positions and I re-adjusted the seat to fit me. Pulling past the porch, I could see the salespeople scanning my action. We picked up Marlese then rolled past the customer parking and down into the little back alley that Speck had shown me. Pulling into the little triangular area, I showed them the turning radius trick, although not quite as fast a Speck had demonstrated. Reggie was definitely impressed. Marlese was fondling the leather seats in the back.

"Look, baby." He said as he investigated the dash. "This thing has a Bose Stereo!"

"Oh." She said.

"Yeah." I said, taking his lead, "Check this out."

Flipping on the stereo I asked him what kind of music he liked. He spun the dial to his station and turned up the volume. It was one I never listened to. He and Marlese started moving to the beat, I just kept driving. Pulling around the customer parking a second time I started past the cement porch again. Jaime and Joe were pointing down over the railing at the back of the car. I slowed to a stop, worried that something was wrong with the vehicle. Facing Colfax, I got out of the car to see what the matter was. I walked around the back of the vehicle then looked up at the guys.

"You forgot your plate, genius." Jaime jibed.

"Oh." I laughed.

Sneaking back up to the driver's door and leaning in, I explained my misstep, "I've got to grab a license plate." Reggie and his bride were still enjoying the music. Shutting the door, I hopped up the stairs for the third time. Ignoring the jabs of my new best friends, I slid back into the showroom. Ned looked up from his desk.

"That was fast."
"I forgot my plate."
"Of course you did." Brick needled.

Striding into the cubby, I reached under Speck's desk and loosed the magnetized plate from its 'hidden' spot.

"Need your plate." I said quickly. Speck looked at me tiredly, saying nothing.
Opting for the ramp, I slapped his plate on the back of the Pathfinder and jumped back into the driver's seat.

"Ok." I breathed, "Let's go." Reggie and Marlese smiled at one another. "Would you like to go up I-70 or take it down Sixth Avenue?" I asked.
"6th is fine." Reggie answered.
"Great." I said, nudging up to Colfax. As I started to pull out, some punk kid switched lanes abruptly in a hopped-up little Celica and nearly plowed into the nose of the Pathfinder. I slammed on the brakes, thrusting Marlese forward into her seat belt.
"Sorry." I apologized.
"It's okay." Reggie answered, "That kid's got a death wish." I laughed nervously and looked both ways again twice before proceeding again.
Driving past the K-Mart parking lot, I asked Reggie if he'd like to see a demonstration of the unibody construction of the vehicle.
"The uni-what?" he retorted.

I decided to forgo that part of the demo drive.

I continued down Colfax, spouting whatever facts I could remember about the Pathfinder. Reggie and Marlese were thoroughly disinterested. Seeing the Taco Bell coming up on the left, I veered into the parking lot.

"How about I let you drive?"

"Ok, then." Reggie cheered.

I hopped out and ran around to the passenger side again.

Reggie got everything readjusted and smiled over at me.

"So you can take it up the hill, or just cut over to 6th from here." I said, assuming he knew where he was.

He circled the Taco Bell and opted for the latter. We drove toward 6th, with the music pumping through the speakers. As we pulled up to the stoplight in front of the overpass, Reggie put the vehicle in park. I remembered the dual climate control.

"So this car has dual climate control." I stated as if reading from a textbook. "So you can adjust the temps differently for the driver and passenger."

"Some A/C would be nice, Mark." Reggie said, a few beads of perspiration sprouting on his brow.

I flipped it on, trying to remember how it worked. A couple green numbers glowed to life on the dash

'Oh yeah.' I thought.

Pressing various buttons, I adjusted his side to sixty-five and mine to seventy-two. The fan whirred to life and started bathing us with almost instantly cool air.

"Nice." Reggie purred again. I was just glad I'd remembered how to work the damn thing.

"So now it will adjust your side to 65 and mine to 72." stating the obvious, verbatim from the dashboard readout. Mercifully the light turned green. Reggie slipped the gearshift back into drive and we sped across the overpass and down onto the onramp for 6th Avenue. He stamped on the gas pedal and we were tipping seventy-five by the time we got to the freeway.

"Oh yeah." He growled happily, "That's what I'm talking about."

The car was as good as sold.

"Nice, huh?"
"Yeah," Reggie agreed, "That'll do."

I directed him to exit at Kipling and finished the squared loop back to the dealership. We entered the lot again at the middle entrance and I had him pull in next to his trade. There were several more cars in the customer parking.

"So you wanna go look at some numbers?" I asked nonchalantly, already knowing the answer.
"Well, Mark," He said, "If you can get me a great deal, I'll take it."
"Let's go do that then." I returned, this time making no effort to contain my excitement.
I walked them briskly up the ramp to the showroom and into the Speck's office. There were only a few salespeople left on the porch, and none in the showroom. It seemed much cooler inside than I remembered. Reggie let Marlese enter the office first and find herself a chair. Then he pulled the other one out a little bit and deposited himself in between the armrests. The chair strained a bit under his weight but held him up sufficiently.

"I'll be right back."

I walked quickly to the tower, smiling brightly. Rounding the corner, I hit my head on the 'Employees Only' sign again. It bounced on its wires in my wake, I'd hardly noticed.
"Whoa." Ned stopped me, "Looks like someone's got a car deal. Is he trading the Camry?"
"The what?" I asked without thinking.
"The car he drove in, is he trading?"
"Oh, whoops."

I stood stupidly at the counter. Ned looked back at me with raised eyebrows.

"I'll go ask him."

Brick looked up over the counter with his faraway stare again.

"Where's the Pathfinder?" he asked curtly to no one in particular.

"Are talking to me?" I asked, curling my hand at myself.

"Didn't you just go on a demo in the white Pathfinder?"

"Yeah?"

"Well where is it?"

His tone was aggravated.

"Uh, it's in the customer parking?"

"It goes back on the line until you sell it."

I looked back at Ned. Not sure what to do.

"So should I move the car back before I ask him about the Camry?"

Ned turned his chair toward Brick, arching his eyebrows once again.

Brick didn't look back. He reached forward and picked up his phone, flipping the handset around. Pressing a button angrily he blew into the upturned mouthpiece. The sound of his breath echoed over the loudspeakers.

'JEREMY SPECK TO THE NEW CAR SALES DESK. JEREMY --- SPECK, NEW CAR SALES DESK.'

There was no *'please'*.

He hung up the phone and waited patiently. Turning his gaze slightly to look at me; his eyes were those of a hungry lion. I looked back at him, waiting impatiently. Then I looked at Ned. He leaned back in his chair and stretched his arms in front of him, fingers interlaced. Nobody spoke.

The doors whooshed open and Speck appeared at the counter next to me. I could see the sweat patches already forming beneath his meaty arms.

"Yeah, boss?" He asked.

"Where do we park cars after we're done with a test drive?" Brick asked him in an accusatory tone.

"Back on the line." He answered.

Brick looked at me.

"Did you share this information with our new friend, Mr. Stapleton?"

"Yes." He stammered, "Well I showed him."

"Then how come he's parking one of our demos in the customer parking on the busiest day of the year?"

Speck blinked and reached up to clutch his tie.

"I'm sorry," I started.

Brick raised his hand abruptly at me, his eyes locked on Speck.

"I'll get to you in a minute."

"I guess I should've explained the procedure more clearly." Mumbled Speck.

"Get the keys from Mr. Stapleton here and park the car back under the tent please."

"Yes sir." He said turning to me. I extracted the keys from my pocket and handed them over; my eyes trying to look apologetic. He took them and slunk out the front doors. I barely had time to feel sorry for him before Brick was right dead in my shit.

"Stapleton." He waited for me to acknowledge.

I turned my eyes to meet his, confused by what had just happened. He looked at me like I was a complete retard.

"Didn't we just go over this last night?"

I looked into his cranky face.

"What?" I said, feeling a little like Joe Pesci's character in *'My Cousin Vinny'*.

"You've got another customer with a trade, you didn't do a 'silent walk-around' and yet you're up here trying to work a deal."

'What the hell's a 'silent walk-around'?' I thought.

"I'm not sure if he's trading." I said aloud instead.

Brick exhaled through his nose harshly, as if to blow the flies away.

"How do you not know if he's..." he started to say, then stopped himself and looked at Ned in disbelief. I saw just a glimmer of the smile start to curl under Ned's mustache then disappear.

"Go ask him if he's planning to trade the Camry." Ned said calmly.

'Jesus.' I thought to myself, walking back to the office. *'Isn't that what I just asked?'*

I stuck my head in through the office door, it felt like déjà vu.

"Are you planning to trade that Camry, Reggie?"

"Uh-uh!" Marlese spoke up, "That's my car!" I was a bit taken aback by her change in demeanor. Reggie reached over and placed his huge fingers on her tiny wrist.

"It's okay, baby. We're not trading that car."

He looked over his shoulder at me to make sure I was clear.

"Okay," I answered quickly, "no trade."

I walked a bit more slowly back to the tower this time. Ducking the sign, I slid up to the counter. There were a couple of other salesmen waiting to work deals. Ned was busy.

"What's the deal?" Brick demanded, waiving me his direction.

"No trade," I said, "It's his wife's car."

"Cool." He said, finally softening a bit. "Grab a 4-square."

Watching him fill out the numbers in black 'Sharpie' was like looking at a mirage or rather, an optical illusion. First the MSRP, then he crossed it out and wrote 'DEMO PRICE'. The second number was close to $1,200 off the original. He swirled the pen over the worksheet as if stirring a pot of soup. The tip found the paper again and filled in 11000 in the money down box. I heard myself exhale loudly. Brick looked up at me briefly and then back down at the payment box. In that square he wrote 579-589/mo. He thrust the worksheet over the counter at me.

"Ok, Stapleton. Since this is a demo I'm giving him over 1,200 bucks off. With eleven grand down, we should be able to get him a payment of under 600."

I took the worksheet tentatively.

"Just get me some cash, a commitment and a credit app."

"Ok." I returned quickly.

I headed back to the office, head down to avoid the sign. As I entered, I circled the desk too quickly, bumped the corner and jostled the items on top. Reggie and Marlese rose up in their seats, startled to attention.

"Whoop." I said flumping down into my seat for a second. Then I scooted up to the desktop and laid the 4-square in front of us.

"Ok," so my boss already discounted the price of the vehicle since it's a demo."

"What's that mean?" Reggie stopped me.

"Oh, sorry." I fumbled, "A demo is a new vehicle that has a few miles on it because one of the managers drove it for a while.

"I want a new car." Marlese interjected.

"It's still considered new." I backtracked.

"So it's still under warranty?" Reggie interrogated.

"Yes." I guessed.

"K."

"Ok, so you automatically get a discount. With $11,000 down, your payment should be about $579-589 per month."

"Uh." Reggie said in disbelief, "I was thinkin' I'd put like two grand down."

"Ok." I stopped, not sure what to say next. Mercifully Marlese came in again with her two cents.

"Baby, didn't you want your payment to be like $350?" My heart dropped into my stomach. I looked at Reggie and waited for him to answer.

"We could probably do like $400 for this one."

"Ok." I said flipping over the worksheet like Farm had done.

I will buy and drive today for $2,000 down and $400 per month.

I spun the worksheet around and asked him to sign.

"Hold up." He said shortly, "We haven't even talked about the price or nothing."

Flipping the worksheet back over I pointed out that the MSRP was $34,267.00 but the discounted price was $33,000.

"Oh baby," Marlese spoke up again, "we can't spend that kind of money."

I was starting to like her less and less. Reggie bowed up a little bit and scooted toward the desk a little more.

"I told you I needed a real good deal, Mark. How about we pay $30,000 even for the car?"

"Ok…" I droned back, unsure again of how to proceed. Pausing for a few seconds to think I decided to just do the same thing over again. Flipping the worksheet over I wrote:

I will buy and drive today for $30,000.

"So do you still want to go with the two grand down?" I asked.

"Yeah." Reggie conceded, "Let's try that."

"Ok. So just sign here and write me a check for the two grand and we'll see what we can do."
I felt myself lay the pen down next to the worksheet like Farm had done. Marlese smirked and rolled her eyes up theatrically. Reggie ignored her and looked up at me. Then he picked up the pen and signed next to the thirty grand number.
"Ok and I just need your check."
Reggie turned to Marlese. She didn't make any attempt to hide her consternation as she reached under her chair for her purse. Rifling through the gigantic bag, her tiny hand found the checkbook. She thrust it at her husband stiffly. He looked at her with an expression of pain, like a dog that had just been swapped with a rolled up newspaper. Her wrist bent down slightly and he slid the checkbook from her grasp.

"You said two grand?" He repeated to me.
"That's fine." I urged.

He wrote the check out slowly and methodically.

"Make it out to you, Mark?" he kidded.
"That's fine." I jabbed back, smiling.

Marlese sat back in her chair and crossed her arms.

He peeled the check from its perforations with a satisfying rip and handed it to me. Sliding the worksheet quietly from the desk I strode back up to the tower. As I crossed the floor, I noticed that both Cortland and Joe had people in their offices also. Luckily, there was no one at the counter. Brick was looking intently at something on his desk in front of him. I slid the 4-square onto the counter above him. He slid it off without looking up and placed it over what ever else he'd been working on.

"So is he paying cash or financing?" He asked.

"What?" I returned, feeling a bit 'Pesci' again.

"It's a simple question, Stapleton."

"Oh," I said, realizing I was still holding the deposit check in my mitt. "Here"

"Ok." Brick said, taking the check from me and laying it neatly in front of him.

"Whoa, two g's, big spender!" he mocked, once again to no one in particular.

I wondered if maybe he was a little bit crazy.

"What's he want his payment to be?"

"Four-hundred."

"Where's the credit app?" he asked, holding his hand up to the counter and flipping his fingers toward his palm.

I was a fencepost.

"You don't have one do 'ya." he grimaced.

"No." I admitted.

"I figured that." He said mockingly with exasperated disappointment.

"Let's just keep this deal rolling; you'll figure it out eventually. At least you got cash and a commitment."

He drew a big line through the two 'commitments' I'd written on the back of the worksheet with his Sharpie. Under which he wrote in large letters:

OK DEAL – YOU NEED 6000 MORE DOWN TO REACH YOUR DESIRED PAYMENT x_____

I exhaled loudly again.

"Calm down, Stapleton." He scolded me, "You've got a car deal here; you just need to bring him down from *'Planet Clown'*."

I laughed. Brick smiled.

"Ok, so try to get some more money down or get him to go up on the payment."

I looked at him fearfully.
"Don't freak out, this is how we do this."
"Ok." I said taking in a deep breath to refill my lungs.
I turned to go and he added, "And don't forget the fuckin' credit app this time."

As I walked back to my office, I could see through the sliding door that Reggie was trying to placate his bride.

'This is gonna be fun.' I thought sarcastically to myself.

Sitting down again behind the desk I steeled myself briefly then delivered the news.
"So my boss is telling me that you need another six grand down to get to 400 a month."
Marlese shifted angrily to the side in her chair and glared out into the showroom. She was not even trying to hear me at all. Reggie looked at me with what seemed to be a little like anger.

"So is he gonna do the $30,000?"

I looked back at him with what I'm sure looked a little like fear.

"I'm not sure we can sell the vehicle that cheaply." I said, grasping. "Can you do any more down?"

He looked over at Marlese again. She continued to stare holes through the glass door.

"Could we do $3,000, baby?"

"You go on ahead and do what you need to do." She said, clearly annoyed.

He looked back at me, I felt his pain.

"See what he'll do with three down." He said quietly, it was almost a whisper.

"Great." I returned in a slightly louder voice.

I strode quickly up to the tower; Cortland and Joe were both working deals now. Standing quietly in the background I waited my turn. Joe was in front of Brick and leaning hard on the counter. His bony shoulders strained the fabric of his yellow dress shirt. They were talking about his customer's trade-in. The tall Arabian gentleman I'd seen earlier ducked his way around the sign and stood next to me. I noticed that we were almost exactly the same height. His shirt was the color of ripe cantaloupe and looked like it was made of silk.

"Hi." He said, leaning back against the glass windows. I nodded and smiled. It felt a little like we were in church.

"Take that turd down to Mik and see what it's actually worth." Brick said to Joe. Joe rose from the counter and inhaled; his eyes bugging out a bit as he did so. Brick glared back at him, with his hungry savannah stare. I wondered if lions ever took down ostriches in Africa.

"What you got?" Brick asked me impatiently.

"He can do three grand down." I announced.

"Where's the credit app?"

"Uh."

"You say that a lot." Brick said tersely, his lidless eyes now glaring into mine. "Didn't I tell you not to forget the credit app; I thought I'd specifically reminded you."

I fought the urge to say *'Uh'* again.

He turned his chair to Ned.

"Did I or did I not tell Stapleton to not forget the credit app."

"You told him." replied Ned, handing a worksheet to Cortland.

"I'll go get it," I started, hoping to bypass the subterfuge.

"No you will not!" Brick stated tersely. "Ned, I may need you to close this deal."

Ned looked at him with mock exasperation then pointed to the Arabian man with two upturned palms. Brick opened his mouth into what looked like a giant yawn, like he was trying to pop his ears or something. Reaching into his pocket he extracted a can of chewing tobacco and crammed a sizeable pile under his lower lip. I could smell the sickening minty aroma over the counter.

"You know what you've got here?" he asked acidly.

"What?" I asked back.

"Reach into your pocket."

"What?"

"Just reach into your pocket."

"Okay." I said robotically sliding my hand into the pocket of my khakis.

"Now reach over a little bit."

"What?"

"Reach over a little bit."

I looked at him quizzically. The sideways smile broke out from under Ned's moustache.

"That's what you got." Brick punctuated by picking up an empty soda can from beneath his desk and spitting into it.

"Very funny." I grumbled, not sure what else to say.

"Gimme your 4-square." He said more calmly, point made and taken.

I watched him fold the paper over in some weird triangular fashion so that all you could see was a blank trapezoidal shape. On this he wrote again with his Sharpie:

"OK DEAL - W/ 3000 DOWN YOUR PAYMENT WILL BE 489-499/mo w.a.c."

x_____

"He's never gonna do that." I blurted without thinking.
"Don't worry about what he won't do, Stapleton, just strap a pair on and go see what he *will* do."

I walked slowly back to the office. My legs felt a little bit rubbery, like an impala that had been running at a full sprint for too long. The worksheet dangled from my clutch like a wet rag. Marlese was still sitting sideways in her chair but Reggie was waiting patiently. I wondered if he'd ever done this before.

"So." I breathed heavily, placing the now oddly shaped worksheet in front of us again, "With three thousand down, your payment is going to be 489-499 per month."

Marlese turned her perfect nose up toward the glass door again, as if the paper had an offensive smell. Reggie dropped his head between his hands and scratched both sides of the back of his hair. It was cut very short, and his neck was very muscular, it looked like a pack of bratwursts. I considered that it wouldn't be very nice to be punched by him.

"You're not helping me out much here, Mark." He whined at the floor between his 'gi-normus' knees.
"I know man." I said back, truly empathetic.

He sat up and pulled his huge hands down his face, stretching the skin into an oddly comical expression. Looking at his lady again, she raised her hand and turned even farther toward the door. I wondered how it was physically even possible. The silence in the room was thick.

"You're gonna have to give me and Marlese a few minutes in private if that's okay?"

"No problem." I said, almost jumping up from my seat. "I'll be right back."

Exiting the office something compelled me to turn around.

"I'll just shut this door to give you two some more privacy." I said, clamping it shut.

I could feel both Brick and Ned watching me through the glass. Walking back to the tower was like treading over broken glass. My feet felt as though they'd fallen asleep in the two minutes that I'd been seated in the office. Their heads were on synchronized swivels as I circumnavigated the glass wall and positioned myself back again at the counter. It was clear that I'd done something wrong, but I had no idea what.

"What are you doing?" Ned asked immediately, Brick just leaned back in his chair and piled his hands atop his head.

"They wanted to discuss something privately." I stated protectively.

Brick swiveled his chair a bit and looked through the glass wall at the office. I turned my gaze that way as well. Reggie was now as sideways in his chair as his immense frame would allow. Marlese was talking with great gesticulation, clearly reading him the riot act.

"Oh, fuck." Brick said warily. "That bitch is queering your deal."

Ned turned his head over his shoulder to see what was going on.

"Oh, fuck." He parroted.

"You need to get in there, like right now!" Brick commanded Ned.

Ned looked up at me sternly as he exited through the little half door at the back of the tower; there was nothing at all sunny about his expression. Striding around the tower he reached over and grabbed my shoulder.

"Don't you say a fuckin' word!"
"Ok."
"Come on." And then; as we approached the door. "So it's Reggie and... what's her name again?"
"Marlese." I said with an annoyed tone.
"Introduce me then stand quietly and watch."
"Ok."

The door slid open as though it were vacuum-sealed.

"Hi guys." I said with as friendly a timbre as I could muster. "This is Ned Strong, the new car sales manager. He is gonna try and help us out here."

Ned's face lit up with sunbeams as he extended his hand, first to Reggie, then Marlese. Whatever Reggie had been talking to her about must've softened her up a bit because she shook Ned's hand and smiled. Ned sat down in my seat and looked across the desk at the two of them. His painted-on smile was infectious. They waited patiently to hear what he had to say.

"Looks like we are having a little trouble with the math here." He stated matter-of-factly.

"I'm just trying to get to 400 a month." Reggie exhaled.

"I understand." Ned returned empathetically, "It's really all about monthly payments these days."

I stood quietly against the grey wall; my jaw set and knees locked.

"Do you like the vehicle, Reggie?" Ned asked.

"Yeah, I do." Reggie admitted.

Ned looked at Marlese longingly.

"So is the car for you?" he asked Reggie specifically. Of course, he already knew the answer.

"Yes, I've always wanted a Pathfinder."

"Did Mark do a good job demonstrating the vehicle?"

Reggie looked up at me.

"He did a great job."

I smiled back.

"So you feel like this car meets your needs?"

"Yes."

"So it looks like at this point, it's just a question of math."

"We didn't think it would be so expensive." Marlese interjected.

"I understand." Ned said again, holding up his hand at her, then turning it outward to the side, palm up.

"What year is your Camry?"

"It's a '94." Marlese added.

"So it's paid off I assume?" Ned conjectured, looking squarely at Marlese.

"Yes," she sat up a bit taller in her seat, "We paid it off last year."

"So you had a five year loan?"

"Yes."

"What were your payments on that car?"

"About $300 per month."

"Okay," Ned smiled again, "Now you said about 300, that's a great low payment. Did you put a lot of money down to get such a low monthly?"

"Well," Marlese looked up, calculating in her head, "the payments were 340 something and we traded our Honda in."

"Oh," Ned pounced, "so you had a trade last time, did you put some money down also."

"We put like two grand down." Reggie offered. Marlese shot him an icy glance.

"Ok," Ned continued, "so what model was the Honda?"

"An Accord." Reggie blurted. Marlese turned in her chair with a disbelieving glare. Ned smiled up at me briefly.

"So how much did they give you for the Accord, Marlese?" Ned redirected.

"I'm not sure," she pretended, slowly turning her daggers away from her husband, "maybe like, four thousand."

"Okay." Ned said with just a hint of smugness.

Sliding the worksheet toward himself on the desk he started writing down some figures with a regular ball-point.

4000 trade
+2000 down
340/mo x 60 mos – '94 Camry

He looked down at what he'd just written as though he were examining the diagram of a nuclear power plant. Then he looked up at Marlese and Reggie slowly. The expression on his face was one of confusion.

"So you basically put six thousand down on a car six years ago and financed it for five years."

As the two of them listened, I could almost see the wind ruffling out of their sails.

"Was the Camry $30,000?" he knew it couldn't have cost that much.

"Well, no." Marlese answered, her shoulders slumped a bit.

"So what you're trying to accomplish today is you'd like to buy a six year newer car with no trade, half as much down..." he paused to scratch his head, "and achieve roughly the same payment?"

Reggie smiled at me briefly then turned back to Marlese. She studied the worksheet in front of Ned intently.

"We're just trying to get the best deal." Conceded Reggie.

"I understand," said Ned, "we want you to get the best deal too."

Marlese looked up from the worksheet at Ned. Her eyes had regained their original doe-like softness. Ned smiled at her again and raised his eyebrows. His hair was standing on end above his furrowed brow; the strands flickering like fiber optics.

"Let's do this," he comforted, spreading his arms and upturned palms out as though soliciting a group hug, "why don't you guys fill out a credit application with Mark here and we'll see if we can't get you a little closer to four hundred? Fair enough?"

We all looked at Marlese with anticipation. I felt like we'd just come inside from a game of touch football and were asking her for some cookies and milk. She rolled her eyes at Reggie and smiled.

"All right then."

"Great." Ned brought his palms together softly and pointed his steepled hands at me. "Come on up with me and get a credit application and we'll see what we can accomplish for these nice folks."

He put his palms on my desk and pushed himself up slowly; doing his best to maintain eye contact with Marlese. It was like a magnetic shift was occurring as he rose, both Marlese and Reggie seemed to relax and settle back into their chairs. Ned started out the office door and set a soft hand on the back of Reggie's shoulder, just out of Marlese's view. Reggie relaxed a tad bit more into his seat. I followed him out silently.

As we crossed back to the tower, Ned smiled at me.

"Now you have a commitment."

Ned entered the tower through the little half door at the back and I circled around to the front again. Brick watched us both intently.

"Got 'em?" he asked Ned, before he'd even sat down.

"Mark's gonna go fill out a credit app, but we've definitely got a car deal."

"Just take the whole deal jacket in with you." Brick said to me.

"Really?" I asked, not quite as certain of the deal as Ned.

Brick just stared at me.

"Ok." I said and traversed to the deal jacket stand.

By the time I'd finished the credit application, Joe was back with his trade appraisal and working his deal with Brick again. Cortland and the Arabian guy weren't around. As I made my way up to the counter, paper in hand. Ned picked up his phone and blew into it like Brick had earlier.

"ABOUD TO THE NEW CAR SALES DESK, ABOUD, NEW CAR DESK, PLEASE."

He reached his hand out for the credit app and snatched it from my fingers. As he began typing the pertinent information in his computer, the Arabian guy ducked the sign behind me,

"Yes boss?" he asked in a deep voice. He pronounced it *'boose'*.

"What are you doing?" Ned asked.

"What do you mean?"

"You got back from your test drive like twenty minutes ago."

"Yes." Aboud returned softly.

"Are you working a deal, or what?"

"Yes."

Ned finished typing in my credit app and hit enter. Then he looked up at Aboud in very much the same way Brick had just glared at me.

"So did you want to write anything down, or are you just going to shoot the shit with these people before they leave?"

Aboud looked back at him with something like confusion.

"*Joost* a second *boose*." And off he went.

Ned shook his head briefly then focused on his computer again. The dot matrix printer behind him sprang to life and started noisily ejecting several pages. Ned wheeled back to it in his chair and curled his hand behind the spooling paper.

"Yes." He exclaimed. "Where's your worksheet?" he hustled me, holding up both hands and flicking his fingers at me in a 'gimme' motion.

I handed him the folded up sheet that I'd actually remembered to grab this time.

"Watch this." He crowed, pushing up his already rolled up sleeves.

He wrote:

<u>Great Credit!</u>

w/ 3,000 down - 464-474/mo x_____

w/ 5,000 down – 433-444/mo x_____

He handed the now tri-folded worksheet back across the counter to me. I reached for it and he held it for a moment in his grip. As the paper stayed in the air between us he looked me dead in the eyes.

"Go tell 'em how the cow ate the cabbage."

He let go of his side of the worksheet and I stood there for a second with it in my grasp. I had no idea what the words really meant, but the message was clear enough. Stalking back to my office I felt a renewed vigor. Cortland and Joe passed me on either side as I crossed the showroom. They both exhibited the sense of purpose that I now felt. I was not going to take 'No' for an answer.

Entering the office I held the worksheet in front of me as though I were reading it for the first time.

"Great news!" I announced.

"It looks like your credit is really good. So with the initial 3000 you were planning to put down, your payment will be here. Or if you want to put 5000 down, your payment will go down to about here. I held my finger on the page like Cortland had shown me during the quick training session we'd had a few days prior. This time I understood partially why he'd done the gesture.

Marlese flipped her head at Reggie. Her expression said 'I told you so.'

"So after your boss went over the numbers, Marlese and I have been talking." Reggie started. It was difficult to glean from his tone what direction he was going. My breath caught in my throat.

"We decided we'd like to put a little more down and get the payment lower."

I exhaled, "So you'd like to go with the second option then?"

Reggie picked up the pen off the desk and looked one final time at Marlese.

"This one okay with you, baby?"

Marlese leaned forward and studied the numbers again.

"Yeah, I guess that's okay."

"Ok Reggie," my finger still stuck to the paper, "just sign right here, write out a check for the additional 3000 and we'll get the vehicle cleaned up for you."

Nearly running this time, I slid up next to Joe at the counter. Ned looked up and smiled as I handed him the check and signed worksheet.

"We got a deal!" I almost giggled.

Brick grabbed his phone and announced louder than he needed to:

"LOT TECH TO THE NEW CAR SALES DESK! WE HAVE A CLEAN FOR DELIVERY! LOT TECH TO THE NEW CAR DESK! WE HAVE A CLEAN – FOR – DELIVERY!!"

As the words echoed over the porch, I watched Jaime and Random's heads jerk around to see who'd sold the car. It was the first of the day. I looked at my watch, it was 10:33.

Chapter Eleven

Hat Trick... Almost.

The twenty minutes I'd waited with Marlese and Reggie to go into the finance office dragged on for what seemed like hours. We talked about everything from where they grew up, to what they did for work, descending eventually onto the weather. Finally, Mel's voice came over the loudspeakers and urged us to retire to the finance office.

I ushered them into Mel's killing room and sauntered back to the tower. My feet no longer felt tight in my shoes; in fact it felt a little like I was walking on air, or perhaps water. As I approached the tower I noticed that there were now five salespeople waiting at the counter, including Random. I figured my dice roll could wait a few minutes and slid out onto the balcony for a smoke. The porch was mostly empty, except for Jaime and Speck. Their round bodies were parked on the small bench under the roof of the showroom. It was the only part of the porch that offered any shade at midday.

"Got another one huh?" Speck droned at me, squinting with one eye up into the bright May sun.

"Yep." I answered. "Sorry about not parking the car back on the line."

"It's okay." He returned, "I should've told you."

I shook a smoke from my pack of Camels and lit up, inhaling deeply as the end crackled to life.

"I can't wait to sell another one."

"Just remember that you can't take another up until you deliver the Pathfinder." He warned.

Jamie looked up at me with a smoke hanging from his lips and wrestled his lighter from his pocket.

"You get a pull."

"A pull?" I asked.

"See those envelopes taped to the glass next to Ned?" he motioned with his head. I noticed that his hair was cut very short. It accentuated the roundness of his head and made him look a bit cartoonish. He couldn't have been a day over twenty-two. Before I had a chance to ask him his age, the loudspeakers erupted again.

"RANDALL TO THE USED CAR DESK, WE HAVE A CLEAN FOR DELIVERY."

It was Z's calm but exigent voice. He only said it once. Jaime and Speck both slumped into the back of the bench a bit more. Having located his lighter, Jaime lit up and squinted with both his child-like eyes as the smoke circled his face.

"You get to pull one of those envelopes since you sold Glinda's demo."

I looked over my shoulder and leaned around the textured cinder block pillar that was blocking my view of the tower. There were five white envelopes taped to the glass wall on Ned's left.

"So what's in the envelopes?" I asked, trying to reign in my anticipation, "More cash?"

"Not exactly." Speck interjected. "It's a spiff; they are usually between $25 and $250."

"So does that go on my paycheck?"

"You'll probably get it in cash today," Jaime added hopefully, "since they're doing the cash in fist thing this weekend."

"Fuck yeah!" I exclaimed, curling my cigarette into my lower jaw like a reptile. I took another huge pull and exhaled a monstrous blue cloud into the air. Jaime and Speck both stared blankly into the lot. The loudspeakers blared to life again.

"MR. STAPLETON TO THE NEW CAR DESK!"

I nearly jumped from my skin at the volume of the page. Peering around the rough edged cinder block column again I saw Brick and Ned snickering behind the desk. Taking another well-deserved drag off my smoke, I crossed in front of the double doors and stubbed it out into the ashtray. A bit of latent smoke trailed into the showroom, I followed it in.

As I materialized at the counter, Brick and Ned were still chuckling about scaring the bejeezus pants off of me. I stood silently in front of them, all coiled up from the startling. Joe and Random were working their deals on either side of me.

"What?" Brick asked up at me, as if he hadn't just paged me.

"What?' I shot back, still feeling bulletproof from the sale. "You paged *me*."

Joe turned to face me, obviously annoyed that I was interrupting his deal. Brick tried again to stare into me with his lion eyes. My rattlesnake stare glazed over and studied him indifferently. He seemed to cower slightly in his chair as I bowed myself over the counter. Then he smiled and turned back to Joe.

"You got nothin' here unless you can bump 'em on the down."

"Come on Man." Joe whined.

"We've already taken all the fun out of this deal!" Brick argued back. "Go get me two grand."

Joe slapped his worksheet off the counter and stormed around me. Random and Ned were having a slightly more friendly conversation. Ned handed the worksheet back over the counter and Random disappeared as well. They both looked up at me now, their catbird grins a matched set. I propped myself up on my arms and smiled smugly.

"Jaime just told me that I get a pull for selling Glinda's demo." I broke the silence. "Is that her real name?"

They both laughed out loud.

"I guess you do get a pull." Brick begrudged.
"Take your pick." Ned promulgated with a flourish of his arm toward the envelopes. There were five.
He reminded me a little of Pat Sajak… and Vanna White. I studied the envelopes intently, trying to guess which one might hold the highest number. An old bar trick leapt to mind where everyone picks the number three.

"Three." I said without thinking.

Ned reached up and peeled the taped envelope from the glass. Brick rolled his chair over and snatched it from him, ripping the end off. I was reminded of Johnny Carson as Carnac the Magnificent. Brick blew the envelope open and peered inside.

"Whoa!" I heard myself exclaim. "Don't I get to do that part?"

Ned looked over at him too, still surprised.

"No." Brick answered. His expression was that of a greedy child.

Ned looked up at me wryly, and then we both waited on Carnac. Brick slid his sticky fingers into the now open packet and began sliding out the small piece of paper hidden inside. He slipped it out painfully slow.

"I see a two," He purred irritatingly. "A five... and..."

Both Ned and I listened impatiently. Joe and Random had joined us back up at the desk. I could see that Aboud was headed across the showroom as well.

"No fuckin' way!" he growled.
"What?" Ned yipped.

Brick showed him the paper, still not allowing me to see. Ned laughed a high-pitched laugh, hyena-like, as he looked up at me. Aboud rounded the corner just as I got the news.

"You pulled the golden egg." Ned said, shaking his head in sunny disbelief.

Brick turned the paper toward me, making sure the other sales guys could see it. It read $250!

"No fuckin' way!" Joe squawked.
"No, fuckin', way." agreed Random.
"Yes." I hissed. "So I get that in cash right?"

Brick's lips retreated from his teeth.

"You pay him." He grumbled at Ned, reaching into his pocket for another dip of tobacco.
"Okay." Ned chirped, drawing a wad of cash from his own pocket.

We all watched him lay the money in front of me, two crispers and a fifty.

"Thank you." I gulped, folding the cash in my hand.

"Does he get a dice roll, too?" Aboud asked in a whisper, his eyes alight with fascination.

Ned turned to Brick again questioningly; his expression again a salacious desert dog's. Brick stared down into his can of chew like it was a black hole. The guys and I stood at the counter with bated breath.

"I guess he does." Brick whined, stuffing a large finger load of tobacco into his cheek. He reached below his desk and spat into a little Styrofoam cup then wiped his lips with a Kleenex and stuffed it into the cup also.

"Come on, Stapleton." He dropped the dice on the counter in front of him, "Let's make this quick, we've got customers waiting."

I scooped the dice up and rolled a three.
"Crap." I hissed again, not really caring what I'd rolled.
"Gonna' double-down, you heartless bastard." Brick jibed, the nicotine obviously easing his consternation.

"Fuck yeah!" I jeered, rolling an eleven.

Brick glanced at the dice for a brief moment then scooped them up knowing his chances were only one in twelve at best. He rolled a nine. I remained mute as he laid out three more twenties in front of me.
"You suck." He murmured and then, "Deliver that Pathfinder then get me two more car deals today."
"Yes sir!"

Tidily shuffling the twenties together I faced them on top of the two hundred and fifty Ned had just given me and deposited the little grip of cash into my own pocket. I calculated in my head as I slid past the other dumbfounded sales guys that I'd just made four-hundred and ten dollars off this deal. On top of the three-hundred plus I'd made the night before, even with the split, that was roughly $125/hour. I decided that I might like this business after all.

The husky pencil was nowhere in sight.

******

Marlese and Reggie emerged from the finance office on a pink cloud, still under the ether of their new purchase. Escorting them outside, I showed them their sparkling new car. As I went over the standard delivery procedure I felt a little like Bob Barker. All that was missing was that retarded wand-like microphone he used to use. As I pushed Marlese's vacuum-sealed door closed, I felt a tingling in my body that traced my spine and tickled up the back of my neck. The guys glared over the balcony railing at me with obvious envy.

I barely had a chance to finger my smokes before two more sets of customers pulled onto the lot. Pausing at the bottom of the ramp, I had to nail my feet to the pavement for want of striking too quickly. As the first couple got out of their car, Joe flew past me with his ostrich stride. I sidled to my left and slithered toward the second set. Coiled in the middle of the customer parking I anxiously waited for them, standing my ground voraciously. Feeling a hand on my shoulder, I nearly jumped from my skin again. It was Farm.

"When's the best time to sell a car?" He asked in his frank style.

"What?" I returned absently.

"When is the best time to sell a car?"

"I don't know."

"Right after you just sold one."

I turned my gaze to him quickly. He was smiling back at me, his hair spiked up into clumps from the blatant overuse of hair gel. I smiled back at him beneath the Arapahoe sun.

"Okay." I murmured.

Two men had gotten out of a rather nice luxury sedan. They appeared to be father and son. As they walked toward us, I extended my hand and welcomed them to the dealership. The younger of the two took my hand excitedly, his father was less enthusiastic. When the older man took my hand, his shake was reluctant and soft, as if he wasn't used to being touched.

"My son is going to CU in the fall and he needs a good, economical car."

"Great." I returned. "Let's take a look."

I had my second up of the day and they looked like buyers too. It wasn't even noon yet.

Starting toward the line of smaller vehicles, I began asking some pertinent questions.

"I assume you're looking for a vehicle that gets good gas mileage?"

"Yes." The father agreed. "But it's got to be safe also."

"No problem." I returned, "We've got some of the safest cars on the market."

The son was walking a few steps ahead of us, eyeing the inventory. He stopped in front of a red Sentra that was equipped with a spoiler on the trunk.

"I like this one, Pop." He announced.

Remembering to grab the stock number this time, I told them to wait while I grabbed the keys. They stood by the vehicle as I trotted back up to the showroom.

'This shit is too easy.' I thought to myself.

Jaime and Speck followed me with their eyes as I shot through the double doors for the keys. I noticed from the corner of my eye that Random and Aboud were on the other side of the porch as well, both smoking. Wondering if either of them had made their deals, I found myself at the reception desk.

"Did you remember the stock number this time?" Cherlie asked without looking up.

"S-5497." I stated proudly.

"Good boy." She said, looking up with a sweet smile.

Snagging the keys from her, I shot into my office for a plate and nearly sprinted back across the showroom floor to the front doors. Farm was parked up at the tower in front of Brick. They both watched me intently as I made my exit.

The boy and his father stood by the car like wax statues as I skipped down the ramp and jogged over to them.

"Is this the most expensive model of this car?" the father asked, his finger pointing to the sticker.

I stood next to him and stared dumbly down at the sticker also. Pasted to the window were the actual *'Munroney'* sticker and a second cardboard tag called an addendum. The second sticker had one line printed on it which read, "Adjusted Market Value" with $1,500 printed on the same line. The bottom figure on the second sticker was the MSRP plus the additional fifteen-hundred. The total was a little over seventeen grand.

"Well, uh. This one is a bit more nicely equipped than some of the others." I stumbled, not really sure what to say.

The young man perked up and the older one's lips drew a bit tighter together.

"I'm sure we can find one that fits your budget." I offered, trying to lighten up the situation. The young man looked at his dad longingly. Dad just stared at the stickers with shock and dismay.

"Let me just pull it out for you and we can go over some of the features."

"Sweet." The young man said, taking three large steps back. Dad unglued himself from the window and watched me pull the car out slowly. I could almost hear the gentle unknotting of the purse strings.

The sporty little Sentra sat between the clean lines of cars with all the doors open. I heard myself yammering on about hood safety catches, pipe-style door beams and twelve-gauge steel construction. Dad listened intently, thankful for my reasoning; the son was thoroughly disinterested. As I shuffled them into the vehicle, the son hopped into the shotgun position and Dad wedged himself into the middle of the back seat. I pointed out the CD player to the kid then flipped on the a/c and started creeping off the lot.

Pulling safely onto Colfax, I asked them if they wanted the city loop or the longer drive up the interstate. They opted for the latter. As we started down the onramp toward I-70 the acceleration of the little car was impressive. It was a learning experience for all three of us as I'd never driven a Sentra before. I decided not to share this information. The young man was visibly excited and I reiterated that sometimes it's better to have the additional power in certain situations. The traffic was insane.

We climbed out of the city and I continued to drive quickly but safely up to the 'Mother Cabrini' exit. Pulling off the highway again I curled into the little dirt parking lot that Speck had shown me the other day. It seemed like it was years ago. Figuring that Dad might be more comfortable up front I got them all out and reconfigured our seating arrangement so that I was now in the back seat. I made sure that the kid adjusted his mirrors and knew where all the controls were. Dad relaxed in the passenger's seat a little bit as we pulled onto the frontage road. The young man was clearly a bit nervous as we headed down the hill.

"Try to keep it under sixty." I offered charmingly. Dad laughed nervously. Son gripped the wheel tightly, sitting up in the seat with his face glued to the windshield. We didn't do more than forty the entire way back down the hill. By the time we'd passed the Conoco station, I could tell that the boy was a bit more comfortable with the operation of the vehicle.

"Okay," I directed, "at the stoplight, you want to turn right and go under the overpass. Then get in the left lane and get back on I-70."

"Okay." The young man answered.

Dad sat up in his seat a bit as his son performed the maneuver. They were both a bit nervous. As we started up the onramp, I urged the young man to feel the power of the vehicle. He merged tentatively into traffic, and I saw his Dad relax again into the passenger seat. The young man let the car go a bit as we descended back into the city. Seeing that his comfort level had returned I had him take the Sixth Avenue exit so that he could get a bit more freeway driving. As we weaved smoothly through the traffic, I felt myself relax as well. The little compact slid easily in and out of the other cars like a shuttle through a loom. Still feeling strong about my earlier sale, I decided to push forward a little bit.

"So you like the car?" I asked.

"It's awesome." The young man blurted.

"Dad?"

"It seems like a very nice car." Dad assisted.

"Great." I punctuated. "Let's take the next exit and head back toward the dealership."

The young man flipped on the blinker and veered out of the middle lane onto the off ramp. We had a green light at the top so he continued through the intersection and looped back to the store. Making sure that they pulled the car back into the line this time, I headed coolly for the showroom. Dad took a more sideways path through the other cars, stopping briefly at a couple to review the window stickers. The young man and I stood at the end of the line quietly. The old man paused confusedly a couple of times and curled his finger over his chin. I had no idea what any of these cars cost, so I just waited patiently. Seemingly satisfied, Dad finally made his way over to us. Not sure if I should ask him the 'closing question' I'd been taught, I just turned and walked them up to the showroom.

The balcony was relatively empty as we climbed the cement ramp. The doors whooshed open at the top and we wound our way through and over to my office. Speck was on the phone in there so we slid past his door and took the next free office. I think it was Joe's. Sitting them down, I realized I was very thirsty.

"Would either of you care for something to drink?" I found myself offering.

"I'll take a coke." said the young man.

"Water will be fine." Dad emphasized politely.

"Two cokes and one water." I responded, feeling like a waiter. "I'll be right back."

Sliding out of the office I realized that I had no idea if we even had a soda machine. Wandering toward the back of the dealership, I rounded the corner in front of the finance offices. I stood in the brightly lit hallway feeling completely lost. The older woman I'd seen in Friday's sales meeting looked up at me from a desk in the second office.

"Can I help you?" she asked curtly, her accent an annoyed Long Island.

"Is there a soda machine back here?" I immediately returned as politely as possible.

"Down the hall to the right." She pointed with her left hand. I half expected her to finish with, 'Now quit buggin' me.'

I looked down the short hallway and realized that a small waiting area was there with a Coke machine humming away quietly beneath the buzz of the overhead fluorescents. The woman had turned her attention back to her desk. I decided not to interrupt her with a 'thank you' and bobbed into the waiting room. Reaching into my pocket, I realized that I didn't have any change. Standing stupidly in the empty room with my hand in my pocket, bathed in the blaring red light of the machine, I must've looked a little like a lost Indian. Another woman appeared at the entry to the room. She was dressed quite smartly in a business suit with a tight knee-length skirt. Her hair was perfect. She looked me up and down briefly, then proceeded to the machine and inserted a couple quarters. She selected a Sprite and bent over gracefully in front of me to retrieve the can. For a forty-something woman, her ass was… quite perfect. Turning in front of me with the soda can curled in her kitten's paw she looked at me oddly, blinking her made-up eyes.

"You lost?" she asked dulcetly. He voice was like buttery caramel.

"Um…" I stammered. Hoping she hadn't seen me checking out her hind-end just now. "Do you have change?" I heard myself say as I pulled a giant wad of cash from my pocket.

Her hair was blonder than I'd ever seen; almost white. She couldn't have been more than 5'5" but seemed somehow taller. She looked up at me with sky-blue, almond shaped eyes. They didn't match her hair really but they were quite beautiful nonetheless. Her cheekbones were high and stretched her mouth into an unintended pout. Her lips were painted with a pinkish hue. Not like eighties video-star pink, more like grandmother's soap you aren't allowed to use pink. Her expression was one of silent mockery.

"The cashier's counter is around the corner." She pointed with her free, Barbie-doll hand. Her suit jacket was cut to hug her ample breasts perfectly.

"Thanks." I said quickly, realizing that she worked here… and was probably also another one of my bosses.

"You better hurry," she smiled. It was one of those smiles where the lips quivered a little bit and the corners of her mouth turned down slightly. "They close at 1:30."

I looked at my watch, it was 1:19.

"Right." I said back quickly.

She laughed and punched me in the chest playfully with her Sprite hand.

"You green-peas crack me up."

Then she turned gracefully on her not too tall, navy stilettos and clicked back down the hallway. Her tight little figure swayed slightly as she walked and I noticed a small slit in the back of skirt above her shapely calves. Then she slipped through a door on the left side of the hall and was gone.

"Mmm." I grunted primally, then found my own way to the cashier.

A young woman sat in a small box that looked like a closet. A thick pane of glass stood between us. A small metallic grate was positioned in the center. The wide hipped girl looked up at me tiredly as I stood at the little counter, it was also royal blue. Her hands were filled with paperwork of different shapes and sizes.

"Yes." She asked; her eyes were ringed in black. The eyeliner curled up at the corners like an Egyptian's.

"Could I get change for a dollar, please?"

Slapping the paperwork down into two piles in front of her, she yanked the drawer open.

"Just a dollar?" she droned impatiently.

"Yes, one." I answered quickly, "No wait, two."

She looked at me wanly as if making sure I was done.

"Two." I said again, sliding a couple crumpled bills under the glass.

She pulled the bills from the metal tray, smoothed and faced them, then put them into her drawer. Scooping a handful of quarters she chucked eight of them into the little metal tray angrily. The coins spun chaotically then noisily flattened themselves on the bottom of the tray with a metallic buzz.

'Who shit in her Easter Basket?' I thought as I turned back to the waiting room.

"Jesus." I whispered as I stuck the quarters into the giant machine.

*

Dad and Son appeared to be in the midst of a very serious discussion when I returned with two cokes and a little Styrofoam cup of water. I felt Brick glaring at me through the glass wall at the tower. Sidling into the office I set the drinks on the desktop in front of us. The boy snatched his up immediately and cracked it open, slurping the foam off the top. His father collected the little cup in his long fingers and took a small sip. Taking the cue I opened my coke as quietly as possible and took a small drink as well. The bubbles bit at the back of my throat.

"Okay," I croaked, then took another big drink, grimacing as the brutal concoction cleared my throat. "So I assume that you're not planning to trade anything?"

"Nope." The kid blurted.

"Let's not put the cart before the horse just yet, Mark." Dad stopped. "I'm concerned about the affordability of this particular car."

The young man set his coke down with an audible clunk and sat back in his chair petulantly. Un-phased by the action the old man continued.

"I saw some other cars out there that were considerably less expensive."

I set my can of coke down also, as silently as possible. Not sure how to proceed. Dad mercifully spoke again.

"We might want to look at one of those."

Since I had no idea how much the others cost. I couldn't really respond.

"Hold on." I said; rising up in my chair a bit and holding both index fingers extended at the pair of them.

Sliding out of the office with my head down, I nearly crashed into Joe and his customers. He glared at me with his buggy eyes as I side-wound around them and headed for the tower. As I passed he noticed that I'd commandeered his office and his glare narrowed to a glower. Curling my gaze away I wove myself through two other salesmen and continued forth. The space in front of the counter was now filled with salespeople. I braided my way into the mass and stood patiently with my back against the glass windows. My back had barely touched the glass before Brick's voice sailed over the top.

"STAPLETON." He spouted sternly.

Merging through the milling salespeople, I rose up at the desk.

"What the fuck are you doing?" Brick intoned.

"I just finished a test drive…" I started.

"Why'd you leave your customers in Righter's office?"

'Who's Righter?' I thought.

"I had to get change for the…"

"Never leave a customer alone during the sale."

"What?"

"When you leave the customers alone, they come out of the ether. If you've got them down, you need to finish the fight."

I shot him a puzzled look, still trying to unravel the mixed metaphors. His gaze came back more reptilian this time.

"Never mind." He spat. "Which car are they on?"

"Well I drove them in the red Sentra…"

"…but now they want to look at some cheaper ones." He finished my sentence for me.

I went mute.

"What's the stock number?"

"Um… wait!" I thrust back, fishing into my pocket for the keys. "5497."

He wheeled his chair across the floor behind Ned and grabbed a large three-ring binder. It was filled with inventory sheets showing the different cars we had in stock. He grabbed the 'Sentra' tab and flipped the book open to that section. Licking his fingers, he sifted through the pages at with lightning speed.

"Fuck." He whispered to himself.

"What?" I whispered back in confidence.

"You've got 'em on the most expensive one."

Peeling a four-square from the pad on his desk, he began to pencil the deal. He wrote the MSRP this time with no discount. Then he proceeded with the down and payments.

"Don't switch 'em yet." He said softly, "Let's see how bad the kid wants this one."

"How much less are the other ones?"

"They're on a fucking Sentra; it's only a few hundred dollars difference between the base model and the hard-loaded 'SE' that your dumb ass put them on."

"So…" I said, trying to calculate payments in my head, "that's like fifty bucks a month difference?"

"More like forty." Brick said even more softly, "But don't worry about that right now. Just try to keep 'em on the unit you drove."

"K."

Threading my way back through the salespeople, I noticed that all the offices were now full. Joe had seated his customers at one of the tables on the showroom floor. He shot me a glance as I looked over my shoulder at them. It was less pointed than before. I wheeled into the office and slid the worksheet across the desk in front of us. As I explained the terms, the cords in Dad's neck stood out in taught strands.

"I think we'd like to look at a less expensive vehicle." He responded immediately after I'd finished.

The young man sighed.

"Okay," I started, "but the other Sentras aren't that much cheaper.

"It appears that there are some that are quite a bit cheaper."

I looked back at him dully.

"Let me check and see what other options we have available."

As I crossed the showroom floor again, my muscles felt like knots had been tied in them. I'd been going nonstop now for about five hours and was feeling a bit drained physically. Wishing I'd brought my Coke with me, I found myself back up at the desk.

"Dad wants to look at something cheaper."

"Of course he does." Brick intoned prophetically.

The three-ring binder was still on his desk and he flipped it open to the Sentra invoices.

"Show 'em 5432." He said quickly. "Let's see if they want that bean can."

I wasn't sure what a bean can was, but it didn't sound good. Nonetheless, I collected the keys from Cherlie and trotted back to Joe's office. Leaning in I informed them that I'd found a cheaper vehicle.

"Great." The young man grumbled, his Dad shot him a disapproving look.

As we walked back out into the wooly heat of the early afternoon, I realized that I'd not yet eaten lunch. My stomach growled lowly and we slid back out onto the glossy blacktop. The sun was well past overhead now, but still high enough to pound unmercifully down upon us. Locating the vehicle quickly I pulled it off the line and immediately rolled all the windows down, at least they were power.

The car wasn't noticeably different from the one we'd just driven, excepting the fact that the interior was a bit more basic, there wasn't a spoiler on the trunk and the wheels were steel with some sort of plastic covers. That and the color; it was a hideous brownish-gold that took on an almost greenish hue. Difficult to describe without actually seeing it, the color was like something you'd see on a plate of Indian food, or maybe in a diaper. It screamed economy. The look on the young man's face bordered on horror, the old man seemed smugly impressed. My stomach grumbled somewhere below again.

"Could you roll up the window, so that we can see sticker, Mark?" Dad asked pleasantly.

"Sure." I said, flicking the button.

The window responded immediately and the father's demeanor improved considerably as the numbers rolled up in front of him. Noticing a blue a/c button on the dash, I pushed it and a little fan whirred to life. The air was already surprisingly cool, so I proceeded to roll up all the windows. The young man stood several steps back from the vehicle; his face had the look of sour milk. But Dad was much happier with the sticker price. This one was in the low fifteen neighborhood, even with the addendum. All I had to do was convince the kid that 'baby-shit' was his color.

Dad decided against taking another drive so we went back inside for some further negotiation. I retrieved another four-square from the desk. This time Brick priced the vehicle with a discount. The down and the payments were lower also. I presented the information quickly. The old man listened intently; his son sat quietly clutching his Coke.

"Looks good, Mark." The father stated. "But I'd like to see the invoice."

I wasn't sure what he was asking so I went back to the tower. Farm was positioned behind Brick this time.

"He wants to see the invoice?" I told them.

Brick flipped the binder open again and handed me the inventory sheet.

"Get me three percent over." He said.

I stood at the counter with the piece of paper in my hand. Brick looked back at me stoically.

"You need me to do the math."

Slamming the buttons on his large ten-key calculator, he ripped the ticker-tape from the top and handed it to me.

"Invoice on that vehicle is 13,127. Three percent over is 13,521. Get me that."

"Ok." I said.

Staring down at the invoice and the little ticker-tape, I ducked under the sign and walked slowly back to the office. Setting the sheets of paper neatly in front of the old man, I explained the deal.

"Here is the invoice," I started, "my boss will sell the car for three percent over, which is 13,521."

Sliding the tape forward, I let him inspect the math. Dad picked up the two sheets of paper and scanned them both. His eyes darted back and forth as he did the math in his head. The young man inspected his soda can dejectedly.

"I'll give you thirteen-three." He offered.

"Ok." I answered looking around for a place to write the offer. Since I didn't have a worksheet, I opted to write it on the invoice.

'I   will   buy   and   drive   today   for $13,300.

X_____ '

I spun the paper around and slid it in front of Dad. Holding the pen out to him, he slid it slowly from my grasp. Pausing briefly, as if doing some final calculation, he reluctantly put the pen to the page and signed.

"Great." I said quickly, pulling the page from the desktop. "I'll go see if that works."

Slinking through three other salesmen I wound my way back up to the tower.

"He offered thirteen-three." I stated, handing Brick the invoice.

"Weak suck." He whispered under his breath. "Don't write on these." He added, seeing my offer on the invoice. "Is he paying cash?"

I looked at him dumbly.

"You didn't ask him, did you?"

My head nodded slowly, no. Brick looked over his shoulder at Farm. Farm smiled down at him crookedly.

I felt a bit of nervousness rise in the pit of my stomach.

"Go get a check." Brick acquiesced.

"Ok." I said quickly.

Sliding back to the office I heard him announce another *'Clean for Delivery'* over the loudspeaker.

"We've got a deal." I announced, extending my arm around and through the door. "I assume you're paying cash?"

"Yes." The old man agreed, shaking my hand briefly.

"Great, so I'll just need a check for the total and we can start the paperwork."

The man was methodical about writing out the check; even filling in the little memo section to denote that is was for a car. As if he wrote huge checks like this all the time and he might forget shelling out thirteen grand or something. He peeled the check slowly out of his book, making sure not to rip the thing. Then he handed it reluctantly over to me. His son was clearly despondent. I slid the check gingerly from his grip and slowly began to exit the office.

"Thanks." I added as an afterthought.

Dropping the check with Brick, I grabbed a deal jacket and filled it out as fast as possible. After checking it off with the tower, I took the folder back to the finance offices. The offices were designed roughly the same way the sales offices were with the sliding doors on the front. Although these cubicles seemed a bit deeper, and the walls were white. Mel and the older woman both had little plastic hoppers stuck to the outside of the glass on their doors. Mel's already had another deal jacket in it and he had a deal laid out on his desk. Before I was within five steps of the door he looked up and saw me coming.

"I'm busy!" he barked, "Take that deal to Brenda."

I pointed to the next office questioningly then answered my own question by following my finger. She had a deal on her desk so I deposited the jacket in her little plastic hopper. She looked up at me briefly then back down at the paperwork in front of her. We said nothing. I looked at my watch, it was 1:44.

**

The third dice roll of the weekend had brought me another eighty bucks in cash and I was ebullient. I'd doubled-down again on a four and Brick was tired of seeing my face. I stood at the far corner of the porch nearest Colfax, enjoying a smoke. The lot was full of people now and salesmen were running to and fro like ants. Cars and trucks rolled in and out below me in concert with the afternoon traffic of the busy city.

"Did you eat lunch yet?"

It was Farm. I took another puff off my smoke and felt the warm swirls fill my insides. Exhaling loudly I realized that I hadn't. My head rotated on my neck, indicating the negative.

"Let's go over to Rubble's."

He motioned to the burger joint across Colfax. I realized that I hadn't noticed the name before.

"K." I said turning to walk down the stairs.

"Let me just tell Brick." Farm said.

I waited patiently halfway down the stairs, watching them through the glass. Brick rose out of his chair briefly then sat back down, nodding. Farm turned back to the door and stormed out in a hurry.

"We've got like twenty minutes."

Jaywalking across the busy four lane street, we had to pause on the cement median before trotting ahead of the oncoming traffic.

The little restaurant was packed. A couple of the other salesmen were standing in the mass of people at the counter. Three cooks were moving frantically around the grill and fryer behind the line. Clouds of black smoke billowed into the stainless steel hood above them. As Farm reached the front of the line he ordered three burgers with curly fries and a butterscotch shake.

"What do you want to drink?" He asked me quickly.

"They serve shakes here?" I inquired stupidly.

"You saw me just order one, right?" He shot back sarcastically.

"Uh, yeah." I giggled back. Nothing could sap my mood at this point, I'd already made over eight-hundred bucks in less than twenty-four hours, five-hundred and fifty of which was in cash.

"I'll take a chocolate one."

He finished ordering then turned to me.

"This one's on you, moneybags."

I looked at him with mock dismay then reached into my pocket. It was thirty-three bucks.

The mustachioed clerk gave me my change then handed me a greasy ticket and told us to wait. A young, dark-haired woman in a white, a-line t-shirt set our shakes and a third drink on the counter. Her skin had an olive tinge and her long, charcoal colored hair was pulled tightly into a sleek pony tail. She seemed a bit out of place amongst the bearish men that were slaving away around her. Perspiration glistened on the bare skin of her arms and forced the ribbed cotton of her t-shirt to cling to her perky breasts. The black brassiere she'd mistakenly chosen to wear was clearly visible through the stretched thin fabric. Farm motioned me over to an empty space by the gumball machines, which was less congested. I grabbed the drinks in my claws and followed him over.

"You'd be smart to stay away from that one," he warned quietly, "she's only sixteen."

"I'm married, dude." I returned with a mixture of embarrassment and shock.

"Yeah." He intimated, "Me too."

I looked at the girl again briefly.

"She's only sixteen?" I asked in disbelief. My tone one of disbelief.

"Yeah," he shot back in a sharp whisper, "they're Greek or something."

"Oh." I mused disconnectedly, enjoying the eyeful for a few more seconds.

"Infidel." He hummed into my ear.

Within five minutes, our burgers were sufficiently charred and the girl called us back up to the counter. Grabbing the three bags, Farm ducked out the door. I followed him out. The sun glared off the white wall of the bowling alley across the small parking lot. It blinded me momentarily as I fumbled for my shades.

"Whose lunch am I buying?"

"Ned's."

"Cool," I said genuinely, "that's real nice of me."

"Yeah." Farm smiled. "The least you could do."

I shook my head as the gravelly asphalt of the decrepit parking lot crunched beneath our feet. The cars shot past us on Colfax and we were forced to play a 'real' game of Frogger in an attempt to get back to the lot. Safely on the other side, Farm headed for the Hogan. The Ute sun was a fireball high in the western sky. Ned had already emerged from the showroom and was angling to meet up with us. We met at the side door and entered the building together. A narrow staircase wound up through the center of the building and led us into a small lunchroom. I inhaled a large glop of shake into the back of my throat. It was cold and sweet and refreshing.

"So I guess you're feeling about ten feet tall." Ned said cheerfully as he snatched one of the bags from the lunch table.

"And bulletproof." Farm added, extracting a pile of fries from his bag and stuffing them into his beak.

I smiled smugly and grabbed my greasy bag from the table. My stomach growled like a grizzly as the smell of meat curled up into my nostrils.

"We just need to get you one more today." Ned continued.

"That would be nice." I said, unwrapping my burger from its glittery foil package.

"Nice has nothing to do with it." Farm clucked.

We all shared a gruff laugh.

"So what do you think so far?" Ned asked.

"I think this is gonna work out pretty good for me." I answered smoothly. My burger was half gone and my stomach was now gurgling happily.

"Where'd you get weak on the red Sentra?" Farm inquired.

I looked at him questioningly.

"I sold the brown one."

"Brick gave the brown one away so we wouldn't lose the deal." Ned said matter-of-factly. "It had to go bye-bye."

He smiled at Farm, a bit of mustard tainting his neatly trimmed mustache. Farm motioned for him to wipe it off. I looked at them both with a pained expression.

"Always walk 'em to the cheapest model first." Farm said flatly.

"What?" I asked dumbly.

"If you walk 'em to the cheapest ride than you can always get 'em to bump themselves; if you start too high then you're just making it harder on yourself."

"Oh."

"That's exactly right." Ned agreed.

I didn't really understand what they were talking about, but again, what the hell did I know. We ate in silence for a while then stuffed our trash into the overfull garbage can. As we emerged from the side door again, our short shadows were pasted against the sidewalk. It seemed like it might never be cloudy again. We all lit up and smoked down our lunches in the afternoon sun. Then we began the slow trek back toward the showroom.

"You should let Farm work with you on your next deal." Ned offered. "It'll save you some pain and suffering."

"Yeah?" I questioned.

"Yeah." Farm finished.

We finished our cigarettes in silence as we continued across the lot. It was surprisingly empty. The porch was dotted with only a couple of salesmen as we slogged up the ramp. My belly was full and I felt like taking a nap. Farm and Ned stubbed out their smokes together and headed back into the showroom. I took a seat on the little bench out front. Joe came out shortly thereafter and slumped down next to me. He was visibly frustrated, his face and neck red. He leaned his head back over the edge of the bench and exhaled a groan.

"What's up?" I asked with genuine interest.

"I fucking hate Nissan buyers." He returned tiredly. "These fuckers will drive fifty miles to save five bucks!"

"Did you sell any of your appointments?"

"Yeah." He whined, "I got one of 'em."

"That's good."

"Yeah." He moaned, "But I lost my dice roll cash when I doubled down."

"Bummer." I sympathized.

"Yeah."

I thought about the little pile of cash in my pocket and decided to change the subject.

"You married?" I asked.

"No," he stated flatly, "I already tried that."

"Oh?"

"Yeah, I've got two kids though."

I examined his profile, a slight scruff was forming along his jaw and the beginning of a dark circle was forming under his right eye.

"So how's that work?"

"I get 'em three nights a week," he answered sadly, "but the my Bitch-Weasel ex-wife worked me for like eleven-hundred bucks a month in child support."

"Jesus!" I said a bit louder than I'd intended. "You make that kind of money here?"

"I was running my own business when we got divorced and I made a lot more than I make now."

"Fuck." I said more quietly.

"Yeah." He said, "I wouldn't recommend marrying a Mormon."

"My wife's a Baptist." I commiserated. "But she doesn't really go to church."

"Just wait dude." He carried on. "How old are your kids?"

"My daughter isn't quite two months old."

"Just one?" he asked.

"Yeah."

"Lucky fucker." He said more to himself than me.

An old Toyota truck turned slowly into the middle entrance and headed for the used car side. We both perked up briefly then saw Tristan walking swiftly toward the vehicle from the used car building. His highly shined shoes reflected the western rays of the sun. We both settled back again. I lit up another smoke, the burger; fries and shake were like a ball of cement in my stomach.

"Are you from Utah originally?"

"How'd you guess?" he droned.

I laughed politely.

"I'm *psycho*." I returned sunnily.

He laughed too.

"How old are you, again?"

"Thirty-three." Joe groaned.

I almost told him that was what I'd paid for lunch then figured that would just sound stupid.

"You?"

We'd both forgotten that we'd already had this conversation.

"I just turned thirty."

"Thirty's the new twenty." He said glibly.

"Let's hope so." I smiled.

"Yeah," he reaffirmed tiredly, "Let's hope so."

Random came out of the double doors in a flurry and stormed past us to the railing. He lit up and spewed a green, menthol cloud into the air. We eyed him coolly from our shady spot. He took another drag and looked over his shoulder. Noticing I was there, he turned slowly and walked toward us. He was clearly perturbed as well.

"So how many you got today, Stapleton?" he asked jealously. "Every time I turn around they're calling 'Clean for Delivery' and there you are."

"Just two." I laughed.

"Fuck."

"You get one yet?" I asked, already knowing the answer.

"Fuck no!" he moaned. "My first guy wouldn't move a lousy twenty-two bucks a month and my second up…" he took another huge puff off his smoke. "Shit, it doesn't even matter."

I took another pull off my own cigarette and realized that the cherry had nearly burned down to the filter. Blowing the sickly sweet smoke from my mouth, I stood up to deposit the butt in the ashcan.

"You'll get one." I said in a big brotherly tone.

"Yeah," he groaned again, "and if a frog had wings, he wouldn't bump his ass when he hopped." His tone took on a southerly accent as he said the last part. I looked down at Joe; he was trying to stifle his laughter. The smell of bacon wafted across the street from Rubble's. I looked back at Random, wondering where he'd come up with that one.

"You're from Aurora, right?"

"Yeah?"

I turned my expression back down at Joe again he was clutching his liver and chuckling to himself.

"Like Aurora, Colorado, right?" Joe added.

Random looked at us blackly.

"Yeah…"

"He wouldn't bump his ass when he hopped?" I asked.

Joe lost it.

I followed him shortly.

Random's face broke into a gigantic smile.

Tears were leaking from Joe's eyes and he doubled over on the bench. I was laughing so hard I had to steady myself against one of the cinder block pillars.

"Fuck all y'all, motherfuckers." Random gurgled, but his smile told the story.

Soon we were all giggling uncontrollably.

Brick burst through the double doors and waddled out to the railing. He turned his back to the lot and folded his arms across his chest, surveying the three of us.

"What are you chuckleheads doing?" he sneered.

Joe was the first to try and contain himself.

"Nothing." He squeaked, and then peeled out with uncontrollable laughter again.

I was still racked with the hilarity of the situation. Random smiled boldly.

"It's nothing." He tried to say, and then giggled to himself.

Brick looked at me, I was laughing so hard I could scarcely breath. He smiled too. Our mood was infectious.

"You guys eat lunch yet?" he asked in a fatherly tone.

"No." Joe intoned, "I missed it."

"I just ate." I said though the remainder of my laughter.

"I got mine." Random said. "Do you guys always buy lunch for us on Saturdays?"

My look was surprised at this. "You guys buy us lunch?"

Brick looked at me like I was a complete idiot.

"How long have you worked here?" He asked.

"Um, two weeks?"

"The dealership provides lunch every Saturday." He stated, "In the lunchroom."

'Thanks for tellin' me!' I thought.

Brick smile/grimaced again.

"Get another up." He directed at Random.

"You too." He said to me.

"Joe, you eat something then see me at the tower."

Joe lifted his lank frame off the bench and headed down the stairs toward Rubble's. I joined Random at the railing and we stared out at the lot. Brick stalked stiffly back inside.

***

My third up of the day proved to be a no-go. I stood on the porch in the waning afternoon wondering if I'd get a third deal. My feet were tired and the husky pencil was inching its way to the back side of my forehead again.

"Brain damage." I heard Farm's voice behind me.
"What?"
"That last deal of yours," he clarified, "brain damage."
"Yeah." I said, again not really sure of his meaning.
"We'll get you a third deal." He assured me.

A rusty old Ford pickup rattled into the customer parking below us. The blue-black diesel fumes leaked up through the rusty holes in its rear fenders.

"Nice." Farm incanted. I was not of the same mind. "That's a car deal waiting to happen." He continued.
"Uh-huh." I mumbled.
"Come on." He said optimistically. "Let's get you that third deal."

Following him reluctantly down the ramp, I watched as the gargantuan behemoth of a truck shuddered into a parking space near the end. It was one of those old two-tone jobs that must've been at one point, red and white. The rust on the lower panels was so bad that I was surprised it had even made it here. It reminded me, sadly, of what my own vehicle might look like in a couple years. The doors popped open together and a country fried couple that looked to be in their mid-fifties jumped down from either side. I noticed that the windows were of the hand crank variety.

'Great.' I thought to myself.
"Perfect." Farm clucked aloud.

He was on them before they could even shut the doors. I put a little hop in my step to catch up.

"Welcome to Centennial Nissan," he crowed, extending his outstretched wing, "you here for parts, sales or service?" He sounded a bit like a Texan, but somehow it fit.

The older man slammed the door of his truck with an annoying squeal. I thought I could hear bits of glass clashing about inside as it met the frame. His woman did the same on her side and then slapped the dust from her hands. They were a slightly rotund couple, their attire jeans and western shirts. Both were covered with dust, as if they'd spent the day in a hayfield. Farm shook both their hands unabashedly as if he were welcoming them to a church picnic.

"I need to get the missus a new vehicle." The man stated.

"Ok." Farm gulped. "We got lotsa those."

It was like I'd never met the kid before. His ability to mimic the customer's speech pattern was astounding.

"Well," Farm drawled on, "I'm Kevin and this here is Mark. He's new so try to go easy on him."

I extended my hand to the man and he encircled it in his firm but quick grip. His skin was calloused and rough but his tone was friendly.

"Nice to meetcha, friend." He said proudly. "I'm Ken and this lovely lady here is Eileen."

I felt like I'd been transported back into the seventies momentarily. An old joke played in my head from elementary school.

'What do call a woman with one arm and one leg?
-I lean.'

Smiling at both of them I found my voice.

"Nice to meet you too." I shook Eileen's hand also.

Farm looked at me with a comical smile and I had to turn away to keep from laughing. I was a bit delirious from the day's events. Ignoring me he turned and began a slow walk toward the used vehicles.

"So are you interested in a new vehicle or a used one?"

"Not sure," Ken spouted, "We haven't bought a vehicle in twelve years."

Farm's hair seemed to stand on end at the comment.

"Okay." He condescended, "Well are you looking for another truck, or would a car do?"

Ken stopped briefly and scratched the side of his head, leaving his hat cocked to the side. It was one of those styles that farmers and truckers wear. The back was made of that plastic mesh stuff and the front was adorned with what looked like an infinity symbol lying on its side with a plant growing out of the middle. It was green and white, although the foamy front was tinged around the edges with years of dirt and grime. Farm stood beside him and I was a couple steps to his side observing at an angle. We were both mute.

"I guess a car would do, but it'll need a big trunk."

"Will it be used on the farm?"

"Not really," Ken answered, lifting the hat of his head briefly and combing his fingers through his rapidly thinning hair, "but it would be nice if we could throw a bale of hay in the back every now and then."

I saw Farm's face flicker with understanding. He stood with one foot cocked to the side and curled a finger over his lips. Crossing his left arm under his right, he scanned the lot for a few seconds.

"I've got an idea!" He said enthusiastically then made a bee-line for the used Pathfinders.

Ken and I looked at each other then followed along behind. Eileen walked slowly past the new cars in our wake. Her face had the awed expression that displayed 'culture shock'. I wondered if these two had ever owned a Japanese car and how they'd even found their way onto a Nissan lot. It seemed that they might be more at home at the Ford store a couple blocks down. I just kept walking.

Farm was looking in the back window of a three to four year old Pathfinder by the time we neared the used side. Eileen was still halfway through the new lines and was gaping at the window sticker on a nicely equipped Maxima. As he saw me and Ken approaching, he rotated around to the windshield and pulled the stock number off of the plastic tag that was pasted inside. When we were within earshot, he yelled the number at me and told me to grab the keys from the used building. I was halfway there before I realized that I had no idea where they even kept the used keys. Stopping briefly I turned to ask, and then realized I could just figure it out myself.

I circled around to the eastern entrance of the building. A few of the used guys were sheltering themselves in the shade of the entryway. I recognized Milo and Tristan; the surprise on their faces at seeing me over here was apparent. Putting my hand on the door I asked them where the keys were kept. They both looked at me like I had three heads. I asked again, telling them that Farm had sent me over. Tristan stubbed his cigarette out into one of the garbage can ashtray tops and blew a cloud of smoke over his head. Milo looked at him nervously then said,

"Go ask Z."

"Thanks." I returned, yanking the door open.

It felt heavy in my hand and a blast of icy cold air rushed out. It was seemingly much colder than the new showroom. An old Phish tune echoed in my mind.

"Won't you step into the freezer…"

Though I rarely came into the building from this side, I recognized the door to the meeting room on my right. Through process of elimination, I could only assume that Z's office must be to my left. My neck was stiff as my head rotated that direction, my bionic body followed. Walking in slow-motion down the hallway so I could glance into the offices, I felt a bit like Lee Majors in the 'Six Million Dollar Man'. I passed one door-less office that was shaped a little like *Veeg-tor's*. There were a bunch of those little black-faced plaques on the window sill. The next office had a door and as I peered in, I saw Z sitting there. His hands were on the desk in front of him, palms down, his eyes were closed. I could see his eyeballs moving back and forth beneath them.

'Is he sleeping?' I thought. *'Meditating?'*

Unsure if I should disturb him or not, I decided just to darken his door for a minute. The grass grew a dark, thick green in the long shadow of the roof overhang outside the window. Milo and Tristan were talking fervently about something on the sidewalk. The parking spaces behind them had a couple cars of various shapes and sizes. A chain link fence edged the neat corner of the parking lot, beyond which…

"What are doing!" an agitated voice barked behind me.
I turned to see Mik standing in the shadowy hallway.
"Um." I stammered, shaken by the intrusion.
"Um what?" Mik billowed back. His hair was a messy whirlwind atop his dome.
"I need the keys to the red pathfinder."
"Which one?" he asked coldly.

'Seize her with a tweezer…' the song continued in my head.

"Uh, the '07?" and then I vomited up the stock number.

Mik's luminescent blue eyes swam in their icy sockets. His hair seemed statically charged; like the tentacles of some long forgotten jellyfish. He loomed above me with an expression that was slightly more indifferent than hate. The hallway seemed suddenly darker. Blood rushed into my feet like wet concrete.
Z's eyes had fluttered open and he looked up at me tiredly. I repeated that I needed the keys to the red pathfinder. His gaze stayed locked on mine, unblinking. It felt a little like I'd entered some forbidden chamber at Giza.
"Farm sent me." I blurted, not sure what else to say.
"Oh." Z rotated in his chair toward the key board behind him.
Locating the correct set, he slid them slowly off their little gold hook and dangled them in front of me. I reached into his tiny office.
"Make sure these come right back to me."
"Ok." I whispered.

Mik stood in the door for a second, blocking my egress. I looked up at him questioningly. He was maybe half an inch taller than me. He glared stone-facedly into me. My lips fell open and I inhaled through my mouth. Then I dropped my gaze to his shoes. They were probably at least a size eleven and had extra thick soles. They were worn on the sides from his bow-legged usage. If we were barefoot, I probably would've had that half-inch back... if not more.

Swinging out of my way like a stone slab, he continued to eye me coldly. I slithered out the door and back down the hallway. I could feel his chilly stare on the back of my neck as I made my way to the exit.

'Won't you step into the freezer...' yowled Phish in my head again, *'Tease her with a tweezer.'*

Pushing through the double doors, it felt as if the air conditioning ushered me out.

'It's gonna be cold, cold, cold, cold, cold.'

The warmth of the remaining daylight warmed my arms as I circled the building again. Milo and Tristan were sitting on the bench in front now. I passed them quickly, following the sidewalk to the curb. The blacktop felt soft under my feet and Farm smiled as he saw me hustling toward them. Ken was standing several steps back from the vehicle with his arms crossed over his chest. He looked like a rumpled old flag. His wife had finally made her way over and was listening to Farm prattle on about something or other.

"Here's the keys." I said, still a bit frozen from my foray into the Hogan.

"Great!" Farm announced as he snatched them from me.

Unlocking the driver's door, he punched the unlock button and immediately went around to the back. As he opened the lift-gate, I realized that the hydraulic shocks extended a bit too slowly. It was a defect with which I was all too familiar; having owned and/or driven no less than six old Subarus. Farm paid no mind as he pushed the gate open above his head.

"One of the nicest things about these rigs is the cargo capacity." He spouted, motioning for Eileen to look inside. She leaned in a bit closer and looked around the back of the vehicle. Once he'd drawn her attention inside, he went on about the sixty-something cubic feet of space, the rubberized cargo mat and numerous 'tie-down hooks'. She seemed at least momentarily interested. Ken took a couple steps forward and scanned the frame on the back, touching it in an odd way. Farm felt his presence and extracted himself to let him inspect the vehicle. Then he pulled me to the side a bit.

"When you sell a used car you're selling the *sizzle*, not the steak." He shared with me in a low tone.

I watched the couple tentatively circle the vehicle. Ken traced the rear quarter panel with his calloused but wise hand. It stopped at the right rear door and he opened it quickly, again inspecting the frame. Then he slammed the door, hard, and craned his neck as if listening for something. Eileen looked at her husband and his expression rumpled slightly.
"I think this one's been hit." He called over to us.
Farm stepped forward with mock concern painted on his face.
"Really," He clucked, "What makes you say that?"
"Well..." Ken hooted softly, "this here door doesn't quite match up, and the screws on the trunk door aren't painted so I suspect they're new."
Farm's head retreated on his neck as he inspected the rear door and the screws holding up the lift-gate.
"They did a decent job on the body work," Ken drawled on, "but I don't think we want this one."
"Ok." Farm conceded, slamming the lift-gate shut. "Do you like the vehicle otherwise?"

"Maybe so;" said Ken. "got some other ones we could look at?"

Farm stepped back and curled his curled his finger over his lip again. There were like eight or nine used Pathfinders parked in the line, they all looked the same to me. On the end of the line were a few other brands of SUVs including a Ford and what looked like an Isuzu. He walked slowly down the line as if studying each vehicle methodically. I wondered why he didn't just pick the next Pathfinder since they seemed to like it well enough. But what the hell did I know. Eileen and Ken watched Farm go for a while then followed on behind.

Farm sensed them out of his periphery and turned slightly sideways, now walking and watching at the same time. Eileen perched her elbow on her palm and rested her chin between her thumb and forefinger as she perused the inventory. I could tell that Farm was gauging her movements. His head was bobbing back and forth at each vehicle as they passed. As they neared the Isuzu, she stopped. He paused for a second then sidled forward in a stilted fashion. I was again reminded of Foghorn Leghorn.

"You like red don'tcha." He drawled again.

"You caught me." She chattered back sweetly.

"Well," He continued smoothly, "I do this for a living."

I noticed a bit of a shiver and perhaps the slightest change of color in her cheeks. Ken drew his attention away from the line and stepped toward them a bit more quickly.

"An I-suzu?" He drawled skeptically, his redneck roots showing through a bit.

"You say that like it's a bad thing." Farm rolled on. "Did you know that the first engines for this vehicle were actually built by General Motors?"

Ken cocked his head a bit at this and Farm puffed his chest out slightly.

"This model year was actually built in Indiana."

I gaped at Farm with something like awe.

"Huh." Ken said, as if putting a voice to my thoughts.

"I like this one." Eileen said meekly.

"Go grab the keys for this one." Farm whispered into my ear.

I trotted quickly back to the Hogan to retrieve the Isuzu keys. Crossing in front of the building I passed by Tristan and felt his eyes on me again. Milo was nowhere in sight. Around the side my hand fell on the door handle again.

'It's gonna be cold, cold, cold, cold, cold.'

Walking briskly into Z's office I could hear Mik lambasting another salesperson in the next office over.

"I need the Isuzu keys, please."
"Where's the Pathfinder keys?"
"Um." I stammered, realizing that Farm still had them.

Z slid the keys for the Rodeo off the hook and held them up to me. As I went for them he pulled them back just out of my reach.

"Bring the Pathfinder keys back before you go on a test drive."
"Ok," I said quickly reaching further out.

He pulled back a bit more and looked at me sternly but tiredly.

"Ok." I said again.

Dropping the keys in my mitt he kept his gaze locked on mine. I wheeled about and dashed back out to the SUV line. Handing the keys to Farm I got the Pathfinder keys back and returned them to Z. Then I trotted back out again. I was learning the system and getting a good workout at the same time. My feet were sweating in my leather shoes and my socks felt a bit scratchy. The walk-around on the Isuzu Rodeo was shorter this time and Farm hustled them into a test drive quickly. Eileen seemed less than impressed with the vehicle after driving it and it felt as though they were slipping through our grasp.

The shadow of the vehicle was cast in a long charcoal smear across the orangey-grey pavement. We exited the truck simultaneously and stood together in a clump as the sun descended behind the mountains to the west. It was a blinding ball of light. The mixture of clouds and pollution was making for a rather beautiful sunset. Golden rays shot brilliantly upward off the peaks into the steely purpling sky. The billowy thunderheads were layered above like orange sherbet. Farm didn't seem to notice and I could tell that he was agitated.

"What about your truck?" He blurted from out of the blue.

"My truck?" Ken questioned back.

"Aren't you about ready to trade that old thing?" Farm probed, clearly grasping now.

"Uh, well, hadn't thought about that…" Ken wavered, thrown a bit off his guard.

Eileen stood silently. I was unsure of where Farm was going with this. Suddenly I was very dry and thirsty. The husky pencil was making its way to the back of my forehead again.

"Let's go take a look." Farm said, walking back toward the customer parking.

Ken, Eileen and I all shared a confused look and then followed after him. As he reached the other side of the lot, he walked up to a truck that was sitting out in front of the service bays.

"We just took this one in on trade." He announced. "If you want to trade that old truck in; maybe we can put both of 'ya into newer vehicles today!"

He explained this as if he'd just had a revelation. The excitement level he exhibited was over the top. His arms waved back and forth from the 'new' truck to the old with wide theatrics. We were completely in the shade of the showroom now and the afternoon was a now a saggy purple. Ken and Eileen stood tiredly in their work boots watching Farm's show. The husky pencil was in full scribble now and my teeth began to clench on their own.

Farm ripped the driver's door open and popped the hood on the truck. Propping it open he implored them to take a look. More out of politeness than interest, the two of them shuffled forward. I was very unfamiliar with this method so I just watched uncomfortably. Farm looked at me with a knitted brow as if I should be doing something to help. Since I had no idea what he was trying to accomplish, I just looked back at him confusedly. As Eileen and Ken poked around the truck, he took a couple of steps in my direction and put the back of his hand in front of his mouth.

"We're gonna make a two-car deal here." He hummed confidently.

I looked up at the porch and saw Brick watching us from the railing. Then he turned and headed back inside. Farm walked back over and began extolling the benefits of the now third vehicle he was trying to peddle. Their eyes had the glazed-over look of information overload. I felt about as close to a deal as the moon. Brick's voice mercifully broke over the loudspeakers.

"Mark Stapleton, please report to the sales desk. Mark." It felt as though he were talking directly to me.

I gave a cursory glance to Farm and he waved me off with a quick, back-handed sweep. Squirting like a watermelon seed, I shot up the ramp. The doors whooshed open and I caught the last bit of the blinding sunset through the far windows at the back of the showroom. Blinking my eyes a bit to get rid of the green spots the blaring sun had left, I slid under the sign and over to Brick's side of the desk.

"What are you guys doing?" he asked exasperatedly.

"They didn't like the first two cars we showed 'em." I said, then with my own exasperation, "So now Farm is trying to get the husband to trade his old truck in on one we just took in on trade."

"The F-350 in front of service?" Brick asked dumbfounded.

"I guess." I said, "That's a Ford, right?"

Brick put the heel of his hand to his right eye and groaned. Then he picked up the receiver and paged Farm to the tower also. Turning to Ned he exhaled and said, "Sometimes I wonder about that kid."

Ned rolled his eyes back and arched his brow.

Brick kept on, "It's like one minute he's a fuckin' genius and the next he couldn't find his butt if it had a bell on it!"

I covered my mouth and looked over his head at the dark mountains in the distance. Farm stormed through the doors and under the sign, the impatience was evident on his face. Receding into the corner I looked on dazedly. Farm opened his mouth to speak and Brick cut him off.

"Dude, you can't show those people that F-350, it's got a bad tranny."

"Shit!" Farm retorted, his hyperactive eyes flitting back and forth.

"Do you even have a deal with these people?"

"She didn't like the used vehicles we showed her so I'm trying to flip the deal around to him."

"Why?"

"I figure if I can get him interested, then I can put together a two-car deal!" He was talking very fast. Brick examined him like a shrink might examine one of his patients.

"You okay?" He asked pointedly.

"I'm fine."

"Do you really think you have a deal here?"

"Yes."

"Kevin?" Brick droned suspiciously. It was the first time I'd heard anyone use his real name.

Farm looked back decidedly, his eyes seemed square shaped.

"Okay," Brick conceded, "Go ahead." Then to me, "Stapleton, you stay here."

I nodded and Farm shot back out through the doors.

"He doesn't have a deal." Brick confided to Ned.

"I know." Ned agreed.

I felt the same way.

"How many you got out today?" Brick asked me.

I was still pressed into the corner, my sagged shoulders leaning up against the opposing window panes.

"Uh, two." I said.

The lights in the showroom seemed brighter as the daylight faded away.

"You look like buttered toast."

"I feel like a piece of bacon."

"Why don't you call it a day and be here bright and early on Monday."

'Thank the gods.' I thought.

Chapter Twelve

Home again, home again.

The moon hung in my rear-view like the nub of Bob Barker's microphone. As the city fell away behind me the cool foothills reflected its light with a bluish-white glow. Sage bushes stood at attention, stock still against the coming night. Shaggy green junipers, equally stoic, stretched their shadows across the crabgrass under the cosmic blue twilight. Cool air rushed in through my cracked window and soothed my bleary eyes. The sticky lifters on my engine ticked away softly under my hood like summer crickets from my far-away youth. I breathed deeply of the mountain air and I hogged the middle lane all the way up to Evergreen. Snapping on the stereo, *'The Who'* yowled raggedly forth from my scratchy speakers.

'Out here in the fields, I fight for my meals…'

Wailing proudly with the ancient tune, I barely felt the sway of my little station wagon as it followed the giant curves of the super-highway. Sixty-three miles mph might just as well have been a hundred and three. With a pocket full of cash I was feeling *'Navajo Nation Rich'*. Shaking another smoke from a now nearly empty pack, I lit up and exhaled voraciously. At the crest of the hill under the Mt. Vernon underpass, the still snow covered peaks laid out to the west before me.

'Yeah, yeah, yeah, yeah, yeah...'

Using the downhill slope, I pushed the little Subaru to her limits. The needle crept fluidly past eighty.

'Let's get together, before we get much older...'

Townsend's guitar rang through the speakers boldly, erasing the scratchiness for a brief moment. The rapidly cooling air blasted me in the face and sent ashes buffeting against the side of my head. I could've cared less. Carrying my speed around a broad corner, I raced onto the new exit they'd built. In the offing, I crossed three lanes of traffic like I'd somehow been granted ownership of the federal highway. Letting off the accelerator, I traversed back over the interstate on an immense bridge, dumping my speed like a downhill ski racer on the finishing flat. The stoplight turned green just as I approached and I blasted on through, easily a good twenty miles an hour over the speed limit. *Daltrey* and the boys would've been proud of me.

Rounding the next corner, my little wagon began to shudder a bit and I let off the gas. Flicking my butt out the window, I let the car slow back to a less chaotic pace and enjoyed the blackening evening as it enveloped the ponderosa pines. *The Who* gave way to some other classic band that I couldn't remember name of, so I turned the volume back down. The rooftops of the King Soopers in Bergen Park sped past on my left and the recently cut through hillside rose steeply on my right. Soon I would be in North Evergreen. As I passed Means Meadow, boulders and pines stood stolidly in its midst, Barker's microphone-moon was now climbing amongst the stars. The old Hiwan homes dotted the hillside to my left. It was the neighborhood where the Hinckley's had lived...

I could almost see the lights of the cop cars that had surrounded the place back in the eighties when that psycho son of theirs had tried to off Reagan. I wondered where they might be living now.

The light at the bottom of the hill was green, so I wheeled through the intersection and down onto the frontage road that led to our townhouse. The night was inky and the street signs were blaringly reflective. My contact lenses felt hard and tight on my eyeballs. My throat was hot and tired from too much smoke and talk. It would be good to have a nice meal and drink a huge glass of water. I was glad that tomorrow was Sunday. The 'Blue Law' restricted the sale of booze and cars on the seventh day in Colorado.

'The MADD ladies must be overjoyed about that law.' I mused disconnectedly.

Pulling into the second parking space in front of our duplex, I let the engine run for a couple seconds to cool down, then shut it off. The inner workings settled themselves with their usual shudder. As I opened the door and swung my leg out, an old ski injury caught flame in my right knee. It was achy and dull but still present. It had been seven-plus years since that fateful day in the Butte, but my thirty year old body wouldn't let me forget about it yet. I sat quietly for a second with one leg on the gritty pavement and the other immobile in my past. The pain subsided finally and I hauled myself out with the assistance of the steering wheel then walked gingerly down the little wooden staircase to our deck. The porch light wasn't on, so my steps were deliberate.

Pushing the sticky front door open with my shoulder, I stepped over a collection of shoes and onto the crappy linoleum landing that served as our mudroom. I kicked my shoes off and let my feet enjoy the coolness of the floor for a moment. Then I slowly turned up the staircase to the living room. My wife was sitting on the couch with the baby in her arms. A baby blanket was draped over her shoulder and she was staring blankly at the television set. Dealin' Doug was blaring out of the box at her about how, *'Nobody beats his deals, nobody!'*

I found the remote on the coffee table in front of her and turned the volume all the way down.

"How's it goin'?" I breathed tiredly.

"We're fine." She smiled forcedly.

I could tell it had been a tough day for her too. Flumping down on the couch next to her, I leaned my head back and exhaled at the ceiling.

"Long day." She stated.

"Yeah." I agreed.

"All this baby does is eat and poop and sleep."

My laughter rolled out easily. Tilting my head forward I looked into the kitchen.

"You hungry?" I asked.

"Yes."

Lifting myself off the couch and plodding into the kitchen, I poked through the cupboards. Everything looked dry and old. The freezer and fridge revealed the same. I stood in front of their open doors deliriously enjoying the mixture of cold and frigid air.

"Wanna order a pie?" I offered over my shoulder.

"Sure." She droned, still staring at the television.

I scanned the counter for the phone book to no avail.

"Do you know where the phone book is?" I tried to ask politely. The thought of food was bringing on my too-long ignored appetite.

"I don't know." She intoned disinterestedly.

My cloudy eyes scanned the rest of the room, searching for the phone book.

"Okay…" I droned to myself.

It was sitting on her computer desk, right next to the mouse pad. Snapping it up quickly, I thumbed to the pizza section. The Pizza Hut people answered quickly and I offered to over-tip if they could have it to us in a hurry. It was there in less than twenty minutes. Less than fifteen after that, we both sat on the couch in a food coma. We enjoyed the blissful pause for about ten minutes more, and then our baby girl awoke. She was hungry and cranky, so my wife took her downstairs to our bedroom.

I flipped through the channels lazily, looking for something funny. TBS was running an edited version of 'Tommy Boy'. I stretched out my tired limbs and let Farley and Spade roll over me. My eyeballs felt like peach pits as my lids shuttered up and down over them. The boys in the movie had just plowed into a deer and were sobbing in the middle of the highway. I chuckled to myself gruffly and then slid into an exhausted half-sleep.

***

When I awoke, the deer in the movie had ripped Spade's car to shreds and Farley was commenting on how awesome it was. I looked around the room dumbfounded, not sure where I was. My wife was still downstairs. Pushing the heels of my hands into my eye sockets, I arched into a twisted stretch then rose from the uncomfortable sofa. Snatching the remote from the coffee table I offed the TV, doused the lights and stumbled down the stairs to our bedroom. My wife and our baby girl were passed out together under the glow of the bedside lamp. My wife was still propped up in her nursing position and the baby lay open mouthed under the swell of her bare breast. Sliding her gingerly off of her mother, I stole some of my wife's pillows and built a little wall around her. Then I stripped myself, clicked off the lamp and lay down in the bed next to them.

The baby's breathing was so small and perfect. Her tiny back rose and fell blissfully. She smelled like sugar cookies. The little 'onesie' she wore already seemed a bit tight on her miniscule but rapidly growing frame. The mini snaps that held it together at the bottom were strained by the puffiness of her diaper. My hand seemed immense as I stretched it out over her back lightly. I surveyed her perfect little face in the glow of the streetlamp that permeated our cheap, plastic blinds and pushed it's way through the slats. The light painted her with alternating stripes of orange and shadowy charcoal. Against the stark white of her little jammies it resembled an old prison uniform. I tried to breathe as calmly as her but my stressed-out lungs could only drag the air in and out forcedly.

My mind raced with desperate thoughts. The treatment center where I gotten sober was still seeking payment for the two-plus grand I still owed them. When we'd moved from my sister's basement to this duplex, the deposit and first month's rent had nearly tapped my savings. Then of course there were bills, diapers and food. There was also my wife's car payment; with which her Father had seen fit to saddle me; shortly following our shotgun wedding. The miniscule wad of cash that sat crumpled in my khakis on the floor next to the bed suddenly seemed inconsequential. I needed a serious shot in the arm.

Lying in the early night for what seemed like hours, I listened to the even snores of my wife and felt the innocent rise and fall of my baby's back. How was I going to make the ends meet? Rent would be due again on Tuesday and I wasn't sure I'd even be paid until the fifth. My back was itchy and my neck had a deep soreness that crept up and clutched the right side of head. It seemed that sleep would never come. Rolling over on my left side, my stomach gurgled angrily. Perhaps I'd find another pot of gold on Monday.

Chapter Thirteen

Like a fish in the sea all the time.

On Sunday I'd reviewed my finances and figured I was going to come up about $600 short on rent. I knew that even with the cars I'd sold, it wouldn't be enough. Sitting on our tiny back deck I watched the Monday daybreak as it broiled up over the foothills to the east. A newspaper rested on my lap, open again to the help wanted section. When I was a ski bum I'd often worked two or three jobs to support my lifestyle. I would just have to do it again. The rumpled pages felt loose in my fingers and I had to keep licking them so I could separate the thin newsprint. I needed to find a night job or an early morning gig.

About halfway down the third page was an odd listing. In the tiny town of Kittredge there was a place that smoked salmon. They were looking for someone to help with the preparation. It was just after six in the morning. The hours that help was needed were from 4 to 7 am. Folding the paper down into a sloppy quarter, I flipped my half smoked cigarette over the balcony and slid my way back inside. After unsuccessfully trying to dial the numbers with my thumb twice, I slapped the paper down on the cluttered dining table and used two hands. Someone answered after the third ring. He seemed unusually cheery for the earliness of the hour.

"I'm calling about the part time position." I stammered.
"Awesome." The man responded. "Ever work with fish before."

I tried to remember if I ever had. Memories of my Father flooded forth. I could almost see him laying there half-drunk in a crappy old lawn chair next to my grandfather's pond. A litter of Stag beer cans and cigarette butts collected on the muddy earth around his tackle box. Stringers of bluegills and crappie sucked in their last dying breaths in the mucky water next to the shore. An offending turtle squirmed slowly toward his grisly death in the hickory leaves of the previous autumn; spilling blood from his neck where my Dad had thrust in his rusty old bowie knife. I remembered asking him why he'd stabbed the poor creature and my Dad had mumbled something about him stealing his bait. The humidity of those old summer days stuck to my skin like rotten chicken livers.

"A little bit," I answered, "not much lately."

The man laughed.

"Can you come by this morning?"

I looked up at the clock that was pasted to the middle of the high wall.

"I guess."

"Cool." He finished, "I'll see you in a bit."

The line went dead and I realized that we hadn't even exchanged names. I pulled on a sweatshirt and some jeans then headed out into the thin morning. The condensation on my windshield was eradicated easily with one swipe of the wipers. Backing out slowly through the blue fog from my exhaust pipe, I lit another smoke and headed up the hill to the main road. It was only about a ten minute drive to Kittredge but I'd have to navigate through town; so I rolled my eyes around in their sockets and blinked the film off my aging contact lenses. As I headed through North Evergreen, I trundled under the stoplight by Olde's Garage and passed the gigantic post office. Misty clouds trailed in front of the dark emerald foothills as fountains of fog emanated forth off Evergreen Lake. Passing the equally gigantic Catholic Church, my brakes squealed gratingly as I slowed through the bottleneck in front of the entrance to Dedisse Park.

The road traced the circumference of the lake and soon I was in Evergreen proper. Water poured dutifully over the dam and a single stoplight dangled from the cables that stretched across the middle of my old hometown. It was green so I continued down past the Baskin Robbins and the Little Bear Saloon. I could almost smell the stale beer and decades of biker 'b.o.' through the tightly closed wooden doors. A couple of magpies danced on the rising morning air in front of me as I rounded the corner past Seven-Eleven. I wondered if the high school kids still met up there on Saturday nights before they scattered off into the hills for keg parties and pot smoking. The curves of the little highway were exactly the same as I'd remembered. Bent pines arched in twisted pain between the road and Lower Bear Creek, their solid roots clutching the jagged sandstone pebbles that eternally spilt themselves off the narrow, steep embankment.

A series of odd cabins were still stuffed into the hillside on a sliver of land that the creek had thrown up so many years prior. I remembered living there back in '78 when my Father had decided to move us to Colorado. It was the first of many excruciating ear-infections that I would experience; living in that crappy little cabin just past the water treatment plant. Sleep had come hard those nights of my early youth too. Onward I rolled, following the wandering asphalt thread; weaving my way down memory lane. It was ironic that I was looking for yet another job in this tiny little burg. The first 'real' job I'd ever had was here. I'd been one of three dishwashers at a cruddy little barbecue place that served the best ribs you've ever put in your mouth. Few people understood that the recipe for great barbeque had less to do with the wood you chose for the smoker than the amount of old sauce caked on the inside of the smoking bins.

I could almost feel the soaked, denim apron that had cloaked me from my ankles to my clavicle. The taste of Texas Toast with too much butter was still palatable on my tongue. Of course there was the time that Jimmy and me almost got arrested in the parking lot, puffing down a giant bowl of Mexican weed, too stoned to see the cops that had pulled in right next to us. Thank the gods that one of them was his cousin or uncle or something. I could still hear his fateful words carving their way through the dusty, green smoke into our spongy bells.

'Jimmy! Put that shit away before you get busted.'

But that was over thirteen years prior, before we had expectations and responsibilities. The eighties were long gone and the new millennium would prove to be a bit less tolerant.

*****

The fish place was easy to find because it had a giant, multi-colored sign with a huge golden salmon painted on the front. The ramshackle building in which it was housed was a faded baby blue and stuffed up against the wall of the canyon. The parking lot slanted away from the door and was just wide enough for my car to fit in front. Brightly lit inside, I could see a couple men working away behind the counter. The glass door opened smartly and an electronic bell dinged once as I entered. Both of the men looked up with a start and then the furrier of the two looked back down at his work. The other one met me at the counter fresh-facedly. His hair was close-cropped and a neat mustache covered his upper lip.

"I'm Mark," I said tentatively, "we just spoke on the phone?"
"You're fast." He said, not introducing himself.

We stood in a brief silence, surveying one another in a classic Rocky Mountain standoff. After the brief, uncomfortable silence, he extended his hand.

"I'm Tony." He smiled.
"I'm broke." I returned without thinking.

His smile broke into hearty laughter.

"C'mon back." He continued, lifting a horizontal door that was built into the countertop.
"Great."

Leading me into the back rooms of the establishment he began the nickel tour.

"So we've been here about two years now and the business has been growing like crazy."

My gaze traced the interior of the operation. The first room had two large stainless steel sinks bolted against the side wall with an industrial sprayer dangling above them. These were flanked on the left by a medium sized walk-in freezer. The walls were stark white and it had a cold, surgical feel. The back room was basically a cement box with two stand-up smokers, each as tall as me. It was much warmer. He smiled lovingly at these and continued with his pitch.

"We've been putting up roughly five-hundred pounds of fish a day with these guys. But hopefully with your help, we can do seven-fifty to eight-hundred."

"That's a lot on fish." I commented.

"Yeah." He mused.

Walking me into the front room, he continued.

"This is where the magic happens." He glittered.

The third room ran parallel to the first and was divided by a thin wall. A long window filled up a full third of it between the two rooms. Against the white wall at the back was a large table that was topped with butcher block. It had wheels on the bottom but they looked like they hadn't ever been used. About three feet in front of that was a large contraption that resembled an old air hockey table. It was actually a bit larger but it had a white top that was some sort of conveyor belt. A long machine overarched the table in the middle and fed strips of plastic onto the back side through a series of odd looking rubber cylinders that were attached to spring-loaded arms. On our side of the table were neat lanes of fish that had been portioned into what looked like half-pound slabs. Thoroughly smoked, they smelled delicious. I realized that I hadn't yet had breakfast and began to salivate. Pressing my lips together I swallowed quietly. The chunks were in odd shapes and sizes. The bearded dude flipped a switch under the 'table-top' and the fish began rolling slowly into the machine. Out the back side came neatly bagged portions that the machine somehow magically produced. The whole process took maybe three minutes but it was nothing short of amazing. Beard guy flipped the switch again and the machine shuddered to a halt. Pushing past us to the other side of the table, he pressed another switch that lit up with a soft green glow. Almost immediately there was the pungent odor of molten plastic. I crinkled my nose spasmodically.

Tony laughed and explained that the machine on the back of the table was the sealer. My hunger became paramount and I began to feel slightly sick. The bearded man began sealing the little bags of fish. It was quite an ingenious machine that seemed to not only melt the bags shut, but it sucked all the air out as well. The finished product left the small pieces of fish impermeably encased in plastic. It only took the man another three minutes the finish the entire process. His manner resembled that of a worker on a Japanese assembly line. After the bags were sealed he set about labeling them from a series of rolled up stickers that were bolted to the opposing wall. They all bore the same golden salmon logo that I'd noticed on the sign out front. The whole operation was a sight to behold. I found myself mesmerized by the methodical efficiency.

Tony walked me past the odd table and through the door from which he'd initially emerged. We were standing by the cash register again behind the long counter under which I now realized was a giant refrigeration case. Several different flavors of the finished product were displayed neatly inside on frost covered leaves of kale, lemon slices and crushed ice.

"Nice." I whispered to myself.

"So you want to start tomorrow?" Tony asked.

"Yes." I droned, again without thinking.

"Awesome." He returned quickly, "Any problem with the four am start time."

"Uh…" I groaned briefly, returning to the reality of the situation, "I guess not."

Flipping my wrist over I looked at my watch. It was 7:11.

"Shit!" I exclaimed. "I gotta go."

"No problem." He answered with a knowing smile. "So I'll see you tomorrow bright and early?"

"Yep." I returned, extending my hand curtly.

He shook my hand smartly, pulling it toward him ever so slightly, and then released me. I thanked him and bolted for the door. The audible ding went off again as I reemerged back into the day.

"Dress warm…" I heard him yell after me as I scuttled around my bumper and ripped open the door to my car.

****

I had roughly sixty-nine minutes to be at the dealership and I hadn't even showered. It was easily ten to twelve minutes to home if I drove like a bat out of hell and fifteen to eighteen more to the store if I did the same. I hit the gas, hard. Robert Plant yowled forth from my speakers with *'Immigrant Song'*, the insanity of his voice was strangely pacifying. The wobbly little wagon took the corners back up to Evergreen a bit wider than I might've liked but I had no time for such trivialities.

> *'Ahhhh-ahhhh-ahhh!*
> *Ahhhh-Ahhhh-Ahh!'*

Pine trees and spruce flew past my windows. The nippy morning had succumbed to the Hiroshima sun that was now flooding the canyon with its orange light.

> *'Come from the land of the ice and snow…'*

I decided to take the back way up to North Evergreen to avoid downtown and hopefully any cops that felt like pulling people over this early. Cutting the corner by Seven-Eleven, my nearly bald tires skidded across some gravel that was left over from the winter and I basically had to perform a controlled slide through the intersection. All four tires chirped as they met the clean pavement again and the wagon lurched angrily against the maneuver. Slamming on the gas, the vehicle righted itself and I spun my head around left and right to make sure that nobody had seen me. The little village was still sleeping peacefully. Finding her speed again reluctantly, my little wagon rocketed up the hill past the hardware store and the old movie theater. They were both shaped like barns.

> *'Hammer of the Gods.'*

I wove my way past Hiwan Hills and the Homestead then down the high road that would eventually spill back out onto the parkway. Scoping the traffic situation from above I noticed that it was clear sailing so I flew down the hill and blew right through the stop sign without losing momentum. I remembered one of my friends from high school saying that the stop signs with the white lines around them were 'optional'. A grinchly smile curled on my lips as the raucous music spurred me on. There wasn't another car in sight. I assumed everyone was still sleeping off the extra weekend night provided by the holiday.

By keeping my flow going I was able to get the wagon up to sixty in no time, even though I was climbing. The purplish morning was giving way to steel-blue and silver. Feathery white clouds spewed up off the hilltops and dissipated into the highest regions of the sky; the fireball sun was steadily climbing over Denver to the east. The stoplight by Olde's Texaco was mercifully green and I pushed the needle to just below seventy as I raced past El Pinal then sidled onto the frontage road. Letting the hill slow me down just enough to make the corner, I careened onto the home stretch. As I crested the last little rise before my 'neighborhood', I nearly clipped a dually flatbed truck that some redneck asshole had left parked by the side of the road; its fat-welded-ass proudly spilling into my lane.

"Jesus!" I whispered harshly to no one as I swerved to miss the behemoth.

Pressing hard on the brakes, I dumped the nose of my Subaru into the community driveway that serviced our townhome. Then I sport parked next to my wife's Chevy. Dust and exhaust followed me down the little stairs the led to our deck as I trotted down them. Ripping open the crappy screen door I pushed through the metal front door. Flipping off my sneakers I started to pull off my shirt as I stumbled down the interior staircase to our tiny bathroom. My jeans fell in a pile at my feet and I leaned over to crank on the water. My neck and right arm were stiff from lack of sleep and overuse. Pausing briefly to flip down the toilet seat quietly, I sat, peeled of my socks and took a cleansing breath. It ended with a wet cough as the steam billowed over the shower curtain. I stood again and lifted the seat to hawk a 'loogee' into the little bowl.

The pounding water felt good on my head and neck as I let the ropy streams pummel me. Opening my mouth I inhaled the hot vapor into my lungs and let my hair drain about my face.

"Ahh..." I exhaled, lingering for a few blissful moments in the onslaught.

Not wasting time with soap I squirted a giant handful of dandruff shampoo into my palm scrubbed my hair angrily, digging my fingernails into my lumpy scalp. The tingle was sanctifying. Spilling the lather onto my shoulders, I rubbed a cursory paw under each armpit then aimed them at the spew of the showerhead, first right, then left. Dunking my head into the spray, I let the soapy water spill down my back and legs then spun around again quickly to finish my three-minute cleansing. Punching the plastic spigot back into the wall I stood for a few seconds in the steam-filled solace of the tub. The remaining water swirled and gurgled down the drain. I ripped the curtain back and stepped gingerly onto the cold tile of the floor. Flipping the towel off the rack, I snapped it open and pushed it hard into my face.

Beads of water wound their way down my legs and puddled onto the floor around my feet. The sickening smell of soap and toothpaste swirled in the closet-sized room. I reached for the switch and flicked on the fan. Stepping in front of the mirror I dried it with the towel poorly and stared at myself through the streaky swirls. Needing a shave I grappled for the slender can of shave gel. The pile I squirted into my hand was enough to shave a Sasquatch. No time to argue with myself, I slapped the goonge onto my face and slathered it up with both hands. Deftly pushing the handle of the faucet up and left with the back of my wrist, I rinsed the excess from my mitts and snagged the razor from its spot on the sink. Bits of old hair swirled in rusty little puddles were it always sat.

Stroke, rinse, stroke, rinse, stroke, rinse.

I was reminded of some old cop show I used to watch with my Dad where the bald middle-aged detective was showing his young son how to shave.

'The key is to rinse between every stroke..." he'd coached, or something to that effect.

The mirror had sufficiently fogged itself again as soapy steam roiled up from the sides of the sink. Setting the razor back in it's place I bowed my chin up and examined my neck and jowls. Satisfied with the mow job, I wiped my face with the towel and deposited it on the floor where I'd left the puddle earlier. Still steaming from the shower I rounded the corner into our bedroom and straight into the 'walk-in' closet. Yanking some clothes from their hangers, I took a half-second to steady them and limit their jangling to a dull jingle. Hopping on one foot then the other I wrestled the slacks over my still wet frame and buttoned them around my waist so they wouldn't fall down. Then I selected a tie and crept over to the mirror to don my shirt. My wife and the baby were both still dead asleep.

I watched them in the reflection of the mirror, my baby girl's stumpy little arms and legs jutting from her tiny shirt and poufy diaper, my wife's open maw was stretched across a mashed-potato pillow. They were beautiful. I looked back at my tie, the knot looked like shit. Glancing down at the bureau my watch glared up at me from it's place next to my wallet. It was 7:54.

"Fuck!" I hiss-pered. Snatching them both from the dresser I raced back up the stairs two at a time.

My car was still warm from the Andretti impersonation I'd tried to effect earlier, blue steam rose from the hood. Dropping my ass in the driver's seat I cranked on the ignition and rocketed back out of the parking space. The intro song to 'The Muppet Show' began rolling crazily through my head. I hummed along innately.

Rolling through yet another stop sign, I trundled down the frontage road and onto the parkway.

'It's time to put on make-up. It's time to light the lights...'

Billions of cars raced up behind me as my little wagon strained up the hill to the interstate.

'It's time to get things started...'

The exigency of the Monday holiday enveloped me. Suburban wanna-be's hemmed me in with their selfishness and pinched faces as they angrily jockeyed for position to pass.

'Why don't you get things started...?'

The little four-banger in my ride found it's stride again and I melded in with the much bigger and faster vehicles around me. I watched the needle climb up to 44, 45, 46. The traffic made its way around me and freed me from their impatience, 47, 48, 49. I crested the hill at fifty and gave it some more gas. Bergen Park sailed past me as the stoplights stayed mercifully green. As I reached the next hill a giant Chevy truck raced around in front of me and I followed his draft, 51, 52, 53. I glanced at my watch again, it was 8:08.

'No time to hate...' my mind recalled randomly.

Some Deadhead in Boise had once shared this quip with me in a past life. I looked up at the truck's bumper in front of me. A sticker on it displayed proudly that the vehicle was 'Protected by Smith and Wesson'. Snickering to myself I let off the gas a bit and continued in his slipstream. By the last corner before the interstate we were doing well over sixty. I lit up a smoke and flipped on the radio. The sun rested on the brown cloud over Denver like a giant Day-Glo golf ball on a New Mexican desert bunker. I hacked up part of my lung and launched it out the window. We rolled through the man-made canyon that eventually spilled us onto the on ramp for I-70. I took the opportunity to ratchet the speedometer up to seventy and catapulted myself past the truck. The highway was surprisingly empty so I traversed three lanes and pushed the little wagon to her limits. Cresting the hill at Genesee I could basically roll to work without using any gas. I slipped the car into neutral. 'Lewis and Floorwax' were yammering inanely about some silliness as I used the laws of gravity and physics to save some money. Cars and trucks drifted past me as I flew down the middle lane. I looked at my watch again briefly, it was only 8:12, I'd make it on time.

****

It was 8:19 when my tire met the curb at the back of the employee parking. Springing from the seat I sprinted across the little lot and into the Hogan before the engine had ceased it's shudder. I flew through the door and toward the back room, it was empty. I looked at my watch again. It was 8:22.

"What the fuck?" I whispered to myself.

I heard shuffling in the hallway and turned to see Z heading toward me, a tiny Styrofoam cup clutched gingerly in his mitt. The gaudy gold watch on his wrist seemed huge.

"What are you doing Mr. Stapleton?" He asked quietly with a look of tired surprise.
"Uh," I stammered confusedly, "I'm here for the meeting."
"We don't have meetings on holidays."
"Oh." I returned with an annoyed tinge.
"I guess Brick failed to share that information with you."
"Uh, yeah."
"Well, as long as you're here. Come into my office."

His middle-eastern drawl made the word sound a bit like *'Orifice'*. I tried to hide the smile on my face. Luckily he'd already turned and started the other direction. I followed softly behind him.

"Have a seat." He offered, extending his palm flatly toward the chairs in front of his desk.

I chose the one near the window.

"Do you want to get some coffee?"
"No, thanks," I said quickly, "I've been up for awhile."

He eyed me quizzically for a moment then decided it was no matter.

"So what do you hope to accomplish here?" he continued.
"Accomplish?" I repeated without thinking.
"Yes," he asked again, "What do you hope to accomplish?"
"I need to make money to take care of my family."
"So it's about the money?"

'No it's been my lifelong dream to be a car salesman." I mused zanily.

"I need money." I opened up.
"Haven't you made some money this weekend already?" He asked.
"Yeah, but it's not enough."
"Enough for what?"

It was my turn to give him a quizzical expression. He raised his eyebrows and lifted his hands questioningly in front of him. I wondered if he really cared to hear the truth.

"Well I reviewed my financial situation yesterday and figured I'm still gonna be short about six-hundred bucks."

Z exhaled through pursed lips and looked about his right angled desk.

"What about the 'CiF' and dice rolls?"
"I've done great on those so far, but it's not enough."
"You really are broke." He exhaled again. "I guess you better figure out how to sell some cars today, somehow, some way."

His redundancy was far from comforting.

'Tell me something I don't know.' I thought crankily.

"You need to exert some control." He stated blankly.

I knew he meant 'assert' but I was too tired to argue. Trying to appear attentive, I gazed back with equal blankness. Maybe I did want that coffee.

"This business…" he continued, "is all about control."

His meaty hands brushed across the smoothness of the giant paper sales log in front of him. The sound was swishy and irritating. I noticed that his wedding ring seemed a bit tight on his finger.

"You have to direct your customers to what you want them to see."

I wasn't sure that my psyche was sharp enough yet this morning to engage in a philosophical discussion.

"I'm not sure I follow." I mumbled.
"What do you say to your customers when you first meet them?"
"Welcome to Centennial Nissan?"
"Is that a question?"
"What?"

"Are you actually welcoming them to the dealership or are you asking them a question?"

"Isn't that what I'm supposed to say?"

"Would you agree that it isn't so much what you say, as how you say it?"

"What?"

"What you are actually supposed to say is; *Welcome to Centennial Nissan, are you here for parts, sales or service?*"

"Seems a bit contrived."

"Yes," he hissed slowly, "but it doesn't really matter what you say."

The husky pencil was inching it's way up from my brain stem.

"So what should I say?"

"Say whatever you like, Mark." He exhaled discontentedly. "This is not the point."

I could feel the dull point of the pencil beginning it's scribe on the back of my forehead like a remedial *Spirograph*.

"So what's the point?"

"You begin to exert control the first minute you engage a customer."

"Okay…"

"By welcoming them to the store you take control of the situation and catch them off their guard."

The pencil began a slow spiral on inside my skull. His limited grasp of the English language left me quietly annoyed. I wished he just make his point and let me go have a cup of Joe and a smoke.

"Think about it, Mark." He expounded. "Are you really welcoming the customers to the dealership, or do you just want the money in their pockets?"

I looked him up and down briefly. He wore another starched dress shirt, this time a light blue job with a white collar and cuffs. The tie that dangled from his neck was an eighties-style multi-colored print pierced with a gold stud, off-center near the bottom.

'Who dresses this freak?' I thought sarcastically.

But what the fuck did I know? He was probably the king of the gypsies back in Lebanon or Lybia or whatever godforsaken place he was from.

"Jordan." He said.
"What?" I asked.
"You were wondering where I'm from, right?"

'How did he fuckin'…"

"I'm from Jordan." He said matter-of-factly.

'Christ on a cracker!' I thought freakishly, *'Is this whole f'n place full of mind-readers?'*

"Mark."

He stopped my mind scream.

"We get paid very well to know what people are thinking, before *they* know what they're thinking."
I stared at him sheepishly, hoping that my embarrassment wasn't too apparent.
"What did you drive to work today?"
"What?"
"What kind of car did you drive to work today?"
"You mean you don't know?" I crowed smartly.

He smiled broadly, his gargantuan teeth emerging brightly from his neatly trimmed goatee.

"It doesn't matter." He shot back, "Guess what I drove to work today?"

The pencil was starting to scribble a gray crescent moon on the interior of my skull.

"I don't know," I whispered, still irked that he'd read my racist mind.
"Guess." He kept on, his smile growing a bit more.
"Guess?"
"Guess."
"A Maxima?"
"Very good, Mark. Give the boy a bag of peanuts."

I shot him a disgruntled 'Charlie Brown' expression, my exasperation readily apparent.

"I drove to work today a hard-loaded Maxima SE."

'Well, congratulations Sheik Mohammed!' I thought angrily.

"Relax Mark, this is an illustration."
"A what?"
"I'm demonstrating how to control the conversation."
"Oh."
"I haven't owned a car in almost fifteen years." He said this as though it were some sort of great accomplishment.
I looked at him tiredly, the lack of sleep beginning to vex my eyes.
"The dealership provides me with a car because I make them tens of thousands of dollars every month."
I leaned forward in my chair and rested my elbows on my knees. My dazed and confused noggin fell forward with exhaustion. The pencil had colored the grey moon completely black.

"Want one?" Z asked.
"One what?" I whined at the floor.

"A free car."

The husky pencil flipped around inside my brain, its eraser poised for action. I looked up from underneath my furrowed brow.

"Does a bear wear a funny hat?" I groaned.

Z's brow furrowed back, the mixed inference clearly lost on him.

"If you sell fourteen cars per month for three months in a row, the dealership will give you a driver."
"Really?" I said, my excitement returning.

His smile dissipated as quickly as it had emerged.

"Yes," he intoned slowly, "but there is a catch."
"Of course there is…" I started.
"You have to sell at least three new cars and three used. Also, once you start selling that many cars, you have to keep a rolling three month average of fourteen or they take the car back."

I looked at him with genuine surprise.

"I guess Brick didn't share that with you either."

It wasn't a question, but my dark-eyed expression gave the answer anyway.

"So how many do you have to sell?" I asked Z deridingly.

Half a smile cracked on the right side of his face again.

"Eighty-five."

I smiled back as much as my tired face would allow.

"You'll be fine, Mark." He advised, "Just take control."

I looked at him admiringly for a moment then out the window. Victor and Tristan were shuffling about on the sidewalk, smoking and having an animated discussion. They looked like adopted brothers from two different continents, and generations.

"Now get the hells out of my office before any of these Mother-Bitches see me talking to you."

We shared a secret smile, one that was reserved for jaded intellectuals and wise guys.

****

I tromped down the narrow hallway from his office and into the even narrower one that went past the bathrooms. Turning the corner too sharply I inadvertently slammed my shoulder into the wall and stumbled wildly back and forth for a moment, the lack of sleep already catching up with me. Righting myself, I made it to the end of the hallway and found the coffee makers. The pot that Z had made earlier was beginning to reek from the stench of the too-hot burner. Fumbling a Styrofoam cup from the top of the stack, I dumped way too much sugar and non-dairy creamer into the bottom. Lifting the pot from its hotspot I shakily poured some java into the tiny little thing. The sugar and creamer reacted with a chemical sizzle and I stared into the sputtering beige potion for a second before stirring the concoction with a stupid, tiny plastic straw. Turning mechanically for the outside door I emerged from the other side of the building.

Sun glints reflected off the windshields of the cars like salt off a steel hammer. I squeezed one eye shut against the sharpness of the glare and reached up to the top of my head for my sunglasses. Sipping the coffee too fast, I burned my tongue and throat briefly then grimaced across the lot. Random and

Joe were walking slowly up the ramp to the new car showroom. A few crows and magpies stalked about in the grass to my left. Exhaling the burn from my tongue, my fingers extracted the pack of Camels from my pocket and I deftly shot a butt to my lips. With the same hand I re-deposited them back into my pocket and slid my lighter out past the pack. The crows started cackling at each other about some latent piece of trash. I wished for a shotgun.

Lighting up quickly, I decided to wander the used lot for a bit just to see what we had. As I circumnavigated the building I noticed that Tristan and Victor had gravitated to the front. Their heads were on swivels as they watched me wander toward the inventory. Even with my shades on, the vehicles seemed ridiculously bright. Most of them were so clean that they didn't even seem like used cars... at least at first glance. As I weaved my way through the rows toward the far corner I felt a bit like the little Chinese kid in a children's book that my mother used to read me...

It was a series of stories about a little boy with like seven super-human brothers that could do amazing feats. The one I was recalling was about the brother that could hold the entire ocean in his mouth. I was the little brother running around on the flood plain looking at the shells and starfish or whatever. I was getting a bit too far out while my big brother was losing his ability to hold all that water in his mouth. As I reached the farthest corner of the lot, I wondered when the impending flood might pull me under altogether.

"MARK STAPLETON! Please come to the new car showroom!" Brick's voice crackled across the air like the announcer from the 'Price is Right'.

"Mark... Stapleton... to the new car showroom."

It felt less like I'd won something and more like crashing waves in my ears.

I looked down at the half-smoked cigarette in my hand and then out over the used car line into Colfax. The traffic was already rushing past like a coal train. Flipping the cancer stick into the street I spun on my rubber heel and began the seven-acre trek back toward the showroom. Walking as slowly as possible I asserted my control over the situation. It took nearly three minutes for me to make my way across the blacktop, up the stairs and into the lion's den. Ducking the sign, I slunk up to the counter. Brick and Ned sat in their usual spots.

"Yes?"

Brick looked up at me from the ad proof he was pretending to examine. A canary-eating grin pasted across his face.

"Oh Stapleton." He began with mock seriousness. "Your wife called."
"Really?" I returned, a sinking feeling of worry dropping into my gut.
"Yeah," he sniggered, "She said I left my belt at your place and you're out of Jack Daniels."

My stare resembled tracer bullets from a Japanese Zero.

"Is that what you paged me up here for?" I stammered, a hot blush rising from my neck.
"Yeah," he guffawed, wheeling over to get a high-five from Ned.

The humor was completely lost on me. Anger swelled in my gullet like I'd never felt before. If I wasn't so tired, I would've launched myself over the counter and stomped his face into a greasy spot. Instead I turned from the counter and stalked into my office. Flumping into the cheap chair behind my desk I rifled through the drawers for my 'three by five'. I wasn't there for thirty seconds before both Brick and Ned were at my door. They stood in the doorway smiling down on me like rabid jackals.

I looked up into their comical faces as they observed me warily. Coiled in my chair like an angry rattlesnake, my reptilian stare surveyed them through my bleary contact lenses. Sensing my dismay they entered my office slowly.

"Come on man," Brick giggled, "we're just fuckin' with ya'."

I felt a tingling at the base of my skull and exhaled slowly.

"I don't need to be fucked with this morning."

Ned slid the door shut behind him.

"What's goin' on?" he asked with a compassionate tone that almost seemed genuine.

"You really wanna' know?"
"Yeah." Brick intoned, "We really do."
"I'm fuckin' broke." I said shakily.

They looked at each other darkly.

"So what do you need?" Ned asked.
"Money."
"That's clear, Mark." Brick dropped, "How much?"

I looked at him questioningly.

"How much?" Ned repeated softly.

"Well I did my finances yesterday and it looks like I'm gonna' be about six-hundred short on my rent. Even with all the bonus dough I've made this weekend I'm still tapped."

They exchanged another wary look but their eyes were both smiling.

Nervously I babbled on, "I got a part-time job this morning so that should help and I've sold a few cars, so hopefully after today I'll have enough sold to cover the guarantee, but I need money now!"

My voice was wavering badly and nearing the verge of rage. What I felt was a mixture of anger, embarrassment and guilt. Brick and Ned sat calmly in the customer's chairs on the other side of my desk. I looked over their heads and out through the glass wall of my office. Beyond the glistening cars of the showroom I could see the neatly cut grass that tumbled down the hill from the front of the store. I wished I was laying on it with a big fatty.

"How 'bout we front you a grand." Brick said from somewhere far away.

My eyes returned to the office and met his. He stared into me with his intent lioness gaze.

"Really?" I croaked. "You can do that?"
"Mark," Brick smiled slyly, "I can do anything I want."

I exhaled again with relief.

"Now why don't you just calm down and sell three cars today." punctuated Ned.

Chapter Fourteen

Up to my ass in alligators.

It was Friday morning and I sat in the drive-thru at the base of the gigantic bank building upon which our paychecks were written. It was just after nine-thirty and I'd already washed three tubs of fish and sat through yet another rat-whipping session at the dealership. I was cashing the thousand dollar check that Brick and Ned had secured for me so I could drive back up to Evergreen and deposit it in my own bank account. I probably could've just deposited the check in my account, but I wanted to feel the weight of the cash on my palm before I handed it over to my landlord.

The teller inside mumbled something about having a nice day over the whoosh and whirr of the tube-sucking machine, then the plastic canister dropped next to me like a stone. I reached over and collected my largess from the receptacle and clunked it back into place. Folding the borrowed grand around the not quite six-hundred dollars I had left over from the weekend, I stuffed the temporary wad into the pocket of my tight fitting slacks. As I crept onto Colfax I noticed the sign for the Westland shopping center. Slowing briefly I went ahead and turned my dusty wagon into the immense parking lot. Santana rolled smoothly from the old speakers as I made my way down the sparsely filled rows of parked cars. Most of them were just slightly nicer than my own.

Reaching the end of the row I saw a discount clothing store called Gordino's. I'd never heard the name before but I needed some new pants, preferably something with a cuff and a permanent crease. Finding a spot near the front, I parked and rolled the windows up, leaving a small gap near the top of each to keep the heat from filling the charcoal grey interior. The engine tinkled at me as I walked toward the series of glass doors and windows that spanned the front of the building. Two gigantic faux marble trash cans stood sentinel at the entrance. I noticed that they also were topped with 'ring' style ashtrays filled with some sort of weird black sand and numerous brands of cigarette butts. I added one to the collection.

The store was ridiculously cold in preparation for the heat of the day. What seemed like a million racks displayed everything from handbags and shoes to slacks and sunglasses. Gravitating to the men's section I found a gargantuan round rack that must've had three hundred pairs of pants. The industrial style hangars screamed their dismay as I rifled around, looking for a decent pair. I selected a couple pairs in my size and wandered to the back of the store looking for a dressing room. Looking up I saw a giant arrow suspended from the ceiling with "Dressing Rooms" in red block lettering below it. I laughed at myself dazedly and walked toward the counter in front of them. A nice Mexican girl stood behind a small counter in front of the louvered doors. She had a monstrous pile of clothing in front of her and a disinterested look on her face.

"I'd like to try these on, please?" I asked quietly.

She handed me a large card with the number two printed on it, she didn't look up. I slunk behind her and pulled one of the doors open. Wadded pieces of pocket trash and discarded product tags littered the floor. Stepping in I pulled the door closed behind me. Dropping my old pants around my ankles, I slid them over my shoes, not wanting to take them off. The tiny closet like room smelled of a thousand years of I don't know what. The first pair of pants fit like a vise and the zipper seemed a little off kilter. I tore them off and threw them in a pile in the corner. The second pair had both a cuff and a permanent crease and fit perfectly. I surveyed myself in the cheap, almost full length mirror and decided they fit well enough for government work. Flipping up the tag that was attached to the waistband I noticed that they'd been marked down from $39.99 to $19.99.

'Works for me.' I thought.

Stripping them off again over my shoes I put on my old pants and headed up to the register. The Mexican chick didn't look up at me as I laid the plastic number card back on her counter. An equally disinterested lady at the register offered me another ten percent off if I applied for the store's credit card so I took her up on the offer and got out of the store for less than twenty bucks.

The ride back up to Evergreen was uneventful and I made it to my own bank by 10:44. After depositing the money in my own account and a check into my landlord's, I found myself with roughly two hours to kill before I was scheduled to be back at work. Friday mornings were such bullshit. Whether I worked the day shift or not, I was required to be at work for the 8:20 meeting so the managers could ask you how many cars you'd sold for the month. After dutifully spouting your number, we'd been either lauded or lambasted accordingly. It was a lot like a military operation. Even though I'd sold two and a half more cars on Memorial Day and earned some more bonus cash, the three days that followed had been as dry as a bone in a paper sack.

I decided to run home for lunch and maybe a quickie if my wife was feeling amorous. The crappy little stairs that led to my postage stamp sized front deck creaked under my feet in the hot sun. I didn't remember my hometown being so hot when I was a kid. Of course I'd grown up closer to the Conifer side of the Evergreen area so the elevation was much higher than where we were currently residing. My wife sat on the deck in a reclining chaise lounge with a pitcher of iced tea next to her. She wore a thin t-shirt and cutoff shorts. Surprised to see me, she dropped her magazine on the boards of the deck and pushed her sunglasses up onto her head.

"What are you doing?" she asked.
"You, hopefully." I charmed.
"The baby's asleep..." she returned with a mischievous smile.
"So what are we waiting for?"

The sex was angry and delicious. I threw her around like a life sized rag doll. Her breasts were swollen and voluptuous, her hips and belly soft and pound-able. It was like eating angel food cake and playing nerf football at the same time. She shuddered with delight as she found her pleasure then I flipped her delectable ass over and found my own. We were young and stupid and blessed by the gods.

As we languished in the afterglow of twisted sheets and mingled musk, the silence was a platinum vapor. I considered how I'd come to be here. Back home with a wife and daughter, twelve years of childish adulthood behind me. Ski bumming my way through the nineties had seemed so difficult. How was I going to raise a child when I was just barely learning to take care of myself? I craved a beer and shot, even PBR and Jameson would do at this juncture.

*** *** ***

There was a pub in Winter Park that had been one of my favorite haunts back when I was still a miserable drunk. The owner was an odd Irishman that shared his name with the coach of the Broncos. But because he was a 'Cheesehead', he rooted exclusively for the Packers. All regional biases aside, he was a righteous dude that always met one with a smile and a free shot of whiskey. I guess I was willing to overlook the fact that the pour spout on top of the Jameson bottle was shaped like a yellow football helmet.

Except perhaps for that one night that I walked in and he presented me with an $88.00 bar tab from the night before…

'I wasn't here last night!' I'd argued.
'Oh yes you were.' Mike retorted. 'You were buying drinks for people like it was 1999! Then there was a puff of smoke and a lightning flash and you were gone.'

'Holy shit!' I'd exclaimed at the oversight.

I had zero memory of even being on that side of town, much less anything that might've transpired in the pub.
'Did anything… else… happen?' I'd asked him, scared to death about what I might have done during the blackout. I'd reached into my pocket and peeled off five twenties.
'Nope.' He laughed, slapping the dough off the bar and pouring me a shot of 'Jam-o', 'but you should've stayed, there were chicks all over you.'
'I guess I was in rare form.' I smiled shakily, wishing I could've remembered.

'You were feelin' no pain brother.' He held up the twenties in front of me, *'I'm keeping this for my pain and suffering.'*

I knocked the shot back and grimaced, 'Well then.' I shot back in my best Val Kilmer-as-Doc Holliday voice, 'I guess my hypocrisy knows no bounds.'

'You're not a hypocrite,' he jibed, pouring me another shot, 'just an idiot.'

'I guess there's no arguing that at this point.' I mumbled, knocking back the second jigger of Black Irish Hate. He pulled a pint glass off the shelf behind him.

'Want a snip to chase that hair down?'

'Mr. S,' I warbled on with my Kilmer-Holliday drawl. 'You are an oak.'

'Say when...' he joked.

'Then again,' I rolled on, 'you may be the anti-Christ.'

He shook his head laughingly and poured me half a glass of PBR.

*****

I awoke from my sex-induced slumber with a start. My wife was gone and the clock read 12:33.

"Fuck!" I exclaimed, jumping up and throwing on my clothes again.

I rounded the stairs in a flash, stuffing my shirt into my new pants. My wife was nursing the baby quietly on the couch.

"Have you seen my keys?" I asked habitually.

"Next to your smokes on the dresser." She laughed.

"Fuck." I hissed, rocketing down the stairs again.

The not quite an hour of sleep had only served to rehash my sordid past, leaving me feeling infinitely dumber. At least the sex was good. Trotting up the stairs a second time I tiptoed past my girls and pulled the fridge door open. Pawing up a couple slices of cold pizza I wheeled again and plunked a kiss on the top of her head.

"Love you."
"We love you too, Daddy." She clucked sweetly.

Trotting down the stairs again, she called after me.

"There's some mail for you in my car."
"Okay." I paused and then unscrewed the knob on the front door.
"It looks, important...."
"K."

Unbuckling the passenger door on her Lumina I snatched the pile of mail from the seat. Ripping my own passenger door open, I threw the envelopes inside and sprinted around to fold myself back into the driver's seat.

****

I drove a bit slower back to work and enjoyed the summer afternoon. The traffic was indifferent. Arriving in the back lot at ten to one, I finished my smoke languidly then walked slowly to the showroom with the mail clutched in my mitt. The sex had smoothed my edges and rubberized my knees. A few of my cohorts were showing vehicles but the day was altogether less agitated than the previous Friday. Even the muzak in the showroom bubbled forth with an old Lennon tune that had touched me at one point.

Wandering past the tower, I entered my office to peruse the stack of envelopes. The first few were bills with due dates that fell later in the month. These were followed by a couple credit card offers that I probably wouldn't get approved for and some coupons for a Pizza Hut and a local car wash. I sniggered a bit at the last one, the faded paint and worn carpets in my ride had long since kissed off the days of even the most masterful of detailers. It was only fifteen years old, but it hadn't aged gracefully. The rust on the steel wheels alone had been there when I bought the damn thing. Placing the bills in my top drawer neatly and chucking the coupon cards in the trash, I looked at the last two envelopes.

One was from AMEX and the other was a cryptically blank white except for the red and black lettering that was made to look as if had been stamped on at an angle. I knew the AMEX letter was another *'Where is our money?'* attempt that I'd been dodging for over two years now, but the other seemed a bit more urgent. The sideways stamp read politely in black; Dated Material: - then in a less cheerful red with larger print, OPEN IMMEDIATELY!! I pondered the use of two exclamation points. Wasn't the block lettering and blood red ink enough? Perhaps I'd won something.

'Yeah,' I reconsidered, *'And if a frog had wings…'*

The thought crossed my mind to just chuck it in the trash along with the coupons. But instead I tore it open and bent the creased folds back so I could lay the letter upon the desk. The page was equally stark except for a small paragraph.

"Mr. Stapleton," It read.

"This letter is an attempt to collect on a debt for which you are severely past due. Please remit the amount of $2,112.00 immediately to the address listed below or you will face legal action!"

The address was for some collection agency in Ft. Collins.

"Awesome." I whispered aloud to myself.

The husky pencil was lodged in my brain stem; etching a frowny-face slowly on the back of my skull. Weaving my black-clawed fingers into my feathery hair I pulled until my scalp tingled. A squawk lodged in my throat like bony road-kill and my breath had the faint smell of vomit.

"What are you doing?" Farm had appeared at my office door.

I looked up at him despairingly.

'Going down in flames,' I felt like saying, 'again.'

His face was pinched under his knitted brow. He looked less like a cartoon rooster than an angry pit-bull.

"There's people everywhere and Gavin's about to have conniption!"
"I just got here." I defended.
"So did three customers." He thrust back. "Let's Go!"

Brushing the offending letter into my top drawer with my bills, I lifted myself from the crappy chair and followed him out the front doors. Jamie and Speck had gotten two of the 'ups' and Random was hobbling down the ramp to pick up the third set.

"Fuck!" Farm snarled harshly.

He slapped his hands together theatrically like I'd seen Milo do that first day. It now seemed like a century ago.

"No one has an up unless you have one!" he growled into my face.

I looked at him with black eyed dissonance.

Brick strolled onto the patio behind him. His duck-footed meander was almost comical.

"What're you guys talkin' about?"
"I'm not sure." I crowed back gravelly.
"I was explaining to Mr. Stapleton that no one should have a customer unless he has one." Farm clucked.
"Makes sense." Brick clucked in agreement.

The Husky pencil came back in full scribble.

I bent my head around Farm's one-eyed gaze and surveyed Brick. His feet were splayed out beneath the cuffs of his tobacco green slacks. They were shod in some odd style of two-tone penny loafer with wide flat pieces of leather on the tops. They were trying to be a variation on the old theme of tassel loafers my Dad used to spit shine in our smoke filled basement; but they actually resembled golf shoes or Hush-Puppies. What was truly hilarious was how small they were, a size seven at best. Farm's shoes were Italian looking and polished to a military sheen that would've been offensive had I not squinted. His size was considerably larger; perhaps a ten or eleven and his feet seemed unusually flat. Like a cop's feet.

"Why don't you guys just say what you're trying to say?" I blurted without thinking.
"What do you think we're trying to say...?" Farm started, but Brick cut him off.
"You need money." He stated flatly. "You think I'm not wise?"

The shirt he was wearing ruffled lightly in the breeze, probably silk. It was an off cream color and appeared to match his socks. I guessed that his wife probably dressed him.

"What time is it?" he continued.
I glanced at my watch mechanically.
"What?"
"What time is it?" he chimed a bit louder.
"1:08." I crowed spastically.
"What time are you supposed to be on?"
"1:00."
"Okay."

I felt like punching him in the face.

"Okay..." I mimicked.

"So I've got three salesmen with ups that couldn't find a hooker in a whorehouse and you're standing here with your dick in your hand."

The sideways complement caught me off-guard and I wavered.

"So how does this work?" I warbled.
"How does what work?!" Farm interjected, his pit-bull spate now frothing in the corners of his mouth.
Brick lay the fingers of his left hand on Farm's crossed arms gently, like a mother duck consoling an agitated chick.

"I've got this." He stated quietly.
Farm wheeled away and stalked to the far end of the porch to light up a smoke.

"Come inside." He said to me.

I was afraid I'd maybe spoken out of turn.

"It's okay." He assured me, "We need to talk."

As we entered through the double doors he turned to the right past the receptionist's desk. We entered a short hallway that led to the General Manager's office. Ribbons of dread rippled through me. I could almost feel the razor edged blade of the guillotine scraping the hairs on my dissident neck. Then Brick stopped in front of a giant dry-erase board that was hanging on the wall. It had been taped off into a grid and ran half the length of the hallway. I didn't know that they even made these things this big. Brick took a step back and surveyed the gigantic thing admiringly. I noticed the names of all the salesmen. Mine was on there also, near the bottom.

"This is how we measure the store." He quacked.

I looked up at the crazy thing with an odd fascination. There were weird abbreviations and fractions, numbers in thousands all scrawled in a rainbow of colors. It might as well have been written in cuneiform… or bird tracks. I exhaled through my lips with a low whistle.

'This is despicable!' I thought comically to myself in a daffy lisp.

"Everything you sell, new and used." he pointed to the first two columns. "What you're tracking," he pointed to the third column. "How much gross you've put up, what F&I does off your deals…" I tried to appear enamored but my day had already been too long and my patience was waning. "What bonus levels you've hit, cars per day…" his eyes seemed to glaze over as he continued. I'd lost my love of numbers in tenth grade, buried under the billow of zero-gravity bong hits and endless pillows of fresh powder snow. The board seemed to vibrate slightly in front of me. The neat columns and rows took on a breathy quality. I wished he'd get to the point soon.

"So you're here." He directed my attention to the row with my name on it. I nodded dumbly. It looked unreasonably blank.
"You've got no cars out." he traced across empty boxes of the row sarcastically with his hand.

"Uh-huh." I stated flatly as if the fact weren't already obvious to me.
"How many did you sell last weekend?"
"Five and a half." I jumped at the chance to crow again.
"And how much cash did you make off those?"
"Roughly $600 bucks."
"You stole $630 from me, but who's counting." He grimaced.
"Whatever." I laughed.
"Not whatever." He punctuated.

I looked at him sideways. He'd turned to face me with predatory eyes.

"Memorial weekend was a gift. Now it's back to brass tacks."

"K." I said succinctly and seriously.

"Good." He assented.

"To get a paycheck, you need to sell eleven new cars this month."

I turned to face him, my sunken eyes blackening again in their sockets.

"Calm down, Stapleton." He continued. "Our best guys sell seventeen to twenty-five cars per month.

It seemed impossible.

"You just sold five and half cars in three days last weekend."

My shoulders relaxed a bit and I felt like passing gas. Considering our proximity to Gavin's office, I clenched my cheeks instead.

"Just do what you did last weekend and you'll be fine."

"Why eleven?"

"Well, there's two break points," he kept on; "when you sell six new cars you get a retroactive bonus of $50 per car. When you get to eleven, the retro is $100/car."

"I see."

"If you haven't figured this out already," he snickered, "a Nissan buyer will drive fifty miles to save five bucks."

"It does seem like they really want to negotiate."

"They could make copper wire out of pennies."

I snickered too.

"Let's go into your office."

His fingers encircled my elbow briefly as he directed me out of the hallway. I turned and walked softly across the tiles. As we walked he leaned into to my ear and gave me the down low.

"Nissan buyers really want Toyotas or Hondas, but they're too cheap to pay up for the brand name."

"So they eventually end up here." I surmised quietly.

"Eggs-actly." He commiserated, following me into my office. I sat down in my chair again. It felt slightly less torturous than earlier.

"They like guys like you because you are nice to them and you don't know anything."

"Thanks." I crumpled my beak.

"Stop." He honked back. Then he whispered gently, "You've got to be an assassin."

My head cocked back and forth, I barely realized I was even doing it, until Brick mimicked me.

"Just walk 'em to a line of cars, let 'em pick the color, then when they're not looking, slit their f'n throat."

"You're losing me a bit."

"It's all about perspective." He paced. "Let me ask you something? How much money do you have in your pocket?"

I'd just deposited most of the money I had into the bank to pay rent.

"I don't know, like eighty bucks."

"You don't know," he asked, "or you don't care."

"I don't know." I said curtly, reaching for my pocket to finger the thin slice of cash that rested there.

"All of your customers care."

"Care about what?"

"Count the money you have in your pocket."

"What?"

"Pull out your money and count it!"

I drug the rumpled pile from my pocket and flitted through it quickly.

"Eighty-seven dollars!" I cackled.

"Okay," he quacked, "Now give it to me."

His predatory gaze was locked on mine again. I looked down at the paltry wad of cash in my hand again. It was all I had.

"I suspect that is all the money you have, correct?"
"Yes." I gulped. The bills lay on my palm like sweat soaked Irish tweed.
"Okay," he conceded, "This is not really fair 'cause I already know that you're broke. But the point I'm trying to make is that this is a game of inches. Don't think for a second that these fuckers wouldn't steal that cash out of your pocket given the opportunity."

I looked down at the paper bills again and then back into his yellow gaze. He exhaled through his nostrils feverishly. I felt that I was starting to glean from his blather the point that he was trying to make.

"Now, you'll get another paycheck on Monday for five-hundred bucks. The 'G' I already gave you will come off the top of your guarantee but I expect you to have at least eleven cars this month, no exceptions."
"K." I answered again.
"Now go get an up before Gavin sees you sitting in here."

As Brick exited my office and waddled back up to the tower, I reached over to my desk drawer and extracted the collection letter and AMEX bill. Depositing them into the circular file beneath my desk I whispered under my breath.

"Can't get blood from a stone…"

Chapter Fifteen

How do I work this?

The following Friday things were not much better. I awoke well before dawn and rolled sleepily down to the fish place. Wiggling the key Tony had given me into the lock of the glass front door; I flipped the dead-bolt and yanked it open. The place was dark save the macabre glow of the fluorescent bulbs in the display case. Reaching to my left I flipped on the bank of switches with a numb arm and waited as the overheads flickered to life. The sinks stood coldly in the back room under the steel purple glow and the sickly smell of bleach and fish intermingled with the smoky spice aroma of the back room.

Unscrewing two of the faucets, the pipes shuddered to life and shot forth blasts of cold water. The sound of streams hitting the deep stainless bottoms of the sinks was almost unbearably annoying. Eventually they pooled and the small room became relatively silent again. I stood in the center briefly and exhaled. A small boom box rested next to the microwave on the upper steel shelf on the back wall. Punching the power button on the front I waited for it to warm up. Classic rock soon flooded the room with its comfortable warmth and I reached above the sink for a pair of industrial rubber gloves that hung from the corner of another steel grate shelf.

The walk-in door opened with its usual clicks and clacks followed by the vacuum hiss and a frosty rush of stale, cold air. A giant baker's rack held six large bins inside. Wheeling the huge rack slowly out, I hefted one of the middle bins onto the stainless table that was formed into the giant stainless steel sinks; then I removed the lid. The pungent smell of lemon and garlic permeated my nostrils as I slid the plastic top back. Pushing the gargantuan rack back into the freezer slowly, I clicked the vault like door back into place.

They generally used two kinds of salmon depending on the current market price. Alaskan, which was a fatter, meatier fish that looked nice in the package but was a bitch to clean. The other kind was Norwegian, which seemed to be a bit leaner and tougher, but to me tasted much better and was way easier to wash. Staring into the meter long bin, I could see that this batch was the former. Slices of wheel cut lemons floated on top of congealed piles of pulverized garlic. The guys used fresh ingredients to make the fish taste better and satisfy the persnickety Evergreen clientele. I wondered how our customers might feel if they actually saw what this crap looked like before we smoked the *buh-jeezus* out of it and put it into its safe little rainbow colored packaging.

The first sink had filled nearly to the top of the brusher. The contraption was a rubberized podium that we suction-cupped to the bottom of the sink and had three bristly brushes that stuck up in a staggered array. They were a little over a foot tall and resembled a cross between the fronds of an Austrian Pine and a Sea Cucumber on Viagra. My job was to extract the fish from the bins, scrub the excess rue and spices from them; wash them in the next sink, and then place them on the smoking racks. It was back breaking work because the sides of fish weighed between seven to twelve pounds each and I had to bend pretty far over to get them through the brushes. But that wasn't the worst part of the job.

The part that sucked the most was that you couldn't use warm or even slightly cool water or the fish would come apart as you washed them. So I had to use bitter cold water on the already almost frozen slabs of fish. Even though the gloves were industrial style and somewhat insulated, the water would invariably spill over the sides and run down my elbows to my fingertips. Now I'd grown up skiing on some of the coldest mountainsides in Colorado, so I guess I had a bit of a leg up when it came to dealing with cold temperatures. But even the most gelid wind across the top of the Continental Divide couldn't have prepared me for this; it was like Siberian water torture.

Staring down into the yellowy pinkish rue, I took a firming breath and plunged in with both hands. The slippery, silver side of fish was large and the pureed garlic rolled like tiny marbles across the slick surface of my gloves. I lost my grip and the slippery bitch slumped damply into the first empty sink.

"Fuck." I exclaimed angrily to the empty room.

Flipping on the the third cold faucet of the morning, I thoroughly washed the rue from my gloves. The side had flopped down scale side up so a little hard water wouldn't hurt it. I just hoped that the tumble it took hadn't ruined the meaty side. Once my gloves were thoroughly scrubbed, I gingerly flipped the eleven pound behemoth over and saw that the meat hadn't broken apart.

"Phew." I exhaled and ran the side slowly through the scrubber.

By 6:48 I'd washed and filled three full racks for the smoker and replaced them in the walk-in. Draining the sinks I turned on the hot sides of the faucets full blast and flushed the bits of remaining lemon and garlic into the great unknown. Stopping the first two spigots, I rinsed my now gloveless arms under the blissfully warm water of the third. The feeling was just coming back into my fingers as I punched the button on the boom box to silence the room again. As I donned my sweatshirt and headed for the front door, Tony pushed through it from the outside... all sunshine and lollipops. He smiled broadly and asked how it was going.

"Great." I returned a bit more acidly than I'd intended. I'd less than an hour and a half to get to the Friday morning sales meeting and was dreading even going.

"Why don't you take some fish with you?"

I looked at him dumbly. The last thing I wanted to see at this point was more f'n fish. He smiled again then started rustling through the display case. He came up with several packets of fish and threw them in a large paper bag. Then he filled a plastic bag with some crushed ice and chucked it in as well. I smiled wanly and took the bag from him. He was just a little too cheery for me this morning. The bags under my eyes felt heavy and cold. He smiled again with something that looked like pity. Then he punched the no sale key on the register and peeled a couple fifties out of the drawer.

"These are for you man," he offered, "give the fish to your wife."

"Thanks man." I returned, feeling a bit guilty about my earlier funk.

"Thank *you*." He said.

I smiled a rumpled Charlie Brown smile and exited through the front door.

***

Sitting in the conference room at the back of the Hogan, flanked by Random and Joe, I dreaded the impending doom that would no doubt be rained upon us. The first week and a half of June had been considerably less fruitful then any of us could've hoped. Both my compatriots were slumped in their chairs with bug eyed dismay. The animation painted on their freshly shaven faces was fueled only by the morning's ration of caffeine and nicotine. Random had that sick, minty smell of menthol and Joe's aroma was an odd mix of musk and tobacco. I wondered what I smelled like.

The door clicked open precisely at 8:30 and in filed the Spanish Inquisition. All but Tristan and Victor snapped to attention. The pall was deafening. None of the managers were joking or smiling. Gavin wasn't among them, but something told me that he was here, somewhere. Brick's gait was unusually stilted, as though he'd hurt his back or something. Z and Mik had positioned themselves at the left corner of the long counter that spanned the wall in the front of the room. Ned and the other managers flocked in a group to Brick's right. Pacing back and forth in front of the room quietly, Brick glanced up at the group about every three seconds or so. His expressions changed from anger to confusion to outright exasperation. Nobody met his gaze.

"This is gonna be a real short meeting." He started in a curt tone.

Pausing again, he paced back and forth with a shorter span this time. Looking briefly at his used car managers then over at the new car managers, he then shifted his eyes downward and kicked at a ball of carpet fuzz on the floor. With his back half turned to the room, he looked up and sighed audibly.

"How many cars you got out Tristan?" he asked to the ceiling.
"Seven."
"Victor?"
"Five."
"Joe."
"Three and a half." He retorted with mock disdain.
"Aboud?"
"Two."

Brick grimaced. I hoped he wouldn't ask me next.

Running through the list of names, he skipped mine repeatedly.

'Maybe he'll forget I'm here.' I hoped against hope.

"Mark?" he questioned, as if in answer to my thoughts. "One and a half."

He turned his gaze theatrically toward our back corner. Random sat up a little straighter, then leaned away from me slightly to his left. Joe pushed two fingers into the furrows of his forehead and slumped away to the right.

"I don't know if you're gonna' make it, Stapleton."

It was a simple statement. The level of sarcasm was pointed but not dripping salaciously. I could still smell fish on my mitts and the hairs on my arms rose defensively. Curling my index finger over my lips, I clenched my chin with my thumb. A latent piece of salmon scale clung to the back of my wrist. I brushed it off then crossed my arms tightly in front of me. Brick glared at me for another couple seconds then brought his gaze back across the room. Leaning my head against the cinder blocks of the back wall, I felt their hollowness. I considered how easily a sledgehammer might find its way through them. Clouds must have run in front of the morning sun outside, because the light streaming through the upper windows dimmed the room for a few seconds.

Brick curled his chin into a profile and locked his one-eyed piercing stare upon the lot of us. He looked like a pirate that had just lain out his first lambasting or more so; an aging prizefighter that had been surprised with an uppercut. I could have chewed cast iron nails and spit cannonballs. My shoes felt tight and I worked my feet around inside them. If I could've made fists with my toes, I would have. My foray into this business had only been a few short weeks, but it might as well have been a century. The light from the outside blasted through the windows again and one of the overhead bulbs started to flicker incessantly. The buzzing and tinkling was enough to draw Brick's lidless eyes away from our corner.

"You got anything." He asked of the other managers in an almost accusatory tone.

They all shook their heads tentatively.

"Okay. We got lots of work to do. Let's go."

Random and Joe flanked me again as we trudged back to the new car showroom. I smoked angrily, hot boxing the tobacco and creating a pointed ash of red and gray and black.

"That must've been fun for you." Joe poked.

I took another giant pull off the cancer stick.

"Yeah," Random commiserated, "you looked like you were going to throw down for a second there."

Taking a final puff off my smoke, I flipped the sweaty butt over the top of the Altima row and into the alley behind.

"Jesus!" Joe warned. "You better hope Gavin didn't see you do that."

"Fuck Gavin." I spat in a low hiss, walking a bit faster to escape their misguided consolation.

They stopped briefly and let me walk on alone. My footfalls were heavy on the soft pavement. Frustration and anger welled inside of me like distilled lava. I felt like running. Almost to the showroom I had to stop as a customer peeled into the lot and rocketed past me into the customer parking. Had I reached out, I could've touched the fender as he shot past me. He was driving an old Pontiac sedan of some kind. A Grand Prix or Grand Am or Sunbird, or 'whatever-the-fuck' nameplate the aging GM brand had decided to paste onto their shitbox that year. Exhaling into the sky for half a second, I turned and stalked after him.

The young man that got out of the car was clad in loose fitting jeans and a t-shirt. His fat feet were stuffed into a pair of K-Swiss tennis shoes with the laces untied. The shirt was a bit too tight and the sleeves were rolled up a notch or two in order to display what the kid must've thought were muscular biceps. He was large in sort of a dumpy way, but certainly not Athenian by any stretch. His blond hair stood out from his scalp in all directions, the hair gel he'd liberally applied earlier just barely doing its job. As he walked toward me with bold intention, I was reminded of Mister Salty from the pretzel box. Laughing inside myself at his comical gait, I extended my hand and felt a slight morning breeze as it slipped under the cuff of my shirt and rippled up my sleeve.

"Welcome to Centennial Nissan." I offered in a dulce du leche tone. The smoothness of my voice surprised me as the anger of a few seconds before began to subside, then dribbled off my left elbow into a steamy pool on the pavement. The young man took my hand with a self-important grasp and he nearly pulled me in a half circle as he slowed his stride for just a fraction of a second. He was clearly on a mission. Turning to match his direction, we walked briskly to the front line of SUV's. Halfway down the row, I could see that he was making a beeline for the solar yellow Xterra that stood proudly at the end. I nearly had to trot to keep up. As we reached the end of the line, he immediately tried the handle on the driver's door. Of course it was locked and he looked at me impatiently. Dispensing with the pleasantries I went right for the throat.

"I guess you know what you're looking for?" I smiled broadly, sensing that this guy might be a slam-dunk.
"Yeah," he offered as he peered through the slight tint of the window. "This is the one."
"I'll be right back." I returned quickly.

The urge to run I'd had earlier was now replaced by a desire to break into a dead sprint. Pushing my feet into the rapidly softening blacktop, I slithered my way up to the showroom as nonchalantly as I could pretend. I gave the stock number to Cherlie in a low voice and slipped silently into my office then slid my plate off the back of the file cabinet. Brick pretended to ignore me as he grimaced out at the lot. Ned was organizing his desk into neat piles and straight corners. Mr. Salty was hopping around the Xterra like a rabbit in heat as I strode across the cement porch and down the front stairs. This was going to be the shortest test drive in history.
Slapping my plate onto the back, I went directly to the driver's side and clicked the key fob twice to unlock all the doors. Hopping in, I started the truck immediately. Mr. Salty took my direction and got into the passenger's seat. Skipping everything I'd learned, I flipped the air on and backed out of the space. I knew that I should be doing the walk-around, but

something told me that I could easily skip that step. Pulling out of the middle exit I rolled easily onto Colfax.

"So would you like to take the truck up the interstate, or a take faster route?"

"I'd like to take it on the highway, but Sixth will be fine."

"Cool."

I veered into the K-mart parking lot and did a couple of slalom turns around some of the streetlight poles.

"The thing I like the best about the Xterra," I started, "is that it is on a truck frame…"

"Yeah," he finished for me, "I like the fact that it has a ladder-rack frame that is bolted to the body."

Slowing the truck to a stop, I turned with mock surprise toward the young man.

"Looks like you know more about this vehicle than I do."

"Yeah, I've wanted one for a while."

"Cool," I said again, "Want to take the wheel?"

He beat me to the handle on the door and nearly crashed into me as we cruised around the front of the vehicle to make the switch. Obviously a local, he deftly maneuvered the truck back onto Colfax and slid into the left lane. Before long, we were trucking down the freeway. He took it up to just under eighty to check the acceleration. Seemingly satisfied, he let the needle coast back down to somewhere in the sixties. The pinkish, brown sun was making its way out of the smog over downtown. It had a pearlescent quality like I'd never seen before. I instructed him to exit Kipling so that we could circumnavigate back to the dealership. As we neared Colfax I asked him if there were any questions.

"Will you guys take my Pontiac on trade?"

The back of my head began to tingle and it felt like an ice patch was just starting to fracture.

"Well…" I paused, "it's pretty old."
"Yeah, I know." He agreed quickly. "I'd just like to get something out of it."
"We'll see what we can do." I assured him.

The green arrow lit up right as we met up with Colfax and Mr. Salty eased through the intersection. No cars were behind us, so he slid quickly into the right lane.

"Take the first entrance." I directed, motioning to the used car turn in.

He went right in and slowly passed the line of used vehicles. I had him deposit the new Xterra in its original spot, which he did reluctantly.

"So no one else can drive this vehicle till we're done right?" he asked nervously.
"I guess you like it?" I returned slyly.
"This is my truck." He challenged.
"Okay," I laughed as I reached over and turned off the ignition, collecting the keys in my fist. Then I looked up at him under cocked eyebrows and let a grin curl up my cheeks.

"Tough guy." I jabbed.

Massaging the steering wheel one more time, I noticed a bit of color rise in his boyish cheeks.

"Let's go make this happen." I punctuated.

We walked akimbo up to the showroom like fighter pilots after a successful mission. The new vehicles flanking us on either side were awestruck children. The sun rose high behind us in its full radioactive glory. I could feel the heat on my neck and back warmly. Our gait was clipped and macho.

All that was missing was maybe a girl in a polka dot dress and perhaps a couple of cigars. We walked slowly up the stairs and through the double doors into the showroom. Jamie and Speck watched us from their standard positions on the bench. I could feel their jealous glares on us as we passed. Jaime said something that sounded like,

"He's got a grape."

Mr. Salty was oblivious.

I walked him over my office and sat him down inside. He didn't ask for a drink, nor did I offer. Turning on my heel I lumbered up to the tower. Ned was watching me the whole time with a gleeful expression. I peeled a worksheet slowly from the top of the pad and slid it over the counter to him. Brick continued to squint out at the lot into the blaring sun.

"Got a deal?" Ned asked with his spritely charm.
"Yep."
"So you walked the trade?"
I started to say, "Ummm..." then caught myself and started to reach for an appraisal card.
"Don't worry about it." Ned stopped me. "What year is it?"
"Ummm..." I droned, feeling stupid and pissed-off at myself.

Brick's expression turned from a squint to his classic grimace. Discontent flowed off him like a wave,

"Skip it." Ned said a bit more harshly than normal, perhaps more for Brick's benefit than mine.

Brick kept his eyes locked forward but I could see his fingers clutching the armrests on his chair.

Ned pulled the cap off his Sharpie and held it in his left mitt as he laid out some numbers quickly on the worksheet. I stood in nervous silence and watched.

He penciled the Xterra at full sticker, including the addendum price. In the trade box he wrote 1000 then 10000 in the down payment box. For the payment he wrote 485/mo. Even with my limited experience I knew that payment with ten large down was way too high.

"Go get it." Ned said sharply.

Turning with the worksheet, I walked methodically toward my office. Ten grand seemed like a lot of dough for this kid. The paper floated in my hand like science fiction. Dropping it to my side I held it against my leg until I was seated behind my desk then laid it out in front of us.

"Great news!" I began with as much excitement as I could muster. "He gave you a grand for your trade. So with ten-thousand down you should be at around four-eighty-five a month."

Mr. Salty scooted up in his seat and examined the numbers briefly.

"The ten grand is no problem, but I was hoping to get two-thousand for my trade."
I was a bit dumbfounded by his response but did my best to appear cautious.

"I'm not sure we can do the two grand," I negotiated, "would you take fifteen-hundred?"

He stared at the worksheet for perhaps thirty seconds.

"I guess that'll work." He assented. "Can I write a personal check for the ten thousand?"

"That'll be fine." I returned as slowly as possible, flipping the worksheet over and writing the offer.

He signed easily then said he had to grab his checkbook from the car.

"No problem," I agreed.

As I brought the offer to the counter, he slipped out the double doors behind me.

Sliding the worksheet over the counter I leaned in to Ned.

"He's in."

"Where's your customer going?" Brick interjected.

"To get his checkbook." I replied smugly.

Ned reviewed the offer and his eyes grew big in their sockets, then he showed the worksheet to Brick.

"Can you even do that?" he asked Ned with questioning eyes.

"We may have to go forty-two months."

"Yeah," Brick laughed, "or twenty-four."

"Good job, Stapleton." Ned continued. "Where's the credit app?"

"Uh, I didn't have time to get one yet."

Brick shot up from his seat to make sure that Mr. Salty was still out front. Then he sat back down slowly as he saw the young man sauntering up the ramp, checkbook in hand.

"Jesus Stapleton." He muttered under his breath.

Ned took his cue and locked me in his directed gaze.

"Get the deposit check right away then do a credit app."

The doors whooshed open behind me and Mr. Salty headed straight for my office. Ned shrunk down behind the counter slightly.

"Take a deal jacket with you." Brick added.

"Already?" I asked stupidly.

"Just take a jacket with you." His expression was one of exasperation.

"K." I answered quickly, tearing a credit app off the pad.

After finishing the credit app and collecting a check, I filled out the entire deal jacket and brought it back to the desk. Ned snatched the application from me and started punching in the info quickly, as if it might suddenly turn to dust without his haste. Brick leaned back in his chair a looked at me with his classic disbelief. I slid down the counter and tried to look at Ned's screen, as if there were something I could do to expedite the process.

"Go sit with your customer." Brick admonished. "We'll tell you if you've got a deal in a couple minutes."

I turned dejectedly and slunk back to my office. Mr. Salty was checking the folds on his sleeves. His boyish jowls were stacked up around his soft chin in gushy rolls. He was clearly living in a dream world of his own design. I wondered where this loser had come up with ten large. I suspected that perhaps one of his parents CD's had matured or maybe his gay uncle died or something. Looking down my less than aquiline nose as I circled the desk, I tried to think of a subject on which we might converse. He didn't look up as I entered. As I pushed my chair back to sit down I was reminded of the *'Trust-a-farians'* I'd known during a three year stint I'd spent in Crested Butte…

They were a funny lot. You'd see them everywhere in that tiny little ski town. Ratty jeans held onto their skinny frames by a worn leather belt or perhaps a shoelace. Feet clad in wool socks and worn out Birkenstock sandals in the middle of winter. White dudes with disgusting Dreadlocks of blond or brown tumbling down to their crusty asses; Dead stickers all over their forty-thousand dollar Land-Cruisers. I'd see them outside the post office as I paid my bills, on the lawn at the park as I commuted to one of my many lame jobs. Their eyes were as red as velvet cake, their interest in me completely non-existent. The female versions were even worse…

****

Turning to sit, with a cat-bird smile painted across my face, I asked the young man if he had his checkbook. He held it up without a word. It looked new.

"I think we may have a deal, so go ahead and write me a check for the ten thousand."

He slapped the book down on the desk and curled his hand out for a pen. I slid a thin, black Papermate into his fingers and he began to fill out a check. Folding my hands neatly in front of me, I tried to act as though this were an everyday occurrence. Ripping the little piece of paper out quickly, he accidently tore the corner a bit next to the check number. Sliding it nonchalantly across to me, I pretended to investigate that it was filled out correctly. It was crisp and flat. The torn off corner hadn't affected the integrity of the check number, which read, '101', definitely a new account. The area where he'd scrawled, 'Ten Thousand Dollars' looked like it had been written by a four-year old. I felt a smile turn up on the corners of my lips slightly before I caught myself. Then I looked up into his concerned gaze.

"I guess I'll need a copy of your license for this one."

As he extracted his license from his wallet, Ned's calm voice echoed over the loudspeakers.

"Mark Stapleton please report to the sales desk, Mark, sales desk, please."

I rolled my eyes for effect then rose slowly from my seat and slid the check and his license into my left hand. Walking to the tower was like entering an Escher print. The tiles seemed to rise in front of me at odd angles and with each step and the twenty-something foot walk seemed to grow longer. The slick feel of the check in my claw felt tenuous, as though the slightest breeze my loose it from my grasp. Both Brick and Ned had their necks craned about to watch my journey. I couldn't tell if I was having a flashback brought on by lack of sleep and overindulgence in caffeine or I'd merely slipped through into some sort of alternate reality... one perhaps where I might actually have some kind of luck other than bad.

As I neared the tower, I noticed that Ned was smiling at me with his patented mock surprise. Brick looked slightly less annoyed than he had earlier, still annoyed, but in a different way. I rounded the corner and bobbed under the 'Employees Only' sign. It didn't move. Positioning myself in front of Ned, but a bit to the left, I set the check on the counter. They were both looking at me pleasantly but their expressions held a note of disbelief. Ned slid the check off the tall counter and showed it to Brick briefly. Brick exhaled and then shot me his smile-grimace.

"Did you run over a Leprechaun on the way to work?" he asked acidly.

"What?"

"I think he walked through a field of four-leaf clovers." Ned added.

"What the hell are you guys talking about?"

"This kid's a 720." Ned let slip.

I didn't know what he was talking about, but it sounded good.

"He's got better credit than most forty year olds."

"No shit?" I returned hopefully, "So we've got a deal."

Ned and Brick both sniggered.

"Yeah," Brick said snidely, like an annoyed older brother, "you've got a deal." Then to Ned, "Now you just have to figure out how you're gonna get up to that payment."

Ned smiled and his moustache twitched a little bit. He looked a bit like Charlie Chaplin.

Brick snatched up the phone and announced, "Clean for delivery!' boldly over the loudspeaker. Then he wheeled back slightly from the desktop and folded his arms behind his head.

"Looks like you got yourself your first three-pounder."

"What the fuck's that?" I spouted out of turn, unable to contain my excitement any longer.

"Pays you a grand." Ned said too quickly also.

Brick shot him a disbelieving look.

I smiled briefly and felt something release its grip on the back of my neck. Relaxation poured down my spine in a tingly trickle. My Cro-Magnon brain had a sudden memory of what it feels like to be a stalactite. The trickle traveled down the length of legs and pooled in my shoes like glittery calcite. I felt like doing a little *'Chaplinesque'* dance of my own.

Chapter Sixteen

Ten Feet Tall and Bulletproof

The next five days I was like King Midas on steroids. Though most of deals were 'minis', it seemed that everything I touched turned to gold. I'd even managed to 'board' a used car. It was just a cheap old '94 Sentra, but it still paid me like a 'buck-sixty' in commission. By Thursday morning of the third week I'd put up seven new deals and had three appointments set up for the weekend. Everyone seemed to hear my words as gospel and had good credit to boot. I'd even made another three-pounder on a minivan of all things and sold the old lady a protection package. My last name crawled up Brick's crazy bonus board like a gecko out of a peyote patch.

I stood on the porch with my right arm stretched out on the railing, a smoke rested between my fingers lightly. Random was going on about some girl he'd hooked up with that was a complete nympho. My head nodded like it was on a spring as I tried to pretend I was listening.

"So she picked me up in this club…" he was saying with his wanna-be ghetto drawl. "Goin' on and on about how she really likes black guys."

Thoroughly disinterested in Random's night crawling activities, I tried to remain attentive. We'd started out together in the business and he felt that we had the sort of friendship that required he share the intimate details of his twenty something ramblings. Since it had been just barely over a month since we'd started, I guess I clung to the instant, pre-mixed fellowship as well.

"So do you like white girls?" I interjected.

He looked at me with a vacant stare. I surveyed him from behind my shades and a trail of smoke.

"I like women," he continued with an irritated tone, "black ones, brown ones, yellow ones and yes, white ones too."
"I like the pink parts." Jamie interjected from a couple feet down the railing.
"Shut up, Hammy." Random jibed, "I'm tryin' to tell a story here."
"I've never had a black girl." I mused.
"They're all right," he answered quickly, "but they don't like it when you touch their hair. Anyway, this chick takes me back to her place and it is on like Donkey Kong. She starts lighting candles, changes into some sexy lingerie…"

Speck pulled onto the lot in a silver Xterra. I turned to watch him exit the vehicle with his customer. He was clearly spouting off in his encyclopedic fashion. His potential sale dwindled with each placating nod of the customer's head.

'Just bring him inside.' I thought to myself.

"So I'm thinkin' I'm in, right…" Random chattered on.

The Arapahoe sun blared down on Speck and his customer. I could almost feel the patches forming under his armpits as the deal slipped further from his grasp. He stood with one arm propped against the back of the vehicle, his tie curled stupidly in his other clammy mitt.

'Just start walking.' I thought at him again.

"Then she lies back on the sofa and starts fingering herself. Pulling her panties to the side you know, squeezing her nipples…"

Speck finally asked his customer some kind of weak closing question and they turned uncomfortably toward the showroom. I could tell by the reluctance in his gait that it was the last thing the customer wanted to do. Oblivious to his customer's body language, Speck yammered on about who knows what.

"At this point, I'm losing my mind…" Random spouted incessantly; completely unaware that Speck and his customer were approaching the stairs.

Jaime slid in a bit closer to the conversation. I removed myself from the rail and walked toward the ashtray to crush out my butt. Random missed the cue and followed me over. Jamie trailed behind like a bulldog puppy in heat.

"So I rip her drawers off and she's shaved!" He shouts way too loudly.

"Keep your voice down, Random!" I whisper warily, seeing the top of Speck's too small head coming up the stairs.

He finally sees that a customer is coming and drops the story down a few decibels. I'm hardly listening.

"Her sweet, little pussy is shaved in the shape of a heart. You believe that shit?" He half-asks, half-crows.

"No fuckin' way!" Jaime spouts too loudly as well.

I punch him hard in the arm.

"Ow!" he exclaims, "What the fuck, Stapleton?"
"Shut the fuck up!" I hiss back, then motion sharply with my head toward the stairs. Thank the gods that Speck was as slow as tar.

Jaime realized that a customer was coming up to the porch and closed his lips theatrically, rubbing his arm through his shirt. We all watched Speck as he passed, the doors opening with their robotic whoosh. They closed behind him and I watched the procession through the glass. The customer looked as if he might turn at any moment and make a break for it. Ned's head was on a swivel as he surveyed the situation. Brick's gaze was locked on the three of us. I wondered how much he saw, or heard. It wouldn't surprise me if he'd been listening, with those lion ears of his, even through the tempered glass doors.

"So I'm going down on this whore." Random continues.
"Did she have nice tits?" Jaime interrupts again.

My head hurt from the inanity. Random wouldn't let up.

"I'm not really thinkin' about her breasts at this point, Hammy!" he chatters, still trying to point the story at me.

Jaime rubbed his arm again.

"So here's the fucked up part, though." Random carries on, oblivious to my disinterest. "I flip her over so I can, you know, do the deed."

"The deed?" I ask sarcastically, wishing he'd just finish the story and leave me alone.

"Yeah, you know, lay the pipe?"

"Lay the pipe." I repeat.

"Yeah," he belabors, "you know jangle her bells."

I look at him from behind my shades, my expression that of one Elwood Blues. I wished I had some dry white toast or perhaps a little Night Train wine.

"Uh-huh." I drone flatly, still feeling Brick's stare upon us.

"So I flip her over expecting to have a nice little white girl ass pokin' up at me and do ya' know what I see?"

"No Random, what did you see?"

"This bitch has got a tail!"

My eyebrows rose above the tops of my shades.

"What?"

"A fucking tail man!" he exclaims. "Some kind of crazy shit growing off the top of her ass like in a fuckin' B-rated horror flick from the 80's or something!"

I turned for the doors to go inside. It was too early and I was too old for this weirdness.

"Where you goin', man?"

"I'm gonna' get me four fried chickens and a Coke."

Random and Jamie stared at me stupidly, the inference clearly lost on them.

"What am I supposed to do about this chick with the tail?"

"Go to a different club next time."

I turned for the doors and they whooshed open; a blast of cool, clean air blew the filth off of me. Entering slowly I could hear Jaime asking if he 'did' her anyway. The doors closed behind me. The image would stick with me for at least another hour.

"Stapleton!" Brick chuffed from behind the glass wall.

Turning to face him I noticed he was motioning me to the counter with a curled up paw. I walked softly over, ducking the sign and resting myself on my folded arms above him.

"Stay right here." He said in confidence.

"Stay here?" I asked, not sure of his meaning.

"Yeah," he reiterated, "Stand right at the end of this counter; I may need you."

Strangely reminded of my football days in high school I turned and leaned back against the front windows of the store, my left elbow still resting on the counter. Brick craned his neck to glare into my office. Speck's customer was leaning back in the chair. Jeremy was obviously explaining something in great detail. Ned looked through the glass wall also. The customer's posture was slack in his chair. He resembled the guy in that old Memorex ad; the one where the dude is planted in a recliner getting blown away by the stereo speakers.

"What is he doing?" Ned yipped, putting the emphasis on the 'What'.

"Fucking up yet another deal." Brick intoned.

I surveyed their co-dependent nervousness indifferently. The sun had warmed the front windows and they felt good through the thin fabric of my dress shirt.

"If he's not up here in three minutes," spurted Brick, "I'm having Stapleton go get the keys."

"Send him now." Ned growled at the floor.

"You know what? You're right."

He slapped a pen down on some papers in front of him. "Stapleton."

"Yep." I leaned in further.

"Go tell Speck that you need the keys to that Xterra."

"What?"

"Go say that someone else wants to look at the truck he demoed."

"Oh," I realized, smiling at the ruse, "I see."

"Go now."

"K."

I crept back under the sign and slithered across the tiles toward our office. Placing my hand lightly on the edge of the door, I leaned in pleasantly. Speck was expounding about gear ratios or something that I didn't understand, or care to.

"Brick needs the keys to the Silver Xterra."

He looked up at me coldly. The verbal fog of his dissertation still hung in a cloud around his customer's head. I held out my hand and flipped my fingers at him.

"C'mon." I snapped a bit more bluntly than I might have intended.

Jeremy's expression was more one of hurt than anger as he leaned back to reach into his pocket.

"Here." He said flatly, handing me the keys.

The customer had come out of the mist and was looking up at me also, trying to decipher what exactly was happening.

"I'll uh, bring them right back." I stumbled, not sure what to say.

Jeremy's expression was one of an elephant in the headlights.

"Whoa." The customer held his hand up, "I'm interested in this vehicle."

I looked down at him, the keys resting on my palm between us like a pile of gourmet jelly beans. The pause was deafening.

"Mark Stapleton, please come to the sales desk." Brick's voice shot nasally through the loudspeaker.

"I'll be back." I said quickly.

When I reached the counter, Brick flipped his fingers at me as I'd just done a couple minutes earlier. Handing the keys over I decided to share my experience.

"Speck's customer seemed a little pissed." I said.
"Of course he is." Brick returned shyly.
"Ahhh." I said, the subversion becoming apparent to me.

He glared at me with the slack eyed, hook nosed frown of a Venetian moneylender; then picked up the handset to his phone.

"Jeremy Speck, please come to the sales desk. Jeremy. Speck. To the sales desk, please."

I looked through the glass wall at our office. Jeremy rose from his desk like a hippopotamus drawn from a mid-summer's wallow. I could almost see the mud dribbling from his arms. His customer had the posture of disbelief. Waddling across the tiles he slowly made his way to us. My teeth felt grainy and wet in my mouth as I ran my rough tongue across them. He ducked the sign poorly and it scraped across his scalp as he entered the salesmen's area.

"What are you doing?" Brick sniped.
"What do you mean?" Jeremy asked, his meaty fingers curling around his silly 80's print tie.
"Are you gonna write him up, or bore him to death with verbal vomit?"

Jeremy stared at him with wary eyes. I could feel his deal getting split. Brick slapped a pad of worksheets from the counter and peeled the top sheet off slowly. The scrape of the paper against the rubbery glue at the top was deafening.

"Gimme the invoice book." He chuffed at Ned.

Ned complied quickly and Brick flipped to the Silver Xterra's page. Handing me the keys, he looked out toward the front porch then scanned the offices. Seeing what he needed to see he spoke curtly.

"Go give these keys to Cortland and tell him to go outside."

Keys in hand, I looked up toward Cortland's office. His and Jamie's cubicle was the one right next to mine and Speck's. The customer was sneaking glances in our direction.

"Go now." Brick growled.

Ducking the sign, I strode briskly across the floor. Cortland looked up at me as I headed his direction. I held the keys in front of me like a bait fish. Cortland smiled at the subterfuge, already aware of what was transpiring. Entering his office, I could sense that Speck's customer was eyeing me warily.

"Brick wants you to take these keys outside." I said in a pointed whisper.

"You should go right back to the tower." Cortland advised back. "Don't say anything, just stand near Brick."

"Okay."

He snapped the keys from my grasp and strode out through the double doors. I noticed that he slowed a bit when he got onto the porch then traversed to the right side stairs where he'd be in full view of Speck's customer. Then I went back to the salesmen's corral and parked myself at the edge of the counter by the front windows. Brick raised a finger to his lips then made a 'stay put' gesture with his right hand. Taking the cue, I did just that.

Speaking to Jeremy very slowly and quietly, he explained exactly what he wanted him to say. Speck's eyes had the wide roll of startled prey beneath the glare of KC lights. Nodding incessantly at Brick's tutelage, I could tell that he was maybe absorbing half of what he said. Brick's irritation was charged with static. I waited patiently, my stomach gurgling with anticipation. Cortland backed the Xterra off the line and headed toward the used car Hogan. Stealthily, he parked the truck out of view on the back side off the building. It seemed like a bit much, his extension of the ruse, but what the hell did I know.

Speck held the worksheet in his limp grasp like a rubber duck decoy. I stood silently to his left against the windows.

"Get me something." Brick warned.

"Ok, boss."

I watched intently as Jeremy reentered our office. He sat down gingerly and laid the worksheet on the desktop. He held it close to him at first then slid it reluctantly toward his customer. Brick grimaced out at the lot. It wasn't three minutes before Speck came back across the floor.

"That was fast." Brick said to him.

"I can't get him to commit."
"No shit."

The worksheet was blank except for the initial numbers that Brick had penciled. I could still smell the sickening whale barf scent of the Sharpie ink. Brick took the page roughly from Jeremy and held it out toward me.

"Go get me a commitment, Stapleton." He said coldly.

I looked across the counter at him questioningly.

"Don't come back without something." he ordered a bit more softly.

Taking the worksheet I reviewed the numbers, and then looked at Speck with something just this side of pity. He'd penciled the deal with eight grand down and payments of 485-495 per month. There was no trade. It seemed easy enough.

"Jeremy," Brick directed, "you go with him and introduce him as the floor manager."
"Ok." Speck capitulated dejectedly.

We walked back to our office slowly. The customer was fully twisted in his chair, watching us as we returned.

"This is Mark, our floor manager."

I extended my hand as I circled the desk and the gentleman shook it warily.

"I can't do eight grand." He spat angrily.
"Ok." I said calmly. "What can you do?"
"Maybe two." He huffed, "But I'd really like see what I can do with nothing down."
"Ok." I advised, "With nothing down the payments will probably go up to close to seven hundred per month, with two grand you'll probably be around the low to mid sixes."

Jeremy leaned against the burlap wall and pressed his hands behind him.

"Fuck that." The customer barked, his fur rising again.

I looked at him with mock surprise, my eyebrows both raised and my forehead a furrowed field.

"Ok," I challenged, feeling that we might actually be getting somewhere. "So if we could get you in the four-eighty to four-ninety range with two grand down would you be willing to do that."

The customer slumped back into his chair roughly and exhaled.

"How about nothing down and four-fifty per month?"

It was more of a statement than a question.

"Fair enough." I flipped the worksheet over and started writing.

Customer will buy and drive today with $0 down and $450 per month.

X_____

Sliding the legal sized sheet of paper back in front of him I asked for his signature. He looked up at Jeremy then back at me. I held a black Papermate toward him, rolling it back and forth in my fingers. He uncrossed his arms and leaned forward slightly, glaring at the worksheet. The stark whiteness of the page glared back up at him beneath the buzzing glower of the overhead fluorescents. I could sense Jeremy's discomfort as he shifted his weight from foot to foot then back against the wall. I felt like saying something more, but something else told me to just keep quiet.

"I guess if you can do that, I'll take it."

He took the pen from me and scribbled his signature quickly on the line.

"Great." I said softly. "Let's go see what we can do."

I slid out the door, Jeremy tromped along behind me.

Back at the tower, I handed the commitment to Brick.

"Good job, Stapleton." He exhaled, "Now we've got something to work with."

He shot Speck a disapproving look and then started punching numbers into his computer. He gazed into the screen when he was done then folded the offer over and creased the paper below his signature. Laying it down on his desk he wrote boldly,

Ok Deal. *You need $4,500 down to reach your desired payment.*

He handed the worksheet up to me and pretended to be examining the math on his computer screen at the same time.

"Go get me a check and a credit app." Then to Jeremy, "You stay here."
"K." he squeaked.

I studied the worksheet.

"Don't think, Stapleton."

I looked at him with disbelief.

"He said he could maybe do two."
"Just present the counter-offer; you have no idea what he'll do."

He gazed intently into his computer screen, deliberately ignoring me.

I slunk back under the sign and over to my office.

Slapping the worksheet onto my desk, I feigned discontent with my boss.

"We can't get to your desired payment with nothing down. But if you can come up with some money we can probably get there."

Speck's customer looked at the worksheet then back up at me. His eyes actually seemed to be looking at my hairline. I wondered if it was receding.

"I told you I couldn't do more than two grand."

"I know." I exhaled. "What if I could keep you under $500 per month with your two grand down?"

Something told me that I might be f-ing the deal up but I had to get something outta this guy.

"Two grand?" he whined out loud.

He looked up at the ceiling and dropped his hands to his sides.

I waited silently. His eyes rolled from side to side as if calculating.

I said nothing.

Finally his head rolled forward.

"Do you really think you can get me under five-hundred with the two grand?"

"I hope so." I chimed optimistically.

"Ok." He agreed, sliding a credit card reluctantly from his wallet.

As he did so, I wrote the new commitment below Brick's counter-offer.

I took the credit card and set it on my side of the desk.

"Just sign here and I'll go to work."

The customer exhaled theatrically then put his 'John Hancock' on the makeshift line I fed him.

Brick glared into his computer screen with a confused look on his face. Speck was sitting on the bench outside staring into the nothingness above the lot. I'd gotten a credit application along with the credit card and the second commitment from his customer. Ned was peeling the credit bureau from the dot matrix printer on the back desktop.

"He's a 682." Ned chirped.
"Dammit." Brick growled lowly from his gullet.
"What?" I asked excitedly.
"You need to get some more money outta this guy." Brick pulled his gaze from the computer screen, "Or you gotta bump him on the payment."
"Jesus." I hissed.
"Calm down." His eyes piercing into mine, "You've got a deal here. It's time to satchel up."
"Ok." I said nervously.

Folding the worksheet down another third, he circled his pen above the page, considering what he should write. My head followed the motion coolly, like a cobra caught in the hypnotic song of an Indian flute player. He tapped the end of the Sharpie on the desk and scowled out at the back of Speck's head.

"Ok." He said to me and himself at the same time. "Do this."

Ok Deal. He wrote a bit larger this time and at an angle.
Then: *You need 3500 down to reach your desired payment.*

*X*_____

"Fuck!" I exclaimed in a scared whisper.
Ned's crooked smile began to emerge from under his moustache as he watched the exchange.

"Don't be a fuckin' pussy, Stapleton." Brick spat back, "You got this."

"I know he's only got two grand." I back-pedaled.

"You don't know shit." Ned interjected quietly.

Brick held up his hand toward Ned as if shielding himself from a blinding light. He reached into a lower drawer and pulled out a credit card slip. It was one of those old carbon-copy types that the guys at full service gas stations used to use. Handing it to me with one hand he held the tri-folded worksheet with the other.

"When you get the thirty-five hundred, fill out this slip and have him sign it."

I turned my head to the side and eyed him with one glazed eye. He shot me a charismatic grin then whispered softly.

"You can do this."

Snatching the worksheet from his grasp, his fingers stood splayed in the air like yucca needles.

"Fine."

I strode back to my office and slid into my chair gingerly, as if there might be a cactus upon it. Setting the folded up worksheet on the desk face down, the credit card slip was pressed against my left leg.

"Ok." I sighed, my consternation apparent. Then I flipped over the folded up worksheet and laid it between us.

"My boss says you need 3500 down to get below 500."

Speck's customer leaned slowly back in his chair and sighed also.

"I told you two grand was all I could do." His tone was less than anger but more than dismay. I shared his grief.

"I know you did, but we can't get the numbers to jive."

My toes were coiled in my shoes as if they were trying to find purchase. If he told me that he didn't have any more money I felt as though I might just blast right through the ceiling.

He exhaled through his nostrils and picked up the worksheet. He flipped it back and forth between his thumb and forefinger. I could tell that he was considering something. I hoped it wasn't a Chevy or a Ford. The silence was unbearable. I pressed my lips together to keep from screaming.

"What if I do 2500?"

I couldn't believe it.

"Hmmm." I snuffed. "Could you do three?"

His eyes were pinned on mine like a mongoose, or perhaps they more like a prairie dog. No matter, he'd already moved.

"I'll do 2750." He acquiesced, "But that's it, if you can't get me under five hundred then I'm walkin'."
"Ok." I gave.

Sliding the credit card slip in front of me I began to fill it out.

"What's that?" he asked.
"It's a credit card voucher." I stated matter-of-factly. "Just a technicality."

His eyes blackened a bit. I kept scribbling. Filling out the slip was like slithering across eggshells toward the henhouse. I could feel him staring burn holes into my scalp as I wrote.

"Just sign here and we'll put this together." I slid the crinkly slip under his nose. I noticed that he had a small moustache and goatee that I'd overlooked before. They twitched slightly as he picked up the pen. He shook his head then put the ball point to the paper.

"I guess you better put this together now." He admonished.

"I guess I better." I mimicked through a muzzle of nervous laughter.

He slid the slip back to me and I avoided rewriting a third offer. My jaw was tight from clenching and my tendons felt like coiled springs as I arose from my chair. He sat prone with his elbows on the desktop as I slid past. I considered giving him a conciliatory slap on the shoulder as I left, then thought better of the gesture. We weren't done yet.

Brick and Ned smiled slyly at me as walked slowly up to the counter for the third time. They looked like puppets as their heads turned to follow me.

"What'd'cha get?" Ned asked.
"I got 2750." I moaned, handing the signed slip to Brick.
"Grrr…" he pretended to be angry.

Punching the numbers into his screen he spoke over his shoulder to Ned.

"You're gonna have to hammer this shut buddy."
"Where we at?" Ned asked excitedly rising from his chair.
"508."

My stomach fell into my shoes.

"He said if we can't get him under five he's walkin'." I squawked.

"Relax." Brick chided, then to Ned "Go close this guy."

He tapped a couple more keys on his keyboard then pushed himself back from the desk slightly and sat up a bit taller in his chair.

"You go with him," he admonished, "listen, don't talk."

I felt somewhat relieved as Ned found his way through the little half door at the back of the tower. He rolled around the other side of the glass partition and met me on the way to my office. Speck's customer was still resting exhaustedly on my desk.

"What's his name, again?"

Realizing that I didn't ever ask, I looked at Ned shamefacedly.

"Doesn't matter," he held up a finger between our faces. "Stand and listen, don't talk."

"Ok."

"Good job."

"Thanks."

Ned strode into Speck's office like a Dr. Suess bandleader. I trailed behind him on tender feet.

"Congratulations!" He spouted, extending his hand proudly.

Speck's customer shot up bolt straight in his chair and looked into Ned's sunny face. I tiptoed in behind and leaned against the wall. Ned shook the man's hand and held it as he slid deftly into the chair behind the desk. Brick paged a clean for delivery over the loudspeakers. Ned's smile became slightly brighter as he looked up at the sound.

"So." He punctuated. "With three grand down you'd have been at around 497."

The customer looked at him icily.

Ned paused briefly, and then continued.
"With your decent credit and 2750 down you'll be at approximately 508 per month."
Speck's customer shifted his steely glare up at me, his whiskers twitching again. I could feel my jaw tightening.

The husky pencil was trying to reemerge.

Ned didn't allow for a response.

"Fair enough?" he half-asked, half conducted.

I could see a myriad of emotions race through the man's mind. His resolve had been worn down to a nub. Finally his shoulders slumped and he shook his head with comical capitulation.

"Fair enough." He agreed.

Part of me wanted to give him a hug.

Ned shot out his glad hand again.

"Congratulations," he sang, "you're now the proud owner of a brand new Xterra."

The man shook Ned's hand and I reeled mine out as well. He shook it with a desolate lack of fervor but I could feel some relief as he released his grip.

"Mark will finish the paperwork and I'll have Jeremy get the vehicle cleaned up for you."

Ned's demeanor was so well polished that Bob Barker himself would've been jealous.

I felt like Dick 'Fucking' Clark.

Chapter Seventeen

I'm in.

The morning was still and bright. I didn't remember Evergreen being so hot when I was growing up there. The bark on the Ponderosas had an orangey pinkish hue that matched the eastern sky. Both seemed to shimmer a bit beyond the smoke of my cigarette. My wife and our baby girl were still both asleep.

Gulping a sweet slug of coffee I took another generous pull off my smoke. Both were divine. It wasn't quite 7:30 but the warmth of the sun on my forehead was energizing. It was Friday and I was actually stoked about going to work. I couldn't remember the last time I'd felt that way. It was certainly never like that when I trudged groggily down to the fish place. Or any of the other numerous employers under which I'd forced myself to be enslaved.

Squinting through the blue smoke as it mingled with the steam from my coffee; I considered my past. From that first day I'd wandered into the temp agency at age thirteen, landing a job shoveling horseshit out of stables; to the admirable pursuit of teaching palsied kids how to ski, it had been a long, strange trip.

Over the years I'd sold everything from advertising to real estate. From slinging drinks and slices of pizza, on up to that stupid job I'd been so 'successful' at after I'd blown off college... pedaling aluminum siding and gutters over the phone. I'd run the gamut from roofing to room service, flipped eggs and burgers, built decks and driveways, painted condos and planted trees. I'd even cleared timber as a lumber-jack one especially broke mud season. I'd made as much as several thousand dollars in one day to as little as a pig-sucking five bucks per hour.

But I'd never actually felt that I'd gotten paid properly for the effort that I'd put forth. The car business seemed to satisfy that mineral need for which I'd been seeking. Somewhere in the mix of gasoline fumes and mental gymnastics, I found the chemical cocktail that filled the gaps between my synapses. Infuriating yet rewarding, these blind mice of the apocalypse had directed me out of the fog of my blue and white and red-collared existence. Emerging into a world of naked honesty and veiled deceit, all wrapped in steel and leather... I felt solid, renewed. It wasn't the money that compelled me; it wasn't the fancy cars or nice clothes, or even the prospect of financial buoyancy for once in my miserable life...

It was the junk.

Who'd have thought that somewhere on the lunatic fringe of Denver, amongst the strip malls and bowling alleys, flashy dealerships and pot lots, crappy restaurants and discount lighting stores, I'd find such an epiphany? Hanging out with a bunch of guys who said things like '*These ones*' and '*supposably*' and '*'member?*' I'd somehow found my brethren. Hewn together by our insecurity, our insatiable need for constant destruction and reinforcement, like Hendrix's 'Castles of Sand' we melted together into the sea of smog each morning. Slugging it out like boxers past their prime, writing out our destinies on the grey and black pages of pavement like misunderstood poets.

Had I found my calling? Finally found the island of misfit toys where I might hang up my elf's hat and become a dentist? It seemed ludicrous and perfect at the same time. As my wife and daughter slept soundly beneath my aching feet, I considered their futures. Would this be my golden ticket, the everlasting gobstopper on which I'd masticate for the next three and a half decades? It sure seemed like something had clicked over in the last week. Or was it just another empty chamber rotating into place on my Russian revolver?

I finished my smoke and craned my neck back to look at the clock on the wall in the dining area. 'Made in England' it read, just above the six. The time was 7:44. Glugging the last of my coffee, sugary grits and all, I rose from my chair and wiggled the handle on the sliding glass door. It sucked loose of the jam and slid open with a dusty grind. The insides of our duplex were shady and cool. I pulled the door quietly behind me and slipped downstairs to get dressed. My pits were a bit greasy from too much coffee and intellectual thought. I grabbed the hand towel off its hook in the bathroom and gave myself a shade tree mechanic's, backwoods pat down. Throwing the now stinky little towel onto the floor I donned the pants, shirt and tie I'd left hanging in the bathroom. It was a trick I'd learned during my restaurant days. Leaving my clothes hanging in a steamy bathroom after a shower, for ten minutes or so, seemed to make them appear less wrinkled.

Or perhaps I was just kidding myself.

*****

Joe and Tristan were shooting the shit and smoking near the back entrance to the Hogan as I arrived for Friday's meeting. I'd sold another Pathfinder after closing Speck's deal and was feeling pretty awesome about hitting the double-digit mark in total sales for the first time. Tristan eyed me coldly as I approached but Joe smiled at me slyly. We still had close to ten minutes before we supposed to be in the meeting so I lit up a smoke myself.

"So you got two yesterday?" Joe asked.
"One and a half," I returned quietly, "I closed one for Speck."

Tristan took a long pull off his mentholated cigarette then scrunched up his face before he blew a chillum-sized billow over my head. Joe and I were both at least a half-foot taller than him.

"Tristan here has already got his seventeen." Joe pointed at him with his hoof.

"Wow," I answered, "I don't know how you guys do it."

"I know." Tristan answered shortly, then snubbed out his Marlboro and yanked the door open behind him, disappearing into the building.

I looked at Joe. His blond hair had been meticulously gelled and blown dry into a wavy helmet. His discreetly patterned tie matched his gold colored pants. The dry-cleaned shirt he wore seemed a little big but the collar clenched his ruddy neck tightly.

"Don't worry about him." He assured me, "He's just jealous."

"Jealous of what?" I blurted, wondering what seventeen cars must be paying him.

"Dude," he continued, lighting a second smoke off his first. It was a Marlboro also, although of the 'light' variety. "His Mom runs Daughenbach Audi."

"Really?" I asked in disbelief, "Why doesn't he work there?"

He sucked the second cigarette to life then squinted at me as he chucked the old butt over the small chain-link fence that bordered the back of the lot.

"Would you want to work for your Mom?"
"I guess not."
"So you're doing pretty good this week?"
"Yeah." I exclaimed, "Hit ten last night."

He paused and looked at me, his smoke clutched between his thumb and two first fingers.

"Ten?" he asked with his own jagged brand of disbelief.
"Yep." I crowed, "Sold eight and a half since last Friday."
"No shit." he exhaled through his perfect teeth.
"I'm crappin' you negative, brother." I spouted in my best Cohen brother's, country-fucker voice.
"Holy sheepnozzle." He returned.
"How many you got out?"
"I'm not tellin'."

We smoked for a while longer then crept into the Hogan. Mik almost plowed into us as we came inside.

"Fuck!" he exclaimed his arms full of logbooks and various other jumbled paperwork. His hair had again the look of a harried college professor. "Look out." He barked, and then strode past angrily and around the corner to his office.

"What's his problem?" I whispered to Joe.
"Very small penis." He whispered back, gesturing its measure with his upturned palms.
"Let's get some coffee." I laughed.

As we entered the meeting room, there was a collection of salesman dotting the chairs. We found a couple for ourselves in the back between Random and Speck. Next to Random were the Finance Managers. They looked annoyed at having to be in the meeting and talked amongst themselves about bank advances and other things I didn't understand. Random shifted away from me in his seat as I inserted myself slowly, so as not to spill my coffee. Speck sat bolt upright next to Joe, his tie hanging like a dead tropical fish from his furry neck.

"What's up buddy?" I whispered to Random. He looked at me blankly, as if I didn't know.

It wasn't long before Brick entered with his entourage. They filed in and positioned themselves at the front of the room as always. Gavin stalked in a few seconds later, all piss and vinegar. Ringing a paper towel over his claws he crumpled it into a ball and chucked it into a tall rectangular garbage bin. Spinning around to his staff, his pin-striped coat tails fluttered up ever so slightly. They reminded me of a magpie's tail, or perhaps a swallow's; I fucking hated pin-stripes. Even on the finest silk or tailored wool, they just looked cheap. Stalking about as he was, gesticulating and emasculating with his harsh whispers, I wondered if he was wearing see-through socks.

My thoughts turned to my 'Uncle' Mario. He wasn't really my uncle, just a friend of my Dad's that had been a car guy for years down in Pueblo. A giant of a man, he had the barrel-shaped chest of his Italian and Mexican lineage. Always the gold chain strapped around his eternally tanned neck, a perfectly trimmed goatee ringing his fifty tooth grin. He was a beacon of machismo. Honest to the point of recklessness yet saltier than the most vulgar ship's mate in Tortuga, he was an interesting role model for me in my young adulthood. There was something supremely frank and honest about his personality, like the way a bull looks at you through strands of rusted barbed-wire.
My Dad had found a good friend in him later in his life. They'd played golf together and told each other racist jokes. A couple of aging salesmen, tough as cast iron lag bolts, blackly rotten to the core. I'd heard he'd once been fired from a Ford store down there in the desert. Apparently he'd hurled his desk through a plate glass window. I didn't know if the story was true, but I wouldn't put it past the guy, he had a temper for which his family was legendary. He would definitely eat Gavin's lunch;, then fuck his wife just for shits and grins.

Wheeling to face us, Gavin's red face seethed behind his yuppie owl eye glasses. His white hair was pasted tightly to his head like a swimming cap. He resembled a strike anywhere match. I covered my mouth with a hand to hide my snicker. Pointing his finger like a saber toward Joe he squawked loudly.

"How many cars you got out?"
"Seven." Joe retorted, bolting upright in his chair.
"Tristan?"
"Seventeen." He droned disinterestedly, his posture unmoved.
"Milo?"
"Fourteen."
"Random?"
"Five and a half."
"Cortland?"
"Seven and a half."
"Mr. Speck?"
"Four and a half."
"Jamie?"
"Five."

Gavin shook his match top head at the floor, I could almost see a spot of red on the carpet, radiating from his flaming face. I wondered about spontaneous human combustion. He turned to Brick and mumbled just loud enough for us all to hear.

"You're clear that this is a *'New'* Car Dealership, right?"

I was starting to understand why he was so spun up. The new car side of the sales staff was clearly floundering. He rotated his bird like head to a profile.

"Mr. Stapleton?"

I paused briefly, hardly realizing that he'd called my name.

"Ten." I answered quickly.

He paused. Turning his white over red match head all the way in my direction, his tiny body followed. Ridiculously pin-striped shoulders rotated around the axis of his pink, print tie.

"Say that again?"
"Ten." I said a bit more quietly than before. He'd caught me off guard.

He surveyed the rest of the sales staff with repugnance.

"You might make it after all, green pea."

Then his lips swirled themselves into something that almost resembled a smile. The managers rolled their eyes at one another behind him. I felt tall and short at the same time, like a male version of Alice in Wonderland that had decided to speedball the cake and the potion simultaneously. Mr. Matchstick swiveled again and nearly caught his managers mocking him. Their expressions immediately stoic, they looked over and around him; toward the lot of us with carrion crow eyes. With that he exited stage left, allowing the heavy door to slam shut behind him.

Brick sauntered forth, his feet clad in yet another pair of two-toned saddle shoes. They looked as if they might be made of suede and were brown over white. His smile was a bit larger than Gavin's had been and he was looking at me also. The other salesmen were looking my direction now too. I slunk down in my chair a bit and wished the meeting was over. Looking down at my own shoes, I noticed that they were black.

"You like niggers, Mark?"

I heard Uncle Mario's voice in my head.

We'd been flipping through the channels on his fifty-two inch projection screen TV, looking for the Bronco game. A basketball game came on briefly and Mario had screamed at the box loudly.

"Get that goddam nigger-ball off my TV!"

My Dad had cackled his approval at the outburst.

"I fuckin' hate niggers!" He kept on, obviously elated by my Father's reaction.

"You like niggers, Mark?"

I was silent, thinking that Italians and Mexicans were two of the most racially disparaged ethnic groups in American history. Not to mention that the game for which we were looking had players that were mostly black.

"I fuckin' hate niggers!"

Two of my best friends in Winter Park and Crested Butte had been black dudes; they both wore their hair in dreadlocks and rode snowboards. I'd declined comment.

Brick continued on with Gavin's tally of who'd sold what. Then he digressed into a diatribe about how we were a new car store and it's what keeps the lights on and blah, blah, blah, blah, blah... I was underwhelmed and embarrassed at being made to be the example. Finally the meeting drew to a close and we filed out. It was weird that my Dad's old friend had crept back into my psychic stew. I hadn't thought about him in years. Joe and Random peeled off from me like angry jackals as we emerged from the other side of the Hogan. I didn't care.

Back in the new car showroom, Ned corralled me at the door.

"I want to show you something."

He held a white three-ring binder in his right hand.

"K." I answered thickly, wishing I'd grabbed a second cup of coffee from the used car building.

"C'mon." he walked briskly toward my office. Speck was already inside and sitting at our desk, his 'three-by-five' in front of him.

"What're you doing?" Ned asked sharply.

"Doing my follow..." Started Jeremy.

"Go get a fresh up." Ned directed dismissively.

"Uh."

"Now!" He said a bit more sternly.

Jeremy lifted himself out of the chair and exited the office. His duck footed stride was annoyed but directed.

Ned deposited himself in Jeremy's seat and dropped the binder on the desk with a clunk.

"Have a seat." He said curtly but kindly.

Opening the binder he found the page he was looking for and then spun it around so I could take a gander. It looked like a spreadsheet. There were a number of columns and rows split into a grid that covered most of the page. At the top were places to put a salesman's name, the month, the year. Then below that were a few other smaller lines to make a forecast; New Units, Used Units, Average Commission, etc. The sheet of paper was gritty and skewed as though it had been copied way too many times. My eyes were crossing a bit as I studied the complexity, although it was actually quite a simple chart.

"Here's how you make the dough, bro." He unfurled his fingers over the page as though it were a signature dish at the Four Seasons.

I looked up at him blankly.

He smiled a genuine smile. It felt like the first one I'd seen from him.

"If you don't plan your work, then you can't work your plan."

"You mean the pay-plan, right?"

"Eggs-actly. How many cars did you plan on selling this month?"

"Well, up until recently I didn't think I'd even sell like 5 or 6."

"Then what happened?"

"I don't know, people just started buying I guess."

"You wish it was that easy."

"I don't follow?"

"Dude, you don't really think you went from one to ten cars in a week because you just got lucky?

"Well it was actually one and a half last Friday."

"Whatever."

He stopped himself and patted the page in front of him lightly. His hand bounced up and down like the page had some sort of magnetic propulsion.

"This," he paused, "this is the difference between an eight to ten car guy and a seventeen to twenty-five car guy."

I looked again at him queerly.

"If you don't know where you're coming from, then you don't know where you're going. Trust me dude, I was blind as a bat for months before I figured this shit out."

"K." I listened.

"Sit down with this sheet for ten minutes and figure out where you've been, then bring it to me and we'll help you find out where you're going."

It seemed simple enough.

"Gotta a blank one?"

"Uh," he flipped through the binder and couldn't find one.

"Here," he said curtly, ripping one from the center of the binder, "This month sucked anyway. White it out then make six copies."

"Okay."

I slid down the hall to the back office where the copy machine was, and hopefully some white-out. The office was guarded by a heavy Dutch door that had a little counter attached to the top of the lower half. Past experience had taught me not to just enter unannounced. The office had a number of desks; behind which sat several ladies that were massively busy all the time. They didn't like to be interrupted or surprised. The first one was a woman named Joanie and she had a haircut like Ferris Buehler's Mom. You know that weird spiky kind that started in the middle front of her head and spun out into a cyclone of spines like a sea urchin. Anyway, she was the Title Clerk and although I wasn't sure what her job entailed, it definitely seemed to put her on edge most of the time.

Standing in the frame of the door like a puppet, I waited for her to acknowledge my presence. Looking up over her bifocals, she shot me a *'What the fuck do you want?'* glance then looked back down at the papers strewn across her desk.

"Well, come in dammit." She drawled with a disinterested wave of her hand.
I pushed the bottom half of the door open and slid into the office.
"Is there a place I can score some white-out?" I mewled.
"Over there." she pointed to a small closet with the corner of title certificate that was clutched in her bony claw. It looked like a stock certificate or some weird form of oversized money.

"Oh," I laughed, noticing that there was an entire office supply closet just beyond the left corner of her desk. I took three quick strides and entered the little alcove.
"Just take one." She yowled after me.
"K." I answered quickly.

Sneaking back to the Dutch door as quietly as possible, I crept back into the hall and over to my office. I shook the little bottle in my hand then unscrewed the lid. The sickly smell of the glue like paint filled my nostrils as I covered up Ned's old sales history and made room for my own. It only took like five minutes. As the sheet of paper dried on my desk I examined the columns. The top of each had simple titles that were hand-written in capital letters. The first four read, 'Customer, Date Sold, Vehicle and New/Used'. The final three were a bit more in depth, 'Boarded Gross Profit, Projected Commission' and finally, 'Cumalitive Commission'. The last one I assumed should have read 'Cumulative', but of course spelling wasn't really anyone's strong suit here.

Shaking my head a bit, I took the sheet back up to Ned. The chart was curled in my fist under the weight of the paint job I'd put on it. Aboud stood in front of Ned, Joe in front of Brick. I leaned back against the front windows and waited my turn. Brick handed Joe a worksheet and murmured some instructions to him in a low voice. Joe took the worksheet slowly and slid past me quietly. I stood against the windows, waiting for Ned to be finished.

"What are you doing?" Brick asked, looking at the heavy paper in my hand.

"Trying to fill out this report." I answered slowly.

"Lemme see." He gestured with an impatient hand.

He reviewed the sheet with an expression of confusion, like he'd never seen it before.

"Nice paint job." He joked, holding the sheet limply in his left hand. "Where'd you get this?"

"I gave it to him." Ned interjected.

"Oh."

"Can I get like a list of my sales so I can fill it out?"

"Use your sales chits."

I looked at them both blankly.

"You know the little pieces of paper we've been giving you every time you sell a car?"

"Oh," I returned, vaguely remembering them handing the little receipts to me over the last couple weeks. "We're supposed to keep those?"

Brick and Ned both looked back up at me disbelievingly.

"Yea genius," Brick mocked, "that's how you keep track of what you're getting paid."

"Oh."

"Do you have any of 'em?" Ned asked.

"Um, maybe a couple."

"Have Carolyn print you out a sales summary and use that." Brick said, handing me back the crusty piece of paper.

"Don't forget to make copies of that before you fill it out." Ned added.

"Oh," I said, staring down at the page, "Right."

I wandered back toward the copy machine in the back office and began making copies. Joanie ignored me on purpose as I did this. Turning with a small pile of warm pages in my hands I felt a bit like the chef on Sesame Street. You remember; the one with all the pies that would always eat it down the stairs after announcing how many he had? I surveyed the length of the large office and tried to guess which one of the busy ladies was Carolyn. I could feel Joanie's impatient eyes sizing me up.

"Are you lost again?" she inquired snidely, with just the slightest tinge of sympathy.

"I need to find Carolyn?"

Her expression was disbelief.

"How long have you worked here?"

"What?"

"Never mind, her office is behind the cashier."

I looked the direction Joanie was pointing and noticed an open door about two-thirds of the way down the large office. There was a little bit of light emanating from the interior of the smallish room. Cocking my head, I pointed silently in that direction. Joanie opened her palms in front of her and her eyes widened with a 'Yeah, duh!' pronouncement. The sea urchin tentacles of spiky hair quivered just the slightest bit above her wrinkled forehead. I turned and stepped quietly through the maze of desks that sat in a staggered layout between me and Carolyn's office door.

As I reached the threshold, I noticed that it wasn't lit with the oppressive fluorescent overheads that covered every other square inch of the dealership. She had a tasteful floor lamp in the corner that threw a comfortable upward glow and a large lamp that bathed the entirety of her desktop in a bright but warm pool. The computer screen into which she was staring was an old school collection of numbers glowing in soft green against a field of black. A small bookcase stood smartly against the wall and was stuffed end to end with large three-ring binders, also black. I could tell that each of them had been labeled on white cards sheathed in plastic. They appeared to contain three month intervals of some kind and went back several years. In the corner to my right was a wide dot matrix printer with the old ledger style green and white striped paper feeding into it from a huge box below.

The office was tiny but neat and scarcely housed the poor woman's desk, let alone the file cabinets that seemed to hem her in from all sides. On top of each of the cabinets rested family photos of the Olan Mills variety. One had her son in a letter jacket against a backdrop of smoky gray, another with her daughter in an angora sweater, her hair done just so. A third showed Mom, Dad and kids against a split rail fence with golden aspen trees behind them. Several other smaller photos stood sentinel at the corners of desk but faced toward her so I couldn't see what they displayed. A ream of folded printer paper stood three inches high on the desk before her. She had another full inch of the report curled back in her fist so that she could review a specific page. Her other hand was tracing the computer screen and she was clearly trying to reconcile some figures. Her robin's head flitted back and forth from the screen to the report. Her pointy nose directed the measured task, her eyes dark black and intently focused.

Standing in the doorway with my own one page unfulfilled report, I felt small and inconsequential. Shifting from foot to foot nervously, I wasn't sure if I should interrupt. She seemed so fully entrenched in her work. Pulling the freshly painted and paltry sheet in front of me, the page crinkled slightly in the grasp of both my hands. The minute noise startled her.

"Oh!" She started, placing a splayed hand against her breast.

'Jesus.' I thought, *'I've given her a frickin' heart-attack.'*

"Sorry." I said a bit too loudly.

"Oh." She exhaled again.

I felt like change for a penny.

"I didn't see you there, young man." She said more softly. "Can I help you with something?"

"Sorry to interrupt."

"It's okay." She intoned softly. "I just didn't see you."

"Um," I digressed. "Brick wanted me to ask you if I could get a sales summary of the last month, on my sales."

"Oh." She laughed to herself. "Yes. Just let me finish this report and I'll get it out to you."

'No hurry.' I wanted to say. But I just stood there stupidly, still feeling bad about scaring the crap out of here.

"Tell Britton that I'll have it ready within the hour."

'Britton?' I thought for a second then I realized that it must be Brick's real name.

"Oh." I stammered, "Ok."

Retreating from the doorway like a clown's shadow from the spotlight, I wheeled around and almost plunged into the platinum blonde woman I'd met by the soda machines in the waiting room a couple weeks prior. It felt like that meeting was ten thousand years ago.

"Whoa, Cowboy." She joked. "Watch those spurs."

"Oh!" I blushed, realizing who it was, "Sorry."

She looked up at me with a mixture of steely coquettishness and simmering disdain. I felt stupid, yet strangely aroused. Her perfectly coifed hair framed her face with just a bit of inward curl at the ends. Her lips parted slightly as I looked into those exotic cerulean eyes of hers. Yet another stylish suit hugged her tight and voluptuous frame. A single, giant fabric button clutched the sides of her jacket smartly together around her narrow waist. I noticed that her lapels, lying stiffly across her full breasts as they were, were pin-striped. My lips smiled slightly at this, I considered that my earlier assessment of the style was a bit too hasty. Perhaps pin-stripes, stretched around the right curvature, had a place in this world after all. Flashbacks of Kim Basinger and Mickey Rourke raced through my mind. What was the name of that movie again? Nineteen-eighty's Basinger had certainly done her best to make pin-stripes appealing… or was it appalling?

It was just a moment; and Glinda was easily fifteen years my senior… but something told me it might be a hell of a ride. Blinking back the filth that I'm sure my own greenish brown eyes betrayed; I apologized again. She was standing too close, so I shuffled back against the door jam. She seemed to glow with a pinkish white hue that permeated her being and challenged the incessant, buzzing downpour of the overhead fluorescents. I felt a bit like one of the *Lollipop Guild.* I almost looked down to make sure I wasn't wearing Lederhosen.

"Hmm." She spouted cheerily, "Don't be sorry," she warned, taking a small step forward, her pointy shoe placed between my own blackly shod feet, "just watch your back."

I looked back into Carolyn's office. She was re-immersed in her reconciliation. Her purplish gray hair was just visible over the top of the upturned report. I was reasonably certain that she hadn't witnessed the exchange. Looking back to my left, I noticed that Joanie wasn't at her desk and the top of the Dutch door had been closed and locked. Glenda and I were basically alone in the back office. She'd narrowed the space between us and my wedding ring felt tight on my finger. Half of me wanted run like a brainless scarecrow and the other half; well let's just say the other half would've been happy to loose a few buttons and rumple some pin-stripes.

"I'll uh, keep that in mind." I exhaled ambivalently.

She inhaled and her perfect lips emitted a slight whistle. A third half of me expected her to tell me to follow the yellow brick road.

"You do that." She cooed instead. Her breath smelled of powdered peppermint and mango flavored smoothie.

A rush of blood left my head and re-deposited itself elsewhere. I wished I had one of Carolyn's three ring binders handy. I dropped the thin sheets of paper I'd copied to my beltline instead.

"Um," I croaked. "I guess I better make some more copies of this."

"Yes." She retreated slightly, "You should do what you, um, came back here to, um, do."

With that, she spun slowly and quietly on her heel and sauntered back to her office. Which I now realized was a glass box stationed at the far end of the large room. She made no effort to hide her hip sway as she disappeared for a moment through her door then slid into a large and comfortable leather chair behind an equally large, glass topped desk. I could feel her eyes on me as I made my way to the copy machine; those lapis almond shaped orbs of her's; examining me, fantasizing, intending.

I left the lid on the copy machine open as I made several copies, letting the bright green flashes blast through my depraved mind's eye. The effect was sufficient enough to get me out the weird Dutch door and back into the hallway. Blinking my way back through splotchy vision I traversed across the tiles of the showroom and jangled into my office. It had the musty stank of old air conditioning, but the coolness eased my demon soul. Laying the still warm copies on the Formica desktop, I placed my palms face down and took several cleansing breaths. My vision cleared a bit and since I didn't have the sales summary yet, I decided to have a cigarette.

Brick decided to join me.

"What the fuck we're you doing back there?"

"You don't even want to know." I heard myself saying.

"Is Carolyn printing the report for you?"

"Yes.

"You have any idea how much you've made so far this month?"

I figured he already knew, but I answered anyway.

"I don't know, like three grand?"

"Is that a question?" He challenged.

"I haven't had much time to figure it out." I shot back with agitation, still shaken from my odd experience with the 'Good Witch of the North'.

"Well you should." He kept on.

"Should what?"

"Know how much you've made."

'Don't should on me.' I thought acidly.

I took a long pull off my smoke and exhaled a pile of blue smoke over the railing. Extracting a thin paper box of cigars from his pocket, Brick lit up as well. It was one of those twig like cigars that Eastwood used to smoke back in all those old spaghetti westerns. My Dad and I used to watch them into the wee hours of the morning. My stomach grumbled angrily, reminding me that I hadn't eaten anything yet this morning.

"How long have you been sober?" he asked out of the blue.

"Just over two years." I decided to share.

"How long did you drink?" he dug deeper.

"Just over thirteen." I groaned.

He took his own long puff off his cigar and inhaled the smoke. The tip of it crackled and tufts of half lit tobacco tumbled down onto the pavement between us.

"I've got just over seven years." He shared.

I looked at him with obvious surprise, not knowing that he was a member of the club.

"Why do we keep track?" he asked reflectively.

"Keep track?"

"Yeah, why do we keep track of how long we've been clean?"

"So we don't go back." I answered triumphantly.

"Really?" he asked, "You think?" and then.

"That's not why I do it."

"Why do you keep track?" I asked, genuinely interested.

He smiled and took another long drag. Squinting through the smoke he rested his wrists on the tall railing, letting his hands hang limply over the edge. He scuffed the bottom of his shoe on the small curb of the porch, as if trying to remove gum from it or something.

"To measure my accomplishment." He said in a faraway voice. "Do you remember the day you quit?"

I laughed and took a puff. Fortunately I had the benefit of a Clear Creek County police report to remind me.

"May 28th, 1998." I trumpeted again.

"I'm not sure what day I actually quit." He imparted sadly. "I woke up on a bunk at Arapahoe House after a multi-day blackout. Somebody had puked in my shoes."

"Gross." I intoned, not sure what else to say.

"Yeah." He continued. "The last thing I remember is pounding on the glass windows of a gas station. The place was closed and the attendant wouldn't let me in; all I wanted was a can of chew."

"So did you get arrested too?"

"Well I hadn't really broken any laws other than being a completely drunk asshole."

"So how did you end up at 'The House'?"

I'd never actually been to Arapahoe House, but I knew that it was a place where the cops took people to detoxify.

"Well, I'm not sure." He continued with a bit of embarrassment, "My brother won't say he did, but I'm pretty sure he dragged my dumb ass there."
"I guess you got lucky that night?"
"Yeah… lucky." He sneered.

I decided to share my own story.

"I spent six days in the Georgetown clink, before my Dad and Sister bailed me out. Then they took me directly to that place up in Estes Park."
"That's lucky."
"Yeah, I'm the lucky one."

We shared a knowing smile then smoked together in silence for a few minutes.

"I guess all's I'm tryin' to say is, if you don't know where you're coming from…"
"…then you don't know where you're going." I finished.
"Yeah." His eyes seemed a bit misty under a sheath of translucent armor. "You can fill out all the 3x5's and tracking reports in the world, just don't forget who you are."
"Don't worry," I laughed, "There's a friendly collection agency in Ft. Collins that is happy to remind me."
"Well then," he pushed back from the railing and stubbed his cigar out in the ashtray by the door, "I guess you better get another up."

I crushed my own half-smoked butt out next to his and looked at my watch…

…it was 11:11.

Epilogue

So that is how we did that. In the late spring and early summer of the year two-thousand. Before the world economy was reduced to powder; leaving the majority of us hanging in the balance.... like blind bats.

~MAC

First of all, I would like to thank the salty dogs that are still on account is this infernal business… this book would not have been possible without you.

Secondly I would like to thank my family members, past and present; that have endured my ramblings… however wayward. In particular, my daughters, who remind me daily of my reason for being.

Lastly, but not *leastly*, I would like to extend a special thanks to my editor-in-chief and special lady. She has the wings of a mighty kestrel and the patience of a Nepalese boulder.

I love you all.

Coming Soon:

Car Store – *(Il Duce)*

17371917R00163

Made in the USA
Charleston, SC
08 February 2013